revenge

a Blood Angel Novel
by Nina Soden

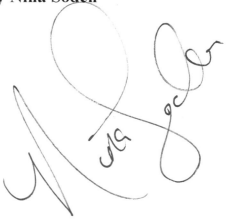

PRAISE FOR THE
BLOOD ANGEL
SERIES

"From the opening scene to the final chapter, the characters in this book dive onto the page and demand your attention."
—Genalmt (Amazon.com ★★★★★ review)

"…It is exciting, twisty, and fun."
—Carole A. Spalino (Amazon.com ★★★★★ review)

"The characters are realistic and compelling, and the author's tone is casual and lighthearted—frequently bringing a smile or even a laugh, or sometimes a tear."
—Ula Manso (Amazon.com ★★★★★ review)

"I quickly inhaled this story. The author has a very easy to read talent that engulfs the reader. I found the pace of the story to be steady throughout. Though, the concept has been done before, the author put her own 'uniqueness' to it that kept be guessing."
—WhisperingWillo (Amazon.com ★★★★★ review

"Excellent vampire story!"
—H.M. Schuldt, Co-Author of Gryffon Master

This is a work of fiction. All of the characters, organizations, businesses, and events portrayed in this novel are either products of the author's imagination or are used fictitiously.

REVENGE. Copyright © 2014 by Nina Soden. All rights reserved.

www.ninasoden.wordpress.com

Editors: Ula Manzo, PhD., Nicole Smith, Clara Tapaninen, and Gena Rawdon

Front Cover Design by: Julie Csizmadia

DEDICATION

For my amazing sister whose determination to succeed inspires me to never give up, and to my parents whose love, support, and guidance have been the most constant things in my life as far back as I can remember. It is because of each of you and the encouragement and love of my husband and children that the Blood Angel series has been possible.

SPECIAL THANKS

I want to say a special thank you to the following Kickstarter Project all-star donors for helping to make the Blood Angel Series a reality:

Bill & Clara Tapaninen *(Mom & Dad)*

Kathryn Dougherty

Harvey Howell

Smith Family

1

The lights dimly flickered in the abandoned ballroom. No movement could be seen. No breath could be heard. And everywhere you looked, bodies lay piled about in pools of blood, amidst broken glass and tables, and fallen chandeliers. There was no way to know which side had lost more lives that night. One thing was clear, though: great tragedy had been suffered by all.

The founders had had reason to suspect an intrusion at this year's annual Celebration, and had taken great care in planning the event, to ensure the safety of everyone in attendance. Checks and double checks had been put in place to prevent the entry of anyone without the official invitation. Twice the usual number of guards had been stationed inside and outside the ballroom. But it was all for naught. The lycanthropes' swift and vicious attack had not been avoided.

As soon as the first drop of blood was spilt, Gregory Davis, the principal of Atlanta High and the oldest vampire still residing in Atlanta, had activated a silent alarm beneath the founders' table, alerting the security office three stories up, and protocol had been followed. Their orders were to evacuate as many members and founders as possible. If evacuation was impossible, containment was the only option. They were to block the two exits immediately and ignite an explosion in the elevator shaft that would eliminate the risk of the threat expanding into the city.

Years ago, for security purposes, the six underground tunnel routes that led to the ballroom had been bricked up and sealed. Few people outside of the founding members even knew they had existed at all. As far as most members knew, the only ways in, or out, were the elevator shaft entrance and the back stairwell behind the founders' table.

Knowing what security procedures were going to be taken, Eric's focus had gone straight to getting his family out at any cost necessary. He knew that the primary exits would be sealed within minutes, but was confident that if he could get them to one of the bricked up underground tunnels he, with the help of others, should be able to break through, and get them out. He hadn't expected to be the direct target of any of the attackers, but Damian had zeroed in on him in seconds, before he could take a single step away from the founders' table toward his family across the room. *'I'm not afraid of you.'* The great wolf form snarled, baring enormous teeth, and growled, but Eric could hear its human voice clearly in his head, almost as if he was thinking the words himself. *'You killed my father! Now I will kill you, or die trying.'* Damian now knew who and what Eric was, and was fully prepared to fight to the death.

The great wolf leapt into the air, and landed with its front paws square on Eric's chest, its teeth only inches from Eric's throat. Eric was too strong for it though, and in mere moments it was on the floor struggling against Eric's grip. Eric gave the creature's throat a quick bite, releasing a small amount of venom from his fangs, and it, Damian, was powerless against him—at least for the short time it would take Eric to get his family to safety.

Eric ignored the chaos before him, looking only for Loraline. He wasn't going to lose her again. Not after just getting her back. He was relieved that when he did spot her she was already nearing the tunnel entrance that they had previously agreed upon as their escape route in the case of just such a catastrophe.

Loraline had Alee and Petra in tow, and Edith, Estelle, and a few others were already gathered at the wall with a young slender boy with dark hair. Eric didn't recognize the boy, but didn't take time to puzzle over it.

However, even over the sounds of screaming and fighting, Eric was able to zero in on Edith's voice as she spoke to the young man, "Your name?"

"Jathan ma'am."

Edith stepped back an arm's length. She wasn't scared. Concerned? Maybe a little. "You're not a dream walker!"

It wasn't a question, but he answered anyway. "No ma'am. I'm not even sure what that is."

Eric would have heard more, but a deafening scream—
"Alllleeeeraaaahhhhh!"—from somewhere on the other side
of the room interrupted his concentration. He heard it clearly
and knew that it was Kyle. Eric had just started moving
toward Loraline, and he saw Alee turn and pull away from
her mother, and run in Kyle's direction. Why Kyle was there
was a mystery to Eric, but as he searched the far end of the
room he saw that Kyle was dressed like one of the waiters
and was trying to push himself through the crowd. *Typical
stubborn boy,* Eric thought to himself.

"Aleerah, NO!" Loraline had lost her hold on Alee's
hand, and was grasping at the air trying to catch her, to pull
her back before she was lost in the crowd. Eric was already
behind Loraline, forcing her toward the wall where the rest of
the family stood waiting as a portal was opening under
Jathan's hand, which he held high against the brick wall.

A foggy mist billowed around Jathan as Edith glared at
him. "You have to tell her. She deserves to know."

"I—."

"You don't know how much time you have left. Tell her,
before it's too late."

Loraline was struggling against Eric's grasp, intent upon
saving her daughter, but as she twisted and slipped free, Alee
turned back, threw her arm up, and with a force that neither
Eric nor Loraline would later be able to explain, she sent a
wave of energy toward her mother that pushed her, tumbling,
across the room and through the black hole that Jathan had
created. Satisfied that her mother was safe, Alee re-focused
on getting across the battlefield to Kyle, with Eric in quick

pursuit. Eric didn't have time to worry about where the black hole would take his family. He just took comfort in knowing they wouldn't be here for the massacre that had already begun.

Eric lost sight of Alee in the pandemonium around him. Only about forty lycanthropes had attacked, but they had the element of surprise on their side, and, with about three-fourths of the guests in attendance being witches, fairies, and other such beings, there were a lot of easy targets. A few witches were casting basic defensive spells, but no one had brought any tools that could have helped with that. Only a few of the fairies engaged in the fights, but those who did tore into their attackers with such fierce hunger it was like watching a starving dog attack a steak. When you live with constant suppression of so much of yourself, it's hard to control your natural instincts when you finally do let go.

The vampires were clearly fighting back. Fear and panic suffused their victims' last breaths, but there was nothing more fearsome than Alee's scream, echoing above all others in the room. "RELEASE HIM!" The lights flashed, the ground shook, and in that instant her blonde hair was a blazing auburn red, her sun-kissed skin faded to pale porcelain, and her eyes were as black and hollow as the black hole into which her family had just disappeared.

Everyone in the room froze in shock—fear—and awe. She was more beautiful than any angel in heaven, and more malicious, at that moment, than any demon in hell. She leapt across the remaining distance of chaos, and was face to face with a huge white wolf with smoky grey eyes. Its muscles were taut beneath its thick fur and its lips pulled back to reveal enormous teeth. It growled a warning.

Eric heard whispers spread through the crowd as people began to recognize who had issued the screaming command and now stood facing the wolf. Rumors had spread throughout the Underground of a dhampir returning to Atlanta, but no one had really believed it. Even those who had seen her glowing tattoo only weeks before weren't truly convinced. Now they all knew that the rumors were true, and, if the legends passed down from generation to generation about the powers a dhampir can hold were also true they all had reason to fear.

A subtle shift in the wolf's posture revealed his recognition as well. Only he didn't know her as the mysterious dhampir. He knew her as Alee, his first and only love, even if she didn't know this herself. Recognition brought instant transformation, and the human Damian stood naked and vulnerable, just a few yards away from Alee, covered in Kyle's blood.

"Alee?" Tears poured down his cheeks as he looked down at Kyle's lifeless body and then back at Alee, realizing what had happened—what he had just done. The pause in the fighting was only momentary, but to Eric the room seemed to be moving in slow motion as fights resumed all around him. His focus was on Alee, and he raced to her, leaping on and over tables, debris, and bodies, aware of no one else. As he closed the distance, he reached out to her with both hands.

"NOOOOOO!" Eric heard Damian's scream, but it was too late. Alee had been hit from behind and thrown to the floor by a huge brown wolf with deep chocolate eyes.

The attack was swift and ferocious, and the wolf disappeared into the crowd. Damian carefully scooped Alee up into his arms and held her close in anguish. "What have I done?"

Eric was fast approaching, and Damian knew that if he was still there when Eric got to him, he too would be lying dead on the floor. Reluctantly he lay Alee down, wrapped himself in a bloodstained tablecloth, and dodged his way past continuing battles and bodies in search of an exit.

Eric ignored Damian's retreat as he finally reached Alee's side. The skin and muscle of her back had been ripped off, down to the bone, and she was drowning in a pool of blood. He pulled her into his lap and held her to his chest, weeping at the loss of his child. The screams and growls and crashing sounds around him slowly faded away and eventually, not knowing how much time had passed, he realized he was alone—alone with his dead daughter and so many other brutally mutilated victims.

Eric remained there with his daughter in the deepening silence, unable to leave her there in that bricked up tomb with death surrounding her. He knew the emergency plan, having masterminded it himself, but there was no room in his mind or his heart to consider the fact that by now he himself might have no escape route.

The longer he sat, empty and aching, the more he became vaguely aware that he wasn't alone. It wasn't the rapid sound of a human heart that tipped him off. In fact he didn't hear a heartbeat at all. It wasn't the sweet scent of fresh blood that triggered his senses. As he turned toward the wall, he could smell nothing but the warm blood, already starting to congeal, that covered the floor all around him. What he sensed was a sudden chill, as if a cool breeze had just drifted through the room—as if death itself were watching over him.

A dimly flickering chandelier on the far end of the room slowly swayed from side to side. Through a thickening fog, Eric caught glimpses of the tall, slender, dark-haired boy standing with his back against the wall, almost completely hidden from sight. Eric had never met Jathan, but he recognized him at once. He lay Alee on the ground and with lightning-fast speed he was face to face, and toe to toe with the boy.

"Did you do this?" His voice was a deep guttural growl and there was no question as to the insinuation in his words.

"No. I came only to help—to try and stop it. I'm sorry. I failed." With that, he put his palm against the brick, ignoring Eric's exposed fangs and flaming eyes, and proceeded to open another portal. Eric could see the genuine pain in Jathan's eyes and, going against his true nature, he didn't push the boy for more.

"What is that?" he asked, gesturing toward the portal.

Reaching toward Eric with an open hand, the boy replied simply, "It's your way home."

Eric looked back around the darkened ballroom with disbelief and sorrow. "I can't leave her."

"Neither could—." Jathan shook his head. "Neither can I, but we must."

Hesitantly, Eric took Jathan's hand and stepped through the portal with him. Vampires have a heightened sense of sight. Like cats, their night vision is just as good as their daylight vision. However, stepping into that portal was like nothing Eric had ever experienced—darkness so black he couldn't even see his own hand two inches in front of his face. It didn't last long. In seconds they were stepping through to the other side.

As his eyes adjusted he looked around, realizing he was standing in the kitchen at The Black Onyx. It truly had been his way home. Jathan, however, was gone.

Loraline sat at the table, her head in her hands. When she saw Eric step through, she rushed to his side, throwing herself into his arms and wrapping her arms around his neck. He felt solid under her fragile hands and yet she knew before he spoke that something wasn't right.

He drew back, and their eyes met—and she realized what that uneasy feeling was. Alee wasn't with him. Not only was she not there, but Loraline knew, with all her heart, that her little girl hadn't made it out alive.

Eric silently shook his head, confirming her fears. Loraline crumbled to her knees still holding onto him as she wept.

Much later, exhausted, her eyes red and swollen, she let Eric help her slowly to her feet. They gazed at one another in misery. "We will get through this," Eric said, with more conviction than he felt.

His own eyes were burning red from tears that he was incapable of shedding, but his voice was steady and she could feel his strength. It wasn't a mind trick. He never used those on Loraline—a promise he had made her long ago—but just then he wished he could. He wished he could make her forget—make the pain go away. It would be so easy, and she wouldn't have to suffer any longer, but he knew it wasn't right. He knew that she would never forgive him and he couldn't stand to lose her too.

"How did—?"

"No." He cut her off. He knew she couldn't handle knowing what had happened. He himself could barely stand to think about his little girl lying there in a pool of her own blood—limp, lifeless, and alone, surrounded by so much death and destruction.

She didn't push him. Maybe deep down she knew she didn't want the answer, or maybe deep down she felt she already knew the answer. Either way she dropped it, for now at least.

Eric suddenly realized that the kitchen was empty, when normally it would be bustling with life. "Where is everyone?"

She didn't answer. So much had happened, so much sadness. She just dropped her eyes to the ground in silence.

"Loraline, what happened?"

When the words finally came out they were abrasive and raw. "Granny Estelle." The tears started again. "She didn't make it—." Then, as if a plug had been released, everything came flooding out of her. "My sis—sister, she's dead, and Petra, I couldn't—I couldn't save her. Then, when you didn't come through, I thought I had lost you too—. Phoebe and Kyle are gone, and we can't find them anywhere—and Granny Edith—she isn't doing well. My whole family is falling apart. They're dying all around me and I can't stop it."

Everything was happening so quickly, and he was trying to catch up. He already knew about Kyle, and with the loss of so many others he thought it best not to bring him up just yet. He knew he would have to deal with Kyle's family eventually, but right now he wanted to focus on his own. "One at a time—what do you mean Granny Edith isn't doing well?"

"The boy—Jathan—he opened a portal to bring us back here. Granny insisted on being the last one through. She said it was her job to protect us. As she was coming through—she was attacked." She was staring across the room as if she were watching it happen all over again. "I saw her, she almost made it, and then she was thrown to the ground. I grabbed her arms and Tom and I were able to pull her the rest of the way through, but not without injuries."

"Take me to her."

She took a deep breath, and led him out of the kitchen and down the hall to the study. "Mom is with her now. I don't know how much longer she has."

Entering the study, he realized that everyone who was left in their family had gathered here together as if it were the only safe place in the world. Maybe it was. Everyone turned to Eric and Loraline with hopeful eyes—as if maybe he would be able to save Edith. He could have, if she would only let him, but she was old and stubborn and he wasn't going to force her if she didn't want his help.

She was losing blood at an alarming rate, and was dropping in and out of consciousness. "Edith, can you hear me?" She didn't respond. Knowing that the only way to help her would be for her to drink some of his blood, he quickly sliced a small cut across his wrist. As the first drop of blood touched her lips, she slapped his arm away.

"Edith, your family needs you and, therefore, you need me." The blood of a vampire has enormous healing powers, and if she allowed him to help her she would recover within days. Without his blood, however, she would probably be dead within hours.

Edith coughed up blood as she tried to speak. "If it's my time to die then it's my time." Then, looking deep into his eyes, she pulled Eric close. "You're a vampire. I accept that. Loraline loves you, and I accept that too. I'm sorry it has taken me so long to see you as the man you are. A good man. A strong man. And I see the love you have for my granddaughter. Thank you, for wanting—." She coughed again, and this time it shook her whole body. "Thank you, for wanting to save me, but it has to be this way. I'm old, and I'm allowed to be set in my ways."

Eric smiled, although her heartfelt admission was not lost on him. "Yes, I suppose you are."

"You can't help me now." She looked out through tear-filled eyes as her family gathered more closely around her. "You help them, and let me go home to my husband—to the one who loves me as much as you love Loraline. That is what you can do for me." He wanted to respect her wishes, and he did, but it wasn't easy. It wasn't only about not wanting to disappoint his wife or the rest of her family—he wasn't ready to let her go either. He wasn't ready to lose yet another important person in his life.

"No! Granny, you can't just give up!" Loraline was kneeling at her side. "You can't let her give up. You have to do something."

Eric just pulled Loraline into his lap and held her like a child. "I can't make that decision for her. I'm so sorry, sweetheart." He kissed her forehead and held her as she cried.

"No," Loraline cried, "she can't die. Not yet, not after we've lost so many." Neither Eric nor anyone else had an answer to that. Eric just continued to hold her. Nearby, Elizabeth and William were comforting their son-in-law, Tom, Jacinda's husband.

A little while later, Eric noticed that the grief in that room seemed to be materializing into a thickening fog. He gently removed himself from his wife's embrace and went to inspect the fog. He went toward the far wall of the study that seemed to be its source. From close up he could see that the fog was coming through the brick wall, and increasing in density at an alarming rate.

Then, in the center of the fog, a large black hole formed and Jathan stepped through, holding Phoebe in his arms. "She's not hurt, only sleeping," he quickly announced as everyone who could jumped to their feet and hurried to him.

Tom carefully lifted his daughter out of Jathan's arms, thanking him over and over again for bringing her home.

Then, without warning, Jathan stepped back into the fog and disappeared back into the black hole.

After the commotion of Jathan's short visit was over, the family's attention went back to Edith, who was holding a shaking hand out to Loraline.

"What is it Granny? What?"

She whispered so softly that Loraline had to lean down, with her ear just above Edith's lips. "She will return, but do not underestimate the devastation that will follow in her wake." Then, she closed her eyes and took her last breath. No one knew what to do or say. Bewildered, they all sat there in silence not wanting, or willing, to accept that she was really gone.

2

The floor was cold and sticky beneath her as Alee slowly started to wake up to a distant, yet steady, dripping sound. Her body ached all over. Her head felt heavy. It throbbed as if something very large had hit her, knocking her down and pinning her to the floor. She had a feeling she was going to have a pretty bad headache for a while, but she couldn't remember what had happened to cause it. In all honesty, she didn't know where she was or why she was lying in what felt like honey and smelled just as sweet.

Not wanting to move too quickly, Alee ran her hand across the floor, grasping in the dark for something to help her up. There was nothing. Her left eye was swollen shut, and since she had been lying with the right side of her face flat to the floor, it was virtually impossible to see anything. She tried to push herself up, but screamed as a burning pain shot through her back and caused her arms to buckle, and she fell back to the floor. She reached a shaking hand around to the back of her body, and felt the deep gashes where the muscle and skin had been torn away.

She tried to remember what had happened—how she had gotten hurt—but she hadn't seen her attacker. She had only felt the pain strike through her like a thousand knives cutting at once. She could still smell the musky animal scent that had surrounded her, suffocating her, as she passed out.

Knowing that she was in no condition to move, let alone stand, she lay there surrounded by the silence for a few more minutes. It dawned on her that even with everything she was going through—serious injuries, considerable pain, obvious memory loss, and who knows what else—she wasn't actually scared. She was mad. No, not mad. Angry! And anger is a good thing in situations like this. It's always better to be angry than scared when you think your life is in danger. Anger can pump up your energy and motivate you to act. Fear only sucks the life out of you and forces you to hide.

Get up. Get up. GET UP! She yelled inside her own head.

She forced herself to focus on what was around her. She needed to figure out what she could use to pull herself up, but her attention was drawn to a burning sensation around her neck and the smell of seared flesh. She reached up and felt something hot around her throat, like a collar of fire, with what felt like charred, scabbed skin stuck to it. She pulled at the unfamiliar object until it broke in her hand, burning into her palm before she let it drop.

In spite of the pain, she reached out and grabbed a table leg, and tried to pull herself forward. But it wasn't just the pain that stopped her. Along with everything else, she was hungry. Not the kind of hungry you get from skipping lunch; it was the kind of hungry you get from being in the desert with no food or water for days.

Alee coughed, and realized that her throat had started to seize up, and she was having difficulty breathing. She rested her head on the floor and took a deep breath, accidentally inhaling some of the gooey liquid that surrounded her. Instantly, the sweet taste of blood filled her senses, and ignited a burning sensation down her throat and into the pit of her stomach. The anger melted away and the only thing she could feel was the hunger. The pain was a distant memory. The pounding in her head no longer mattered.

She started slowly at first, licking her fingertips clean. Then, as her energy and strength increased, she tried, more urgently, to suck the blood directly off of the floor. Soon she was on her knees, feverishly scooping the blood off the floor with her hands and pouring it into her mouth. Looking up, she realized that her vision was returning, revealing masses of lifeless bodies strewn around the ballroom.

Her throat still burned, and she had no other choice. She rushed on hands and knees to the nearest body she could see. It was a girl. She could tell this only by the long black hair and the white lace dress, but the girl's face was mostly torn off, completely covered in blood, making it virtually impossible to tell who she had been, or even how old she had been. She lifted the girl's arm to her mouth, not even noticing the familiar pentagram tattooed on the center of the wrist that marked her a member of the Wenham coven. With fangs exposed, Alee sank her teeth into the small wrist. There wasn't much blood left in the girl's almost-drained body, but the little Alee was able to swallow began to work instantly, dulling the pain.

Within an hour, Alee had fed on over twenty bodies. She was able to walk, and the swelling in her eye had receded. She hardly felt the burning in her back. She moved through the room looking for anyone who might still be alive. She found no one. As she examined body after body she began to understand the enormity of what had happened. Her memories of the evening began to return—slowly, like a puzzle, one piece at a time. It fueled her returning anger, and fed her hate.

Alee surveyed the bodies, the blood-soaked tablecloths, the wilting flowers, the wreckage, and then found herself in front of the statue of the three wiccan goddesses—the maiden, the mother, and the crone—and she remembered it all!

It was as if a light had been turned on in her head, and her memories began to play like a movie in front of her. She saw her mother trying to get her to safety. "—come with me!" Her mother's voice had been so calm and confident.

She saw Petra being grabbed, and Jacinda chasing after her. She heard Kyle's scream from across the room, "Alllleeeeraaaahhhhh," as the large white wolf attacked him. Then, as a dagger to her heart, she saw what happened next. The wolf became human again.

She paused the movie in her head and dashed desperately across the ballroom, trying to retrace the path she had taken during the chaos and confusion of that night. As she leapt over bodies and dodged fallen tables and chairs, she remembered Damian standing before her, covered in blood. *Damian?* She thought to herself. *How could he? Why?* Then, somehow, she tripped, and the pain came back like a wave up and down her spine, and consciousness faded. When she opened her eyes again she was lying on the floor, just inches from Kyle's cold, lifeless body. He almost looked peaceful— as if he had just drifted off to sleep. But Alee knew that wasn't the case. She knew he wasn't sleeping, nor had his death been peaceful.

Her breaths came shallow and fast. She was panicking, hyperventilating, trying to get to his side. "No, no, no— NO—NO—NO! Please don't leave me." She wasn't sure how much time had passed, but *she* had survived somehow, and maybe, just maybe, she thought, there might be hope for him too. She quickly rolled him over onto his back—it was easier than she thought it would be. He wasn't a small guy, and should have been much too heavy for her to move so easily on her own. But she couldn't think about that right then. It wasn't the time or the place.

As soon as Kyle was on his back, Alee started blowing air into his mouth and pounding on his chest in a frantic effort to revive him. With the first thrust she heard a rib crack, and yet she still continued. After what seemed like hours, she finally gave up, falling to a heap on his chest, sobbing into his already blood-soaked shirt. Nothing worked—she was alone.

Then she felt a soft breeze across her cheek. *'I'll always be with you.'*

"Kyle? Is that you?" She franticly searched the space around her, but he wasn't there. He was nowhere. His voice echoed so clearly in her mind, as if he were standing right behind her, but no matter how much she wanted for it to be so, she knew it wasn't possible, not with his lifeless body still cradled in her lap. "And now I'm going crazy." She said it out loud, because there was no reason not to, no one could hear her anyway.

She wasn't expecting a response, but she got one anyway. Her arm, from wrist to shoulder, started to burn. She wiped at the thick tacky blood that covered her arm and realized that the tattoo that wrapped its way around her right wrist was once again glowing. It was an occurrence that she had gotten used to, but it had only happened when she was working on a particularly hard spell, or when she was with Kyle. Eagerly, and hopefully, she pulled at the sleeve of Kyle's shirt, but there was nothing to see. If his tattoo were an indication of his chances for survival, it only confirmed what she already knew—Kyle was dead—whether she wanted to believe it or not.

She looked around the room, trying to figure out what was causing the reaction, and once again felt the cool breeze across her cheek. Then she felt a tingling sensation running up and down her spine. When she reached to tentatively touch her back, she could almost feel the skin moving, mending— healing itself at an alarming rate. *What the hell?* She thought to herself.

She looked around the abandoned ballroom, and spotted a knife on a nearby table. She snatched it up and slashed her left wrist before she had time to stop herself. The blood barely began to line the edges of the cut before the skin began to close up again.

Oh my God! The reality of her situation hit her: instant healing powers, superior vision, heightened hearing, and a ceaseless need to feed. She began slowly at first, searching her wrists then her throat, and finally directly above her heart— trying to find a pulse—but there was nothing. No sign of life. Well, no sign other than the walking and talking, but, where she lived, that just wasn't hard proof of life, these days.

"Listen again. It's there, only much weaker and slower." Her father's voice echoed through her mind, and she sat as still as she could. Trying to stop herself from trembling, she focused only on the sound and feel of her own body.

"Thump-thump." It took a few minutes, but she finally felt it. She collapsed back onto the floor, not knowing whether she should be happy or afraid.

She tried to remember what Eric, her father and full-blooded vampire, had told her, *"—completed the change— reborn— vampire—witch—vulnerabilities and strengths— immortal—"* but none of it made any sense. The only thing she could wrap her head around was the ever-growing hunger that was still building inside her, and the accompanying anger that made her want to rip out the throats of everyone responsible for what had happened this day.

She gave in to the hunger, because it was the only thing she could do. She didn't know how much time had passed when she finally stopped drinking, and even then she was still hungry.

As she finally crossed the ballroom toward the lobby, she fought the urge to stop and drink from every lifeless body that lay on the ground, as if offering itself up to her.

The lobby looked like a war zone. The elevator door had been blown off—exploded across the lobby. The walls of the elevator shaft had crashed in upon themselves. Bodies lay in piles across the floor—bloody, crumpled, and lifeless.

Alee stumbled her way to the bathroom across the rubble that covered the lobby floor. She stared at her blood-covered reflection, and she could almost hear Kyle behind her, "Hey, you look just like Carrie at her senior prom." It would be just like him to make a joke of it, but it wasn't anything to joke about and she knew it.

The mirror reflected Alee's familiar and greatly missed reflection. It had been a while since she had truly seen her real self—auburn red hair, pale porcelain skin, and soft pink lips. It pained her to realize it, but she knew she couldn't stay that way. She had a plan, or at least she was starting to formulate one. She knew her objective at least: to avenge Kyle's death—even if she didn't know exactly how to do it yet. What she did know was that she wouldn't be able to do anything if she showed up in Atlanta in the body of a dead girl, and according to everyone who had ever known her, Alee was six feet under with no sign of returning.

OK, well, maybe a few people had seen her last night at the Founders' Celebration, when she dropped the spell. *Was it really only last night? It feels like weeks—or at least days have passed since then.* She slapped her face a few times, forcing herself to re-focus.

Turning her back to the mirror, she kicked off her shoes, dropped her dress to the floor, and began to rinse the blood off her body from head to toe. It took the better half of an hour, but when she was done she felt clean, refreshed, and ready. Her hand flew to her throat, though, searching for the pendant that she had worn for years. She felt only the rapidly-healing wound around her neck, realizing that it must have been the pendant's silver chain that had been burning her—the necklace that she had torn off and flung to the ground. She wanted to run back to the ballroom and search the blood-covered floor until she found it, but she knew that if she didn't leave soon she never would. The blood smelled too good—too tempting. She needed to get out before it was too late.

She looked, one last time, at her reflection in the mirror, and whispered softly, "I cannot be seen. I cannot be felt. I cannot be heard. I cannot be smelt! I walk undetected, for only those I grant to see. And as I have spoken, so now shall it be!" Her reflection slowly faded until suddenly the room was empty, save for the pile of bloody clothes in the middle of the floor.

When she left for the ballroom, the only traces of her presence there in the ladies' room were her bloody footprints. It didn't take long to find the spot in the wall where she remembered seeing her mother disappear. She pounded on the brick a few times trying to unlock it, but she soon realized that it wasn't actually a door.

She pressed the palms of her hands against the rough brick so hard that they actually started to bleed. She closed her eyes, and her voice filled the room, echoing around her. "Open a door to the other side and grant me access where I can hide!"

The Wenham family was gathered, mourning the loss of their loved ones. Like so many other families throughout Atlanta, they huddled around their television to watch Mayor Albright deliver a live broadcast on the morning of November first. "The storms and tornados last night have caused the deaths of over a hundred Atlanta residents. We have declared a level one state of emergency within our city limits, and a dusk till dawn curfew has been set until further notice."

"What is he thinking? No one is going to believe there were tornados last night! It didn't even rain." You could hear the disgust in Phoebe's voice as she spoke. "People are dead, and he's trying to cover it up?!"

"Phoebe——." Loraline's voice was soft. She knew her niece was in pain; she had just lost her older sister, her mother, her grandmothers, the cousin who had quickly become her friend, and so many others, but this wasn't the time for their community to fall apart, let alone their family. Loraline knew that the Wenham Coven, being the oldest coven in Atlanta and still the largest, would have to be a big part of the relief effort throughout the Underground. "We are all hurting right now, but you know, as well as we all do, how important it is for us to stick together and, most crucial, to protect our identities."

Is she really saying this? Phoebe thought to herself.

Mayor Albright continued, monotone and distant, "— therefore, roadblocks have been set up along the city boarders. No visitors will be allowed to enter the town limits until the curfew has been lifted. In addition, Atlanta residents will not be permitted to leave until all residents are accounted for. Schools will be closed until Monday, November 15th, and we are asking that parents please keep their young children off the streets and safe at home until all disaster relief efforts have been completed." Mayor Albright maintained his composure throughout the remainder of the speech, and expressed sympathy for those who had suffered losses. Everyone in attendance at the press conference was obviously moved by his words, but Phoebe just shook her head, still biting her tongue, trying not to lash out.

When the newscast ended, the family began to disperse, and Phoebe made an excuse to go for a drive. The world seemed to be moving in slow motion around Atlanta, but only the true natives knew the real reason why, and they weren't talking. Everyone else just seemed to be walking around in a fog, mourning the tragic loss of so many loved ones, classmates, co-workers, and neighbors.

Then she saw it. On street after street, large trees lay across the roads, street signs were bent to the ground, and shingles had been ripped off of homes. Storm damage surrounded her, even though she knew not a single drop of rain had fallen. *No wonder no one is questioning anything,* Phoebe thought. No wonder they were blindly accepting the explanation that they had received, and were simply going forward with the search for ways to help rebuild their community.

Was it a vampire mind-game that was making everyone believe the lies? Maybe. But Phoebe didn't think so. Even vampires couldn't have made the trees fall, or caused the damage to the roofs all across town.

No one was talking, but Phoebe knew her family well enough to know that they were the only coven with enough power to have cast a spell strong enough to affect the entire town, both physically and mentally. She sought out Melissa and Michelle, her great-aunt Elaine's daughters, to ask them about it.

"Do you think the vampires could do something like this? Do you think they could actually change the memories of that many people in a single night? Could they cause all that damage?" They didn't answer her. They just busied themselves with their cooking, baking, cleaning—anything to keep their minds occupied.

"You know, I have a theory—." Phoebe continued. "Even without, you know—" she cleared her throat, "—we're still the largest family in town, and by far the strongest. Do you think that maybe Aunt Loraline—?"

"You shouldn't be messing around in things that don't concern you Phoebe. Things are the way they are for a reason, and that should be explanation enough."

"Really? Things that don't concern me! How can you say that? I'm part of this family too, aren't I?" Neither one of them bothered to look up from what they were doing, let alone give her the courtesy of a response. "You know, you two aren't that much older than I am. I don't see why you get—."

"Not that much older than you? You're a child. You're what, fifteen now?"

"Sixteen!"

"Fine, sixteen. Wow. We're nineteen years older than you! Nineteen, and in those years we have seen and been through much more than you can imagine. Things that you don't want or need to know about—and we're not talking good things—things that we hope you never have to see. So, yes, we *are* older than you. And yes, we will continue to protect you, because your mother can't do so any longer. Now drop this and leave it to the adults."

That was the end of the conversation, although it wasn't the end of Phoebe's curiosity. For now, she headed back home, not wanting to press her luck by staying out too long.

On her way home, Phoebe planned her strategy. Since Granny Edith's house was temporarily empty, Phoebe figured it would be the perfect place to do a little digging. Most of the family journals and spell books were kept at The Black Onyx, but Phoebe knew of a few very old journals that her grandmother had kept stashed away in her basement. Technically, it was her great great grandmother's and her great grandmother's home, but Phoebe had always just thought of them all as "the grandmothers." Shortly after Petra had come of age, Phoebe had seen Petra being led by Granny Edith to the basement door. Curious as usual, Petra had sat at the top of the basement stairs, eavesdropping. *"Being a tracker is a great honor,"* Granny Edith had begun, *"but it is also very dangerous, Petra. You are still so young, and ignorant in your craft. You must learn everything you can. Don't be afraid to seek help."* She had lifted the top off of an old metal chest, *"These were written many years ago, by my great-grandmother's Aunt Gilda. She was a tracker too— some say the first. At any rate, she was the first woman to possess the gift."*

"You mean—."

"Before her, only men—warlocks—were trackers. There is no proof that they possessed any powers or special abilities to track, except strength. When Gilda came into her powers, it was obvious what they were to be used for, just as yours are today. Her smaller size and lesser strength never held her back, and neither will yours."

"What's in the books?"

"Tracker spells—but they should only be used in extreme situations—emergencies. They are powerful. More powerful than anything I could create."

Phoebe could remember the conversation like it was yesterday. *I need those books,* she thought to herself. She wasn't yet sure what she would learn from them, but with Petra gone the thought had occurred to her that maybe her sister's powers would stay in the family—maybe even pass on to her.

Her plan to retrieve the books was going to have to wait for a while, though. When she got home, her dad was pacing the floor in the living room, regretting having allowed her to go anywhere alone with things still so unsettled throughout the town. She had a feeling it was going to be hard to get away from her father's watchful eye for a while, and that's exactly what happened.

For the next week, her dad hardly let her out of his sight for more time than it took to go to the bathroom. She couldn't really blame him. Besides, she hadn't really wanted to be alone anyway. However, now she had a mission, and that gave her the strength she needed to move forward. She couldn't necessarily move past what had happened, but after only a few days no one would have expected her to.

Through powers of persuasion that only a daughter can wield, she managed to convince her dad to let her go over to her best friend's house for the night. Tom knew Molly and her parents well, and he trusted that they would take care of Phoebe while she was there. Besides, he wasn't unreasonable. He knew that after losing her mother and sister, not to mention her grandmothers and her cousin, Phoebe probably needed a little "normal" kid time, even if just for a night.

"Sure, you can go."

"Really? Oh thank you Daddy. Thank you so much." Phoebe wrapped her arms around Tom's neck and squeezed as tightly as she could. "I love you, Daddy."

With tears close to the surface he replied, "I love you too, baby girl." He pulled away, holding her at arm's length. "You go straight to Molly's house. Stay there. I don't want you out on the streets after curfew. Do you understand?"

"Of course, Daddy, and I promise to be home first thing tomorrow morning, after breakfast of course. You know Molly's mom makes the best chocolate chip pancakes."

"Of course, after breakfast will be fine." He went to hug her one more time, but Phoebe was already out the door and down the hall. With her alibi in place, she didn't want to waste any time getting to her grandmother's house.

The last time Phoebe had been down in her grandmother's basement the metal chest had been shoved in a corner and covered in dust and cobwebs. She was betting that no one else even knew it was there. Petra had been a quick study and had only taken a week to read, review, and learn all of the spells in the books. Phoebe figured it was going to take her longer. She didn't have the same capacity for memorization that her sister had had.

When she arrived at the house she quickly found the hideaway key that her grandmothers kept under the potted plant on the porch. After slipping inside, she locked the door behind her and made her way through the living room toward the kitchen. As she was about to turn into the kitchen she noticed a soft flickering light coming from the bathroom down the hall. "Hello?" she called out, but no one answered.

Phoebe slowly made her way to the bathroom. Her grandmothers' house had always seemed unsettling to her when she was young and that hadn't changed as she got older. "Is anyone there?" she asked before quickly shoving the half open bathroom door and sending it slamming into the back wall, but no one was there. "What the—?" Phoebe picked up a small glass jar sitting on the bathroom counter. Inside was some sort of liquid with what looked like amber and glowing crystals. "What is this?" she asked aloud to no one. Carrying the glowing jar she made her way through the rest of the house, but all was as it should have been.

She spent the rest of the night flipping through the old leather-bound books, reading spell after spell, and hoping to find anything that might help. It was four thirty the next morning when she finally spotted it. She had brought the journal up to the kitchen, and about halfway through the book she read, in neatly written calligraphy, *A Tracker Awakens*.

She had been quickly turning page after page, not really sure what she was looking for. Then she came to what she had been seeking:

A Tracker Awakens
  Tracking is not only a set of talents given as gifts from the goddesses. It is a skill that has for centuries been taught, learned, and passed down—from generation to generation—in every coven around the world. Although some are better at scrying than others, every witch has in her the power to track those of her bloodline. Others, those we call trackers, develop the gift to track 'those who

must be found' for the safety and survival of our kind. Still others have learned, through the taking of blood, that tracking doesn't have to be merely guided by the calling, nor does it have to be bound by the ties of our relations.

The taking of blood. The taking of blood. The taking of blood. That one sentence would play over and over in Phoebe's mind for the rest of the day. She packed as many of the old journals into her backpack as she could fit and returned home by mid-morning.

"Hey Dad, I'm here," she called out, as she walked in the front door.

Tom was there in seconds. "How did it go? Are you all right?"

"I'm fine. Just hungry."

"Hungry? What about the chocolate chip pancakes?"

"Oh, yeah. Right. They were great. I think I'm just hungry because I haven't really been eating much since the—." She didn't finish her thought. She didn't have to.

"Don't worry about it. I'll put a plate together for you, sweetie." He turned toward the kitchen. "Why don't you go to your room and unpack. I'll have food ready in a few minutes."

"OK." Phoebe watched as her dad started taking breakfast items out of the pantry, and couldn't help the aching she felt in her heart. Their whole family had been ripped apart, and, being mortal, there was nothing her dad could do about it, but maybe she could. Maybe that's what really mattered now.

4

Alee stepped through the portal she had made, unsure of where it was going to take her, and was surprised to find herself standing in an authentic 1940's style kitchen. The walls were painted bright yellow to match the yellow countertops and yellow and white floor tile. White curtains with small yellow flowers were arranged along the window tops. Bright white cabinets lined the walls, and the appliances, likewise, were white. It was like stepping into a museum, or back in time. Alee had never seen a kitchen so organized and spotless, while being, somehow, so overwhelming at the same time.

The lights were off, but that didn't really matter—she was a vampire after all—a creature of the night. She couldn't hear anyone in the other rooms, so she started to move slowly through the kitchen. She recognized a familiar combination of scents that filled the air around her. Curious, she opened the cabinet door over the stove. She found the shelves filled with fresh seasonings and homegrown spices in jars with neatly handwritten labels. When she opened the next cabinet she wasn't at all surprised to see more glass jars and bottles of various sizes. Some were filled with oils, others with stones and crystals, and many were empty, waiting to be filled. It was a typical wiccan kitchen. *Typical wiccan kitchen?* If someone had told her a year ago that witches were living in Atlanta, let alone that she was one of them, she would have thought they were crazy. Yet here she was, drawing the obvious conclusion from her observations, and nothing about it seemed the least bit out of the ordinary. How life can change in just twelve months!

She knew what some of the items were, but certainly not all, or even most of them. There had to be hundreds of different ingredients. Everything looked to have been carefully selected, or grown and stored, by their owner. She searched the shelves, and finally selected a few of the jars. The first was filled with smooth pieces of golden amber crystals. The second contained a clear mineral oil. The last held a finely-ground crystal powder. Alee poured the oil into the jar of amber, whispering, "Bring to life the honey glow,—" Then she added a pinch of the crystal powder. "—through this amber let it flow!" She twisted the lid on tightly, and gently rolled the jar in her hands, mixing the ingredients, as she repeated the incantation a few more times. "Bring to life the honey glow, through this amber let it flow." As she spoke the words, the stones started to shimmer. "Bring to life the honey glow, through this amber let it flow." Then, with a sudden spark, the amber came to life in a golden radiance that filled the room around her.

It still surprised and excited her every time one of her spells worked, but this time she had no one to share her excitement with. Alee turned to where Kyle normally would have been, there behind her, waiting patiently and excitedly, and the image of him lying silent on the bloody floor came flooding back to her. She was alone—completely and utterly alone! The horror of what had happened sent a chill down her spine as she stood in this strange place, surrounded by so many familiar things.

She felt naked and vulnerable—and then she realized that she actually was naked. She quickly moved to explore the rest of the house, in search of something to cover up with. When she ducked into a bathroom down the hall, she glanced in the mirror only to find that there was no reflection of herself looking back. "Oh my God! What the—? Where the—?" She couldn't breathe as she slid to the floor grabbing a towel off the rack and wrapping it around herself.

"Just stay calm. There has to be a reason." Then it hit her. "Dracula. It's because of Dracula. Vampires don't have reflections. I'm a—I'm a vampire, so I don't—" The events of her 'awakening,' if you will, played through her head— drinking blood off the floor, finding Kyle's body, seeing the reflection of her true self in the bathroom mirror, washing the blood off of her body. "No, wait, I have a reflection. I just— ." She started to laugh out loud, forgetting to worry that someone might hear her. "That which is hidden be brought to

light. My image unclear be brought to sight." It worked
instantly, confirming, and reinforcing, her fear of being naked
in a stranger's house.

Holding the towel tightly around her, she left the
bathroom leaving her amber-powered lantern on the counter
and continued down the hall to a small sitting room. There
were afghans on the couch and chairs, and doilies on the end
tables. Although the room was perfectly decorated and just as
clean and organized as the kitchen, the overwhelming smell
of mothballs reminded Alee of her great-great granny Edith.

Why is it that all old people smell like mothballs? She
wondered.

The last time she had seen Granny Edith was in the
ballroom at the Founders' Celebration. As soon as the
lycanthropes burst into the room, Loraline had grabbed Alee
and her cousin and headed to where her family was gathering
at one of the far walls. Alee had seen Jathan create an
opening in the brick wall, and she had paused in her desperate
rush to Kyle to somehow send a psychic force that pushed her
mother through the opening to safety. At least she had hoped
it was safety that she was sending her mother into. The
alternative wasn't something she wanted to think about.

Jathan was there? Oh God, what did he do? She thought
to herself, trying to remember what had happened after she
pushed her mother through the hole he had created.

Jathan was a dream walker, or so she had been told, and
although he had seemed fairly harmless to Alee, everything
she had been told about dream walkers had been bad. They
were said to be manipulative creatures that could get into

your thoughts and dreams, making you do things that you wouldn't normally do.

Alee had never really believed that Jathan would harm her, but she couldn't explain what he had been doing there, at the Founders' Celebration, with her family. At least, from what she had seen, most of them had gotten out in time, but she hadn't.

"I haven't heard of him, but that could be because he's new in town—." Petra's words ran through Alee's mind.

So, maybe he is *a member. Maybe Petra just didn't know him.* She was standing in the entrance to the living room, not really focusing on anything in particular. *I'll have to ask her to look into it when I can go back home.* Alee knew that the constant cravings she was fighting were going to make it unsafe to go anywhere near her family for a while. Even though Eric had told her that he and her mother would be there for her throughout her change, Alee didn't want to risk hurting them. Besides, in that moment she didn't have time to think, or even care, about them. She had something to take care of, and, in her opinion, that trumped everything.

Searching for a clue as to where she was, she went to a bookshelf across the room and picked up the first framed picture she saw. There was a young Edith and her husband John. John, by all accounts, was legendary. He had been the primary negotiator in the truce between the Wenham coven and the Henley clan. Alee had heard the story more than once, and she had seen that same picture every day for months, hanging in the hallway of The Black Onyx. But this wasn't The Black Onyx. So whose house was it? Granny Edith's?

She quickly started weeding through the bookshelves, searching the drawers of the end tables, and finally found a pile of mail on the credenza in the foyer. She sifted through it, looking for only one thing—a name—and she found it! Edith Wenham!

"Wow! So, this is Granny Edith's house." She turned, slowly looking around, seeing the house in a completely different light. When she had thought it was a stranger's house she had been nervous to touch anything—but she did it as a necessity. Now, knowing it was her great great grandmother's house, she was *terrified* to touch anything!

Alee had never been to Granny Edith's house—not for lack of wanting to see it, but because Granny Edith rarely had anyone over to visit these days. She and Granny Estelle had lived there alone since the deaths of their husbands—or rather, the murder of their husbands. When their husbands died, Granny Edith and Granny Estelle transferred all of the necessary family items—spell books, potions, even the family journals—to The Black Onyx, making it unnecessary for anyone to visit their home. It wasn't that no one ever went there; it just wasn't especially weird that Alee had never had occasion to be there. Phoebe had once told Alee that her mother, Jacinda, thought the reason that the grandmothers hadn't wanted their home to become a family hub was that they were trying to preserve the memory of their husbands. *Phoebe* thought there was more to it than that, although she wouldn't say what.

It was clear that no one was home at the moment, but Alee couldn't be sure that the grandmothers wouldn't be home soon. She wanted to gather anything she might need before they got back, and, for starters, that meant clothes.

Searching through the closets in the bedrooms did nothing for her. Everything was too big, too small, or too old. It wasn't that she was trying to be picky—she just couldn't imagine wearing a baby-blue polyester pantsuit while avenging her dead boyfriend. Besides, all the movies she had watched as a child had taught her that vampires were supposed to be trendy—not fashion victims.

Continuing her search, she noticed that the door to what must be a basement was ajar. She made her way down the stairs, where she found boxes and boxes on the shelves lining the wall. The boxes at the very top had the word DONATION scribbled across the front. She quickly pulled one of these boxes down and started scrounging through it. There were skirts, shirts, and jeans, and everything seemed to be in fairly good shape, and, even though they were about ten years out of date, they weren't your typical granny attire—and she could live with that. She pulled on a pair of jeans and a light yellow t-shirt. She also found a pair of flip-flops that fit her just fine, and they actually matched the shirt.

Something of a plan was starting to come together, so Alee headed back to the kitchen. She went through the cupboards, gathering up samples of all the ingredients she recognized and stashing these in an old shopping bag she found next to the refrigerator. She made sure to take from the back, so, at first glance, no one would notice anything missing. She tossed the bag behind a bush just outside the back door, then went back inside and lay down for a short nap. She figured if her grandmothers came home she would hear them come in and be able to slip out the back door, grab the bag, and be gone, without their noticing that anyone had been there.

Her plan hadn't failed; it just hadn't gone quite the way she had expected. When she finally woke up, the sun was already shining brightly, and the clock read eight fifteen. She had slept through the night, and neither of her grandmothers had come home. She was groggy and had to practically drag herself into the kitchen, where the only thing she could find to eat was oatmeal. This was odd—you would think that there would be milk, or juice, or bread, or something. Come to think of it, the whole house was a little odd. It looked as if it had just been professionally cleaned. Not a thing was out of place—even the afghans and doilies in the living room were perfectly placed. Maybe the grandmothers spent more time at The Black Onyx than Alee realized.

To say that she found the mere idea of oatmeal to be less than appetizing would be putting it politely, but since it was her only choice, she prepared herself a bowl. She took the first bite and almost vomited. There was no way oatmeal was going to satisfy the burning hunger that was building in the pit of her stomach.

She knew what she needed, and how to get it, but hunting at eight in the morning wasn't her idea of a good time. However, starving to death wasn't really an option either, if that was even possible for a vampire. She still wasn't a hundred percent sure of all the rules.

Eric had tried to explain to her, as much as he could, what it would be like when she completed her change. But there had never been a surviving dhampir before, which made it rather difficult for him to know for sure what life after, well, life, was going to be like for her. What he could and did tell her was how and what to hunt in order to stay alive. He explained that being immortal didn't mean you couldn't be killed. He hadn't gone into the gory details of how to avoid the "true death" as he called it. That was OK, she knew the basics from growing up watching horror films, or at least she thought she did. Don't touch a cross with your bare skin, stay away from holy water and silver, and, most importantly, don't get staked in the heart. So those would be the ground rules for her survival now. She especially thought the "don't get staked in the heart" rule was a good one.

In an effort to wake up a little more, she headed down the hall and searched though the closet in the guest bedroom. She exchanged her flip-flops for an old pair of tennis shoes and pulled them on, not wanting to run through the woods barefoot. She opened the back door a crack and looked toward the tree line that was only about twenty feet from the house.

There wasn't another house for at least a half a mile so she had no fear of making too much noise and causing suspicion. The problem wasn't that she was afraid of being seen. She could always cast another cloaking spell if she had to. The problem was the sun. She knew she had completed her change, but what she didn't know was the weaknesses that came along with it. Basically, she wasn't sure if she had or hadn't developed an allergy to the sun in the process of her transformation. The last thing she wanted was to become barbeque her first morning as a vampire. Eric had told her that it takes years, hundreds of years, for vampires to even wake up during the daylight hours, let alone walk under the sun. What if she was no different? What if she burned to a crisp the moment the sunlight touched her skin? But then again, since birth, Alee had never been like other vampires. The fact that she was walking around, able to talk to herself at that very moment, hours after the sun had come up, proved that she wasn't "normal," if you can even call vampires normal.

"Just do it!" She said out loud. "It's daylight. You're already awake. You haven't been a vampire for even a week, let alone hundreds of years, so you're already a step ahead." It made sense, and she knew it, but that first step was still hard.

She opened the door a little more, and held her fingertips out into the nearest beam of light, then gradually inched her hand out until it was entirely bathed in sunlight. Nothing happened, which seemed promising, so she pulled the door open and stepped out onto the back porch. When she still didn't burst into flames, she let out a deep breath she hadn't even realized she had been holding and whispered, "Oh, thank God."

She double checked that the bag she had stashed outside the door was still there, in case her grandmothers came home, and she took off for the woods. It took only minutes to catch a small rabbit and even less time to drain it. Feeding increased her energy almost instantly, but the rabbit wasn't going to be enough to sustain her. She hadn't even realized how sluggish she had been until she didn't feel that way anymore. It was as if a weight had been lifted off her shoulders, and she was almost floating through the woods as she ran full speed, hunting and feeding on animal after animal.

When the burning finally stopped and she felt fully satisfied, she rested against a tall oak tree and stared into the woods around her. It wasn't until then that she noticed that it was cold enough that she could see her breath. Yet, with just jeans and a t-shirt, she wasn't cold. *Wow, I could get used to this. I'm usually freezing in eighty-degree weather.* It was only a passing thought, and it was interrupted by the crackling of a branch under the weight of an approaching deer.

She killed three more animals, two deer and a mountain lion. One by one, Alee half dragged half carried the animals back to the house. With her new super-human strength it wasn't that they were too heavy, but their awkward weight distribution made it hard for her to balance them. There was an old storm cellar connected to the back of the house, sealed up with a chain and padlock. Alee easily broke the chain off with her bare hands, and dragged each of the dead animals down the stairs and into a small room at the far end of the cellar. It was November 1, and already starting to show signs of an early snowfall. It was probably cold enough to keep the animals outside, but it was at least fifteen degrees cooler down in the cellar, and Alee guessed that the cold cement walls would help keep the animals preserved for at least a day or two longer. She was hoping she could last at least that long before needing to feed again.

No! She couldn't!

Apparently, the thirst of a new vampire never really goes away.

Despite the fact that she was beginning to have her suspicions about her grandmothers' absence, and, truthfully, deep down, she already knew the explanation, which was soon confirmed, she was will a little worried that they would eventually return home. So, she used some fallen tree branches to disguise the broken lock.

She spent the majority of the next couple of weeks, when she wasn't hiding out at one of a few secluded spots in the woods that she and Kyle liked to visit, feeding at least two or three times a day and adjusting to the changes her body was going through. She had to learn to control both her anger and her hunger if she was ever going to be able to go back to her family, let alone avenge Kyle's death.

She watched the news most nights, glued to the well-written and fully-rehearsed lie-filled speeches that were coming from every official, every reporter, and every bystander on every channel. *It was a great tragedy—affecting so many families—the natural disaster that hit this tiny town—and so on.* Did anyone really believe this? When the names of the dead and missing scrolled across the bottom of the screen she was shocked at how many names she recognized—classmates she never would have guessed were part of the Underground—neighbors she had known growing up as a child. Even one of the nurses who had taken care of Alee a thousand times when she was just a little girl, was on the list. She read each name, wondering if they were a witch, a vampire, or another member of the Underground, or if they had been part of the lycanthropes' attack. Who had been victims, and who had been part of the reason for this needless loss?

Alee had grown up watching movies that portrayed vampires as heartless, vicious creatures, without an emotional connection to anything or anyone; they were soul-less creatures driven by one thing and one thing only—self-preservation! But she didn't feel that way. She was a vampire, and even though the hunger and need for survival was there, she wasn't heartless. She still cared. She still loved. In fact, it was her love for Kyle and her need to avenge his death that was probably the one thing keeping her going.

She wanted so much to go home to her family—to ask for their help. But she knew she wasn't ready. She couldn't control her blood lust enough yet, and she wasn't willing to risk hurting them.

And then there it was—scrolling across the television screen with all the other names of the deceased—Edith Wenham, Estelle Wenham, Jacinda Wenham, Petra Wenham, and even her own name. Alee felt physically crushed by the enormity of it—the unthinkable loss of these people who had come to mean so much to her, and the life-altering losses of the other family members who had survived. She had suspected, even feared this, but the fact, the *finality*, of it was mind-numbing, sickening. She drew up her legs, wrapped her arms around her knees, dropped her head, and wept.

Slowly, even though the tears, through the spinning scenarios of loss, in the depths of her consciousness, the ember that had been driving her survival was fueled by this new level of loss. She was already teaching herself to control her hunger—to control her change—by replacing the hunger for the blood her body needed with hunger for the blood she needed even more. She focused on that. It was all she needed, more than life itself: the blood of those who had slain her family, who had slain Kyle—the blood of the shifters! She was determined, now more than ever, to make sure that everyone responsible for what had happened would suffer.

"Phoebe? Honey, can you come to the kitchen please?"
Phoebe's dad had taken on the roles of both mother and father
since Jacinda died, and he had introduced strict dinnertime
rules. "Phoebe, dinner is on the table!"

"I know, I'll be right there." Phoebe had spent every
waking hour of the last couple of weeks locked in her room
reading through the journals she had managed to get from her
grandmothers' basement. She had meant to go back for more,
but she ended up having so much to read with the ones she
had that there just hadn't been time. Besides, with "drill-
sergeant" Dad watching her every move and regulating her
food intake, she didn't think she would make it out of the
house very long before he would be in quick pursuit.
Everything would have been fine, only he had found out that
she had lied about going to stay the night at her friend
Molly's house. Then, when she wouldn't tell him where she

had really been, she got grounded—for about the rest of her life.

She had already shoved the journals under her bed, thrown her headphones over her ears to pretend like she had been listening to music, and was about to walk out the door when her dad was right there, knocking. She yanked open the door, like a little joke, but her dad wasn't buying it.

"Phoebe, I wasn't kidding," her dad barked, as he stepped back a half step.

"No, I know Dad. You're never kidding." Even as the words were escaping her lips she regretted saying them. She could see it all over his face—pain—sorrow—isolation. "Dad, I'm sorry. I didn't mean—."

"Yes, you did. But, it's OK. We're both hurting and I'm sorry I've been so hard on you. It's just that I can't—. I couldn't handle it if—." He wasn't even looking at her any more.

"Dad, nothing is going to happen to me. I'm right here. I'm fine—. I mean, yeah, I'm hurting too, but I'm here and I'm OK. We're going to be OK." She took a step forward and gave him a quick hug. She had to be the one in control. The strong one. "Listen Dad, it's OK, you're OK. I don't mind eating dinner with you, or breakfast, or even lunch. It's kind of nice actually." She noticed that he smiled for the first time in weeks. "And if it would make you feel better, you can drive me to school and pick me up for the next few weeks."

"Really?" He was watching her now, carefully. Because the Phoebe he knew would never have given up her driving privileges. "You'd do that?"

"If it makes you feel better, sure."

He hugged her, tightly. It was the type of hug only a daddy can give, and even Phoebe had to admit that it felt good. "No, no I don't need to drive you. You're a big girl and I know that. Besides, I'm sure you don't need me hanging around while you scrounge through your grandmothers' house after school tomorrow to look for more of their old journals."

"What?" She tried to act innocent, but she had never been a great liar.

"Don't worry, you're not in trouble. If I had even an ounce of your powers I would be searching through the books too, but I don't. Sometimes being just a normal human really sucks. Just promise me something, OK?"

"What?"

"Promise me that you won't do anything without talking to me first. I may not have powers, but that doesn't mean I'm helpless. Your Aunt Loraline, your Uncle Eric, your Aunts Michelle and Melissa, your whole family is here for you and we all want to make whoever did this pay, just as badly as you do. But they can't do it alone and neither can you."

They stood there in silence for a moment. "Phoebe?"

"Yeah, no, I know. I promise. I won't do anything stupid OK? I promise to talk to you first, no matter what."

"Good. Good, that's good." He stood there for a moment, as if contemplating something before finally speaking again, "You remember your grandmothers' house has a cellar, right?"

"Um, yeah, I guess. I hadn't really thought about it, but it's out back right?"

"That it is." He didn't elaborate, but instead just pulled her in for one last hug before turning to go. "Now let's go. Dinner's probably already cold."

He was gone, and she stared at the empty doorway wondering why he had asked about the cellar. More importantly, she considered what it was that she had just promised him, and how mad he was going to be when she couldn't keep that promise. "Oh well, I can't worry about that right now."

Dinner was good, and after she helped with the dishes her dad left her alone to thumb through the journals in her room. It already felt better not having to hide them from him anymore. Around eleven o'clock she fell asleep somewhere in the middle of reading about 'marking' spells.

Her alarm went off at six thirty in the morning, reminding her that it was the first day back at school, and she realized that somehow she didn't remember having fallen asleep. She was still in the clothes she had worn the day before, and, except for her hair that was sticking straight up on the side where bedhead had set it, she didn't look half bad. She chose her outfit and jumped into the shower. When she came out, she opted for a whole different outfit before she went down to the kitchen for breakfast with her dad.

"Dad?" she called. He wasn't in the kitchen that morning, which was extremely unusual, at least for recent weeks. "Dad, are you gonna have breakfast with me?" He didn't answer as she called down the hall.

Just as she was grabbing for the phone it began to ring. "Hello?"

"Good morning sweetheart. There's breakfast waiting for you in the microwave. It should still be warm. Drive safely to school and I'll see you when you get home tonight."

"Wait, what? Where are you?"

"I'm with your Aunt Loraline and Uncle Eric. But there's nothing to worry about. We're just going over some options."

"But—."

"I only called because I didn't want you to worry, and because I wanted to make sure you eat your breakfast. Now, go eat and don't be late for school." He hung up before Phoebe had a chance to respond.

"Wow. Well, goodbye to you too Dad." She hung up the phone and went to the microwave. Sure enough he had made chocolate chip pancakes and they were still warm. She even had to admit that they were just as good as the ones Molly's mom made.

That wasn't the last call she would receive that morning. Shortly after she left for school she got a voice mail from her grandfather, asking her to call him at The Black Onyx. She did, but all he wanted to know was Damian and Victoria's last name. She told him and he quickly said his goodbyes. It wasn't the strangest thing that had happened lately, so she tossed the phone in her purse and made her way up the school walkway.

At first she thought she had walked into the wrong building. The hallway walls were plastered from floor to ceiling with hand-painted banners calling all students to take action and raise money for those who were suffering from the recent disaster. Phoebe was struck with a sudden chill, and she zipped up her black hoodie wrapping it more tightly around herself. *What the hell--did everyone get up at the butt crack of dawn to come to school and paint posters?*

Teachers up and down the hallways were organizing their homeroom students to create donation boxes for the collection of items for the relief efforts. Even Principal Davis was showing his support to the "storm" victims by allowing relief effort activities to take precedence over regular class schedules for all students willing to volunteer their time.

Phoebe spent most of the morning wandering from class to class, not wanting to participate in the so-called relief efforts. She knew the truth. Even though she hadn't been invited to the Founders' Celebration, she had in fact been there that night. She had seen first-hand the battle that took place. She had heard the crying and pleading of those being attacked. The only reason she had survived was because Jathan had somehow found her hiding, curled up behind a long floor-to-ceiling curtain that hung on the wall behind the head table. Kyle had put her there just after the attacks had started. He had told her not to move, and she hadn't. Well, she hadn't moved until she was startled awake by Jathan's arms wrapped around her, lifting her off the ground.

The next thing Phoebe knew, she was being laid down on a couch at The Black Onyx. Her father was sitting with her. He wouldn't stop crying. At the time she hadn't known the extent of what had happened to her family, but she had already realized that the memory of all those innocent people

being viciously attacked and murdered would haunt her
dreams for a long time to come. Thus, she now knew she
wanted no part of the storm relief efforts taking place at
school or across town. The mere idea that they would lie to
the community about what really had happened made her
sick.

Shortly after she sat down at her desk in third period, a
shrill scream was heard from down the hall. Everyone,
including Phoebe, was up out of their seats in seconds, trying
to see out the doorway and into the hall. "Back to your seats.
I'll be right back," said Mr. Evans, Phoebe's biology teacher.
He left, closing the door behind him. The commotion settled
after a little, and Phoebe and her classmates were back in
their seats talking and doodling on the desktops when Mr.
Evans got back. "All right, let's get started."

"What was it? Who was screaming?" Phoebe wasn't the
only one who was interested, and Mr. Evans could see that
although they were in their seats they weren't going to be
able to pay much attention to the lesson unless he told them
what had happened.

He closed the door and went to the chalkboard.
"Headache is all. Vicki Ward, but she'll be fine. She's going
to see Nurse Green."

"Victoria?" Phoebe interrupted.

Mr. Evan's eyes went right to Phoebe, he wasn't the type
of man that liked to be corrected. "Excuse me?"

Phoebe's eyes dropped to her desk, realizing that she had
just snapped at her teacher, but she was concerned, and
sometimes she tended to speak without thinking. "I'm sorry, I

didn't mean to interrupt. I was just asking if you mean Victoria Ward, not Vicki."

"Yes fine, Victoria not Vicki." Turning his attention back to the chalkboard, he wrote the reading assignment on the board. He had obviously lost interest in the short-lived commotion in the hall. "Now, let's get back to class, shall we? Or do you have something else you'd like to say, Ms. Wenham?" She just shook her head, wondering what could have caused Victoria to scream like that, and knowing that it couldn't have just been a headache. No one in their right mind screams when they have a headache.

Phoebe had been having chills all morning, since she first stepped into the school building, and she was starting to be afraid that she might be getting sick. She stopped by her locker on her way to lunch and exchanged her black hoody for a heavier fall jacket. Then, taking a short detour, she poked her head in the nurse's station to check on Victoria. She was surprised to see that the place was far from empty, but Victoria wasn't there. When Phoebe asked, Nurse Green said, "I'm sorry but Ms. Ward hasn't been to see me at all today."

Why would Mr. Evans have lied about Victoria? She brushed the thought aside as Nurse Green interrupted her thoughts.

"I'm sorry, but is that all? I really need to get back to the others. We've had an awful lot of sick students this morning. But if I see her, I'll tell her you were looking for her."

Phoebe looked around the room again and realized that there *were* an awful lot of sick students today. All of the seats were taken, and, more students were sitting on the floor, lining the walls. She remembered to reply to the nurse, "Oh! Yeah, OK. Thanks." Although Victoria and Phoebe were far from friends, Victoria's reputation, including her stubbornness was well known throughout the school. Phoebe figured that Victoria had probably just decided she didn't want to go see the nurse.

When Phoebe finally made it to lunch, students were sitting silently in small groups scattered throughout the cafeteria. No one moved, spoke, or even looked up at her as she made her way to the back of the room, to her normal table. She set her tray down next to a girl she didn't recognize, wondering why she was sitting at "their" table. The girl turned slightly, but didn't quite make eye contact as she spoke. "Hey," she said. It was little more than a whisper, but it seemed to catch the attention of everyone at the surrounding tables.

Phoebe was stunned. "Wow, Molly, you changed your hair." Phoebe's eyes were wide at the realization that her friend was almost unrecognizable. Molly had, for the longest time, dyed her hair black in an effort to fit in more with Phoebe and Petra. It had never looked a hundred percent natural, but Phoebe had gotten used to it. Seeing her now with her natural blonde curls, looking more innocent and fragile than eccentric and Goth, didn't feel right somehow.

"Yeah, I just—." Tears started to fill her eyes and she couldn't go on.

Phoebe noticed that Kim was nowhere in sight and the cafeteria was so quiet you could have heard a pin drop. She tried to sound strong through her trembling voice. "Don't worry, I get it." Phoebe had done what most girls do. A few nights before school started up again, she had called her two best friends, Molly and Kim, and told them everything that had happened. They already knew she was a witch. She knew it was against the rules, but the three of them had been friends for years, and they didn't keep secrets from each other.

Molly gathered her things with shaking hands and stood up, holding her tray as steady as possible. "I'm sorry. I just—. I can't be here. I thought I could, but I can't." Then she turned and walked away.

It took a lot to affect Phoebe, but Molly walking away like that had a definite impact. She knew that in those few words, one of her closest friends was walking away from their friendship, most likely forever. It wasn't because of who she was, but because of what she was. Molly understood that Phoebe had nothing to do with all of the innocent deaths, Phoebe was certain of that. Phoebe guessed that even the strength of their friendship couldn't help Molly to separate Phoebe from those who were the real villains.

Molly's opinion of The Underground had been tainted when she learned the truth about what had happened to her classmates, her friends, and her community, and Phoebe could see how Molly couldn't help but blame everyone involved, including Phoebe and her family. For Phoebe, the worst part of this bad situation was that Molly still cared. She cared enough to keep Phoebe's secret, and that, too, was eating Phoebe up inside. Sitting there alone, at the empty table, watching her friend walk away without even looking back, Phoebe wished more than anything that she hadn't shared so much. She wished she could take it all back, make Molly forget.

Toward the end of the lunch period, Phoebe, and everyone else, was startled by a loud scream coming from the other side of the cafeteria. A sophomore boy who Phoebe vaguely recognized was sitting on the floor with his hands over his head screaming. *Free headaches for everyone. Come one, come all!* Phoebe thought to herself. A few of his friends helped him up, and off to the nurse's station.

In class after class her teachers assigned free study time instead of doing their normal lectures. Not having a clear assignment or task always made the clock tick more slowly somehow. When sixth period was over and the bell finally rang, it took Phoebe mere seconds to gather her stuff and make it to her car. She was barreling down the road in no time, heading straight for Granny Edith's empty house.

Driving through town, she noticed that all the local businesses had donation boxes of their own set up outside their doors. Restaurants had signs advertising free meals for families who had lost loved ones in the storms. Even the small consignment shop downtown was overflowing with donations. Funeral arrangements were being made all across town for those who had died, even though only a handful of bodies were actually recovered—two of whom were Edith and Estelle Wenham. Obituaries filled the local paper, and for two weeks now the news broadcasts had been streaming the names of hundreds of Atlanta residents who were reported missing or presumed dead.

As she pulled up the long dirt driveway to her great great grandmother's home, memories came flooding back. She had been there less than two weeks earlier to get the journals, but somehow this visit felt different. She parked on the side of the house, out of habit, but instead of making her way to the porch she stood and stared out into the back yard remembering all the fun times she and her sister Petra had had back there when this had been the family hub. Their old tire swing was still hanging from the big oak tree. Off in the distance she could see the small opening in the tree line where the trails started.

As she slammed the car door shut behind her, she could almost hear Petra's voice calling, "Granny's got cookies for us. Come on."

Phoebe took a step toward the back porch and a chill ran through her as a cool breeze brushed her cheek and she heard a door slam shut, almost as if on cue, but no one else was here, and the door had never opened.

"Hello? Is someone there?" She called out into the empty yard, but her voice got lost in the sudden whistling wind that picked up fallen leaves and blew them across the driveway and into the air in front of her. *Of course there's no one there! Get yourself together!* She was thinking rationally, or trying to at least. She tried to convince herself to go on in, but something in the back of her mind wouldn't let her. The house had felt empty when she had been here only weeks before. But now—now there was an energy buzzing around her that she couldn't quite explain.

Instead of heading toward the porch and into the house like she had planned, she went around the patio, and stood in front of a large wooden cellar door. *'You remember your grandmothers' house has a cellar, right?'* It was such an odd question for her dad to ask, but as she stood in front of the door, she was certain that he had had a reason for asking.

The chain on the door had been broken off, and lay in a pile on the ground with the padlock still attached. She hesitated, but then reached out, grasped the rusty handle, and pulled the door upward from its resting position. The hinges were rusty as well, but after a few hard pulls she finally got the door open. It was dark and musty-smelling, but she went down the steep, narrow steps and across to another door that stood slightly ajar. She saw a dim, flickering light through the crack of the doorway, but she couldn't see anything else, even by pressing her face against the sliver of an opening and squinting.

She was starting to feel creeped out about the whole thing, and was about to turn and go back up the stairs when the door behind her slammed shut. Phoebe was left standing in utter darkness, with only the soft light of what seemed to be a candle that was threatening to burn out, in the room in front of her. She swallowed hard, took a deep breath, and opened the door into the small empty room. The outline of a circle of white sand had been laid out in the center of the room and five candles, burned almost all the way down to the ground, had been placed just within the circle's protection.

Of course, having grown up in a family of wiccan belief, Phoebe recognized a ritually cast circle when she saw one.

However, this circle was complete—closed—and the candles were still burning, yet no one was inside. Although Phoebe was still young, she knew well enough that you never exit a ritual circle without performing a ceremonial cutting, and as she circled the sand she saw no indication that a line had been drawn across the sand to break the circle. Phoebe's Granny Edith had stressed, on numerous occasions, the dangers of exiting a cast circle in the wrong way. And now, to find a ceremonial circle left empty, with candles still lit, obviously not cleared at all, let alone correctly, brought Phoebe near to panic.

Her first thought was to just *leave*, but as she turned, the door slammed shut, blocking her escape. She tugged at the handle, but the knob fell off in her hand, leaving the door locked in its place. Phoebe knew it was still daylight outside, but the windows, almost touching the ceiling far too high above her head to reach, were covered in dust so thick that the light couldn't penetrate into the bleak tomb that surrounded her. She looked around, noticing that the cellar was a lot like the one at her house and the one out in the back of The Black Onyx. Phoebe never did understand why her parents hadn't expanded the space, connecting their cellar to their fully finished basement, instead of leaving it separate and so primitive.

Backing up against the door, Phoebe lifted her arms to cover her eyes and took slow deep breaths, trying hard to steady her racing heart, but the flickering candles almost seemed to be dancing to the rhythm of her heartbeat. The more she tried to block it out the brighter they seemed to become—the higher the flames seemed to burn. Then, suddenly, she was being pulled away from the door and into the circle, but by what she had no idea. She tried to fight it, grasping at the doorframe, but it was no use. Whatever had a hold of her was too strong.

As she crossed the circle of sand she could feel a current of energy flowing through her body from her feet all the way up to her head. The heat from the candles was so intense that beads of sweat formed across her forehead, though this didn't last long. Once she was in the center of the circle the temperature dropped at least twenty degrees and she immediately started to shiver. She tried to curl up into a ball on the floor to keep warm, but something or someone was holding her upright, preventing her from sitting. "You aren't safe here." It was a familiar voice that she couldn't quite recognize, and it was more desolate, more desperate than any she had ever heard. Without further warning, a sharp pain penetrated her throat and she collapsed into the arms of her attacker.

As far as Alee calculated it had been a little over two weeks since the Founders' Celebration. But then again she wasn't really sure how long she had been "asleep." In reality she knew that she hadn't been asleep, but it made her feel better to think about it that way. There was no getting around the fact that sleeping sounded better than dead.

She had spent that time hunting, feeding, and alone in the woods remembering her time with Kyle. On the rare occasion when she wasn't doing one or the other of these three new favorite hobbies, she was trying to work on spells at Granny Edith's house. One Sunday night she saw a newscast stating that the local schools were going to re-open the next day. She didn't care if she was ready or not, she wasn't going to wait any longer. Besides, in her mind, the worst thing that could happen would be that she would lose what little control she had gained and end up feeding on one of the animals that had killed Kyle or her grandmothers. *That wouldn't be much of a loss,* she thought to herself.

Early that morning, before the sun had even risen, she slipped into the main campus building through an open window at the back. She went through the halls, placing small potion pouches in discreet places throughout the building. If she had learned anything over the last month or so since discovering the Guardian bands it was how to detect a lycanthrope.

Alee wasn't stupid. She wasn't planning an attack, or even a trap. Not knowing how many there might be, she wasn't going to risk getting herself out numbered in a fight. Her plan was only to identify who they were by utilizing a spell similar to, but not quite as strong as, the one her family had once used to keep vampires out of The Black Onyx. She thought that if she could make them uncomfortable enough, she would be able to identify who they were, allowing her to decide how and when to proceed later, one on one.

Alee used black tourmaline crystals as the main ingredient in her potion. Tourmaline crystals are interesting because they are pyro-electric, meaning that when they are heated, one side of the crystal develops a positive charge, and the other side develops a negative charge. This change can result from a number of things, such as a change in temperature or even vibrations. However, Alee had experienced firsthand that when the crystal comes in contact with a lycanthrope it has the same reaction, and the energy behind the positive and negative charges can lead to pretty severe burns. She hadn't known it at the time, but the scar burned into Victoria's palm was the first of many signs Alee had missed about her friend's true identity.

This seemingly nonthreatening smooth black stone, often used to increase luck and happiness, can also be used to ward off negative energy, thus minimizing the dangers from encroaching shifters and other potential enemies. Alee was hoping that a combination of the crystal and the spell would allow her to identify the shifters, or at least scare them back into hiding.

The morning bell rang just after she had hidden the last potion pouch. The pouches were spread throughout the hallways and a few had been placed in the cafeteria. She quickly tossed the empty duffle bag in her locker, and headed out to do a little recon.

Her plan for the day was pretty simple: follow Damian and Victoria around and see who they were working with. She knew their mother had been involved in the attack—Alee had seen Karen at the Founders' Celebration. Karen had basically *led* the attack, but still Alee didn't believe she could have been the one responsible for it, or maybe she just didn't want to believe it. Karen had always been such a soft-spoken, gentle woman. She just didn't seem the type. That was Alee's impression at least, until she saw her leaping across the head table and transforming into a mountain lion as she launched an attack on Principal Davis.

Alee also wanted to see if she could find out where Jathan had been hiding himself all year. She knew where all of her other friends lived, but everything about Jathan remained a mystery. That hadn't seemed at all strange to Alee until their weird encounter in the cave a few weeks back. Alee figured that with her new stealth-like invisibility spell, and the shadow-weaving she had been practicing as a backup, she just might be able to follow him home without his knowing she was there. At least she hoped so, because she hadn't quite learned how to make her clothing disappear, and being spotted naked was not her idea of a good time.

She waited in the hallway near the main entrance, but Damian and Victoria never showed up. Jathan was missing in action too. Alee was beginning to worry, when she finally saw Phoebe walk in. She felt a wave of relief, and followed Phoebe through the hallways and into her first class. She spent the morning tagging along next to Phoebe, from one class to the next.

Nothing out of the ordinary happened until third period, when everyone heard a loud scream coming from down the hall. "Stay in your seats. I'll be right back," said Mr. Evans, Phoebe's biology teacher. He was a portly man—not someone you would expect to run to the rescue of a damsel in distress by any stretch of the imagination. Alee slipped through the door right behind him. Just because she was invisible didn't mean she could walk through walls. She had to rely on other people to open doors for her; otherwise she would raise suspicion—*random doors opening? Maybe even a few flickering lights. Hmmm, that could be fun.*

Out in the hallway, she headed in the direction of the scream. She could hear students making a commotion in classrooms all around her as teachers urged them to go back to their seats.

When she got to the end of the science wing she turned a corner and saw Victoria curled up in a ball holding her head in her hands, crying and screaming at the same time. *Oops, I guess that one was a little more powerful than I expected,* Alee thought to herself.

She knelt down behind Victoria, and the subtle scent of wolf washed over Alee, thrusting her back to the moment the great wolf had thrown her to the floor. She remembered how it felt to have her back sliced through by claws as sharp as knives. She remembered trying to turn herself around to fight off the chocolate brown wolf, and looking for just a moment into its deep brown eyes before it overpowered her. *It was you!* At once, her fangs were exposed and she fought every instinct not to bite down into the warm pulse just beneath the flesh of Victoria's throat. *I'm better than this. I'm better than her. I need to know more.* The enormity of the revenge she sought sustained her. She needed to find and punish them *all*, not just this one.

Alee tried to contain her rage by biting her own lip and, with shaking hands, she lifted Victoria to her feet. Victoria was in so much pain from the headache that she didn't even notice someone helping her, or even the fact that *no one*, at least no one visible, was helping her. "It's just a headache," Alee called out to the teachers coming their way. She did her best to disguise her voice as she waved Victoria's hand at them. Soon enough, the teachers slowed their steps, and headed back to their classrooms, and Alee was left standing there, holding a crying Victoria, trying to come up with a plan.

Her plan wasn't a good one, but it was the only one she could think of, aside from draining Victoria's blood right there in the hallway, which she really wanted to do. She had to get Victoria out of the school, so her screaming would stop, but what to do with her after that she didn't really know. Then it hit her: The Black Onyx.

She managed to get the suffering girl outside and calmed down long enough to sink her fangs into the side of her neck. She wasn't planning to feed on her; she just wanted to give her a small enough dose of venom to knock her out, but once the blood hit her tongue, she found it hard to stop.

"Victoria? Are you OK?" Dani had seen Victoria leave the building and followed her to make sure she was OK. The fact that she had come out at that moment might have actually saved Victoria's life.

Crap. Alee pulled away as she waved Victoria's arm in the air. "Everything's fine Dani. Thanks. Just a migraine. I'm going home." Alee stumbled their way across the parking lot, trying to make it look like Victoria was walking on her own. Once she was clear of the school and Dani had gone back inside, she heaved Victoria up onto her shoulders and took off running. She made it to the shop in less than five minutes, lay her down outside the front entrance, and started banging on the door.

Alee could have walked right in, but she had just tasted Victoria's blood, and although she had thought she could control herself, she had been wrong. She needed to feed, and if she didn't do it soon she would be feeding on the first person to open the door.

When the door finally opened it was William, Alee's grandfather. The parking lot was empty and he didn't see anyone as he looked up and down the tree line across the road, so he gently lifted Victoria up and into his arms, trying not to wake her. Then he turned, shutting the door behind him.

Alee was able to hunt, drain a deer, and still make it back to school shortly into the lunch hour. Students were already filling their cafeteria trays with mystery meat, mixed vegetables, and God only knows what else. The smell of the overcooked school food was making Alee sick to her stomach, but definitely not hungry. She tried hard not to focus on how repulsed she was feeling, and instead headed to where she knew Phoebe would be. It wasn't hard to find her, considering she sat at the same table every day rain or shine!

As she entered the cafeteria, Alee spotted Phoebe talking quietly to a blonde girl Alee didn't recognize from the back. Phoebe didn't look too happy, but then again she did always seem a bit more serious than a sixteen-year-old should be. Alee took a seat across from them, and was shocked to realize that the blonde girl was Molly, Phoebe's best friend, her black hair transformed into blonde curls. Just then, Molly started to shiver, recoiling away from Alee. Alee started to switch to a seat farther away, but it didn't really matter because two seconds later Molly was saying goodbye, and Phoebe's eyes were welling up with tears. Although Alee wanted nothing more than to give Phoebe a hug, and tell her everything would be OK, she didn't know exactly what had happened and she couldn't honestly say it would all work out, considering everything else that had already happened. She just didn't think Phoebe deserved any more pain.

As she was about to reach out and touch Phoebe's hand, a loud scream came from the far end of the cafeteria. She was there in seconds and knelt down beside a young boy she had never seen before, or at least had never noticed. She sniffed around his head—sweet and musky. He wasn't a wolf, but he wasn't human either. *Definitely a lycanthrope* she thought to herself. Eric had told Alee that once she smelt the sweet odor of a shifter she would be able to recognize them anywhere and he was right. Although, despite Eric's distaste for the sweet scent, Alee was actually drawn to it.

She went to the corner where she had placed the pouch and quickly opened it up, dumping the contents into the trash bin. As the ingredients of the charm separated, the boy's screaming subsided. Alee just stared at him as others helped him up and started walking him down the hallway toward the nurse's station.

The rest of the afternoon was fairly unproductive. Phoebe was quieter than she had been during her morning classes, if that was even possible. By the time the final bell rang, Alee was thankful to finally be leaving for the day.

Alee had hoped to find Damian at school. She wanted to punish him for what he had done to Kyle, and she wanted it done quickly before she lost her nerve. Since she still wasn't a hundred percent sure how to 'punish' him, the fact that he wasn't there was probably actually a blessing. She needed a plan, a real one, and unfortunately that meant that she was going to need to get her spell book from The Black Onyx, and she had no idea how she was going to do that without being detected.

After following Phoebe around all day she decided that it couldn't hurt to hitch a ride back to the shop with her. It would give her a chance to grab the book, find out how her family was doing and, of course, check on how they had handled Victoria being dropped on their doorstep like a gift basket. Besides, she was getting thirsty, and she didn't feel like trying to hunt down another deer when she knew that her father always had fresh blood stored in the kitchen.

As they drove through town, Alee realized that Phoebe wasn't going back to the shop like she did every day after school. She wasn't going to her house either, because she had already passed that about a quarter of a mile back. When the car finally stopped and Alee realized that Phoebe had driven to their Granny Edith's house she had a moment of fear wash over her. Then she realized that Phoebe just might be the answer she had been looking for.

Alee had the element of surprise on her side, being invisible and all, but Damian would be expecting something. After all, his sister had disappeared from school earlier that day. It wouldn't take a genius to figure out that if someone was after her, they were most likely after him too. Alee knew that she didn't have enough power to fight him on her own, nor would she be able to handle anyone else who might be with him—protecting him. However, the thought had occurred to her that borrowing Phoebe's powers for a while might just be the key to success.

Alee squeezed out of the car behind Phoebe, who just stood there, lost in her thoughts. Moving quickly across the yard, Alee made her way down into the cellar where she had been storing the animals she had been feeding on for the past two weeks. In her haste she didn't think to make sure the door eased shut, and it slammed behind her, echoing throughout the cellar. "Hello? Is someone there?" Phoebe called from around the side of the house.

Alee went straight to the back room of the cellar. It was a small room, with barely enough space for the three dead animals, let alone Alee, but she had to tame her hunger, and she knew that the only way she was going to get through what she had to do was by feeding right now. The mountain lion hung loosely in her arms, dangling by its snapped neck as she drained the blood entirely from its already lifeless body and then dropped it to the floor like a dirty rag.

With a new burst of energy, Alee moved with ease and purpose. She had noticed a crate of wiccan supplies the last time she was down here, and she quickly began digging through it. She tossed some old books into a corner, and deeper in the crate she found the things she needed. She used the sand she had found to cast a circle in the center of the main cellar room, and she placed the ritual candles just inside the circle. Although Alee had experience a ritual circle casting during the new moon celebration with her family, she wasn't aware of the dangers of crossing a cast circle, or the pain it can bring to the one who crosses it. She stood in the center of the circle, not breathing, not moving. She would like to have had more time to prepare, but, knowing Phoebe, it would probably be a matter of minutes before her cousin figured out where the noise of the slamming door had come from.

Alee's keenly tuned vampire hearing zeroed in on the sound of the rusty door hinges as Phoebe, hesitantly at first and then vigorously, pulled open the door, fighting against the weight of the wood and the rust of the hinges. "Ignite the flames and draw her near, the fire's power will bring her here," Alee whispered softly under her breath, silently counting the footsteps as Phoebe descended the twelve old, cracking steps that led down into the cool damp cellar.

Alee felt a tinge of excitement as the five candles around her lightly flickered and came to life. She had seen her grandmother cast a circle of sand before, but for the only circles Alee had ever cast she had used the elements, and she didn't have time for that right then. Luckily for her, her natural instinct had kicked in, and she was thankful for the supplies that had been left in the otherwise empty cellar.

Alee assumed that whatever her grandmothers had been up to, living together in that old house for so long, probably had something to do with that room. It was too ominous to just be for common spell casting or potion mixing. This was a place where you came to hide your magic—a place where negative emotions still flowed and black magic lived on. Maybe Phoebe knew about it, maybe she didn't, but at the moment Alee was only interested in one thing—power—and, unfortunately for her cousin, Phoebe was the only one around from whom Alee could steal.

As Phoebe slowly pushed open the door to the main room Alee could hear her heart racing. She could see utter confusion in her cousin's eyes, sudden terror washing over her face. Alee turned slowly, careful not to leave the circle, watching as Phoebe walked the outside perimeter of the circle of sand, searching for any indication that a line had been drawn, cutting the powers that were held inside. Of course, there was nothing and, realizing this, Phoebe started to panic, taking quick-shallow breaths at first, and then turning for the door.

Alee threw her energy toward the door, slamming it shut just as Phoebe grasped the handle. Then the rusted handle fell off in her hand, locking her inside. Alee's focus turned to Phoebe, and she called her closer, pulling her away from the door and into the circle. Phoebe fought hard, but she was no match for Alee. Especially when she didn't even know who or what had her, or why.

As she pulled Phoebe across the line of sand, Alee felt a jolt of energy suffuse her body. For a second, it felt like she was being electrocuted, but it didn't last long. Phoebe kept pulling away, crouching toward the floor, making it difficult for Alee to keep her on her feet. Finally, Alee gave up. She pulled Phoebe close, whispering in her ear, "You aren't safe here!" Then quickly she sank her fangs into her cousin's throat and for the second time that day drank from someone she knew. Instantly, Phoebe collapsed. No more struggling. No more fighting.

Having just fed from the mountain lion, Alee was in more control, and was able to stop herself from taking too much blood. Alee lay Phoebe gently on the ground in the circle at her feet and knelt before her. Her plan was to borrow her powers for a while, something she had been practicing for months, but it had always been while in physical contact with the other person. This time she wanted to use Phoebe's powers separate from Phoebe. She knew it had to be a much stronger spell, and would take a lot out of Phoebe, but she was confident that it was possible. She had to do it!

With one hand holding Phoebe's hand and the other on the powerless girl's chest, Alee began to chant. "Power from mother power from earth I am as strong as she. Power from coven power from birth let her powers come to me." A soft blue glow started emanating around Phoebe's forehead as Alee continued to chant over and over. The light grew into a bright ball of flames above them as Alee continued with intense force and urgency. Then, suddenly, she was thrown backwards onto the ground as the energy ball struck her in the chest with a force even she could not withstand. It hovered there, slowly seeping into her skin. The heat of it burned from the outside in, and she couldn't move—couldn't—fight—couldn't scream.

When Alee woke up, Phoebe was still lying at her feet in the center of the circle. Only her soft, shallow breath indicated that she was still alive. Hesitantly, Alee stood up, unsure of what to expect. She felt great, better than great. She felt amazing.

"I'm so sorry, but I didn't have a choice." Alee cut a line in the sand breaking the power of the circle and left Phoebe alone in the cold dark cellar. She knew she would wake up soon enough, so she wasn't worried about the cold, or what might happen to Phoebe.

Alee got the door open with a spell and then closed it carefully. She rushed up the stairs and into her grandmothers' house. She didn't stop until she reached the bathroom. She stood before the mirror naked and exposed, no longer invisible. Her auburn curls were wild around her face like a blazing fire and her eyes were black as coal. She felt the energy and power flowing through her veins.

Phoebe had been driving Petra's car, and Alee knew that Petra always kept a change of clothing in her trunk, usually something black, tight, and way sexier than Alee was comfortable wearing. Alee never asked why Petra carried an overnight bag in her trunk—sort of a teenage code—don't ask, don't tell. Thinking back now, though, to the way Petra had fought the attackers at the Founders' Celebration, she had a sneaky feeling the overnight bag had something to do with why Petra disappeared every day only to return late each evening.

It took only seconds, with her vampire speed, to find the clothes, get dressed, and be miles away, quickly approaching Damian's back porch.

7

It was early morning. The Black Onyx was quiet except for Elizabeth, William, Tom, and Loraline, who sat talking quietly in the kitchen, laying out a plan for what would happen next. The public schools were opening that morning for the first time since everything had happened. Eric had left early to scout the high school before his niece, Phoebe, went in.

After Granny Edith died, the family had turned to Elizabeth as their new crone. She was third in line, after her aunt Ellen and her cousin Jaclyn, to become the crone. However, her aunt Ellen was too distraught over the deaths of her sister and mother to be of any use to the family. She was glad, and even relieved to be able to hand over the responsibility of crone. Ellen's oldest daughter, Jaclyn, had a family and life of her own, outside of the Underground community. She had no interest in taking over as the family leader. The obvious choice was Elizabeth, and the transition took place with little if anything said about it.

From the moment Edith took her last breath, Elizabeth had been comforting her family and moving forward, instead of allowing them to dwell on, and drown in, their losses. Today was no different. With her mother, her grandmother, her oldest child, and two of her grandchildren as good as buried, she wasn't going to let anything happen to the rest of her family. Of course without bodies as proof, some of the family was still not willing to accept Jacinda's, Petra's, and Alee's deaths, but that didn't change things in Elizabeth's eyes.

"There's no way that this boy Damian and his sister orchestrated the attack," Elizabeth was saying. "They wouldn't have had the resources, or even the knowledge, to accomplish such a task." She took a sip of her coffee and a light went on in her head as she turned toward Loraline. "Did Aleerah mention those children's last name?" Loraline just shook her head, so Elizabeth added, "Would you call Phoebe please? Ask her if she knows what their family name is."

"Why? What are you thinking?"

"I'm not sure yet." That wasn't exactly true. Elizabeth had been around for a long time, and she had known many of the original shifters in the area. If she could figure out what family Damian and his sister were born into, she might be able to figure out who led the attack and, if she was lucky, why they did it.

Loraline just laughed as she crossed the room and picked the cordless phone up from its wall mount and dialed her sister's home number. After three rings, Jacinda's voice sang in her ear. "You've reached Tom, Jacinda, Petra, and Phoebe. We're not home—" Loraline gasped for breath as she dropped the phone on the kitchen floor.

Her father, William, was at her side instantly. "What's the matter honey?" She couldn't answer. She just shook her head. When he picked up the phone and put it to his ear he knew exactly what had happened. "—message and we'll call you back as soon as we can."

The phone beeped in his ear. He took a deep breath, cleared his throat, and left a message. "Phoebe, it's your grandfather. I'm at your Aunt Loraline's. Please give me a call before you leave for school." After he hung up, he turned back to his wife as a single tear rolled down his cheek. "She'll call. Just give her a few minutes." He softly kissed his daughter on the forehead and gave her a gentle hug. "We all miss her and, you know, it's OK to cry. You just have to believe that we will get through this, as a family." He was hurting inside just as much as everyone else, but he was strong, and determined to protect what family he had left.

"You know, I think I'll just give her a call on her cell, too. Just in case she already left the house." He took the phone and quickly dialed. Leaving the same short message he hung up and went to refill his coffee.

The planning session hadn't progressed much further when Eric came through the kitchen door. "The school's secure. No sign of danger." He grabbed a sports bottle from the refrigerator and popped it in the microwave before he noticed that Tom was there. "I thought you were going to drive Phoebe to school. Is everything OK?"

"Everything's fine. I called her earlier to let her know I'd be here. She's going to drive herself. She has a few things to take care of after school."

"After school? Tom, she should come straight—."

"She'll be fine."

"I only meant—.Never mind, you're right. She's your daughter, and you know best." Although Alee had only been in his life for a short time, he had already grown so comfortable in the father role that losing her so soon was taking a harder toll on Eric than he had expected. He looked around the room and noticed Loraline sitting apart from the others, on the other side of the room. "Is everything OK here?" he asked hesitantly.

"We're fine." Loraline had stopped crying and William had returned to the table to sit beside his wife.

"Thank you for checking the school, Eric." Elizabeth's voice was very soft, yet focused. "We should make sure Phoebe knows." Eric started for the phone but she stopped him before he made it. "No need to call. She'll be calling shortly anyway." He hadn't made it back to the table when the phone rang behind him.

"Hello? Hi, Phoebe, are you OK? Yes, he's here, just a second." Eric handed the phone over to William who promptly put it to his ear and walked out into the hallway to talk to her in private.

"How did you—." What was that all about?" Eric leaned down and helped Loraline to her feet. They joined the others at the kitchen table.

"Dad had called her cell a few minutes ago. Mom wanted to find out something about that boy Damian, that's all." At the sound of Damian's name Eric's eyes flashed red. He quickly blinked it away, hoping Loraline hadn't seen, but it was too late. "Eric, are you OK?"

Loraline still didn't know what he had done—how he was connected to Damian's family—and he wanted to keep it that way. If she found out he had broken the truce between the Wenhams and the Cummings, even though the Cummings had broken it first, she might never forgive him.

"No. Sorry. Just hungry I guess." He stood up and downed the last of his drink. Then he rinsed the sports bottle in the sink. "I have a meeting this morning with the remaining founders but I should be back by early evening. For now, please stay inside. We have people patrolling the tunnels and the streets looking for shifters, or anyone who may have assisted them in the attacks. The punishments won't be light for those who are found guilty. Without Petra down there to protect you, I'd rather you all stay clear of the tunnels. At least for a while."

Loraline had never liked rules or being told what to do. "Petra was just a child—."

"One with amazing tracking abilities, and you know as well as I do that she was the only one among you who could take on a vampire and actually have a good chance of surviving."

Loraline couldn't argue with his point, but that didn't stop her from trying. "But we haven't done anything wrong."

"I know that, sweetheart, but they got in somehow. They couldn't have done it alone. They would have needed someone with a lot of pull in the community, or a lot of power. Well, either that or someone very weak, and easily manipulated. I shudder to think who could have done it. However, until we find out, the founders are looking at everyone as suspects." Loraline opened her mouth in protest, but Eric quickly stopped her. "Even those devoted members we know would never have done anything like this, even the founding members are not above suspicion!" Then looking deep into her eyes, he grabbed her hand and kissed it. "Please? For me, just do as I ask this one time." Eric had always been a gentleman. Even as he was giving her a direct order he knew just what to say and how to say it to make everything seem OK, or at least acceptable.

Loraline just nodded. Eric kissed her one more time, then made his way down the hall and through the large wooden door that lead into the tunnels of the Underground.

"Do you know Eric just left?" William came back into the room waving at the empty hall behind him.

Loraline nodded. "Founders' meeting."

"Did you get the boy's name?" Elizabeth was waiting patiently.

"Ward," he said, and Elizabeth's eyes widened. "Do you recognize it?" She didn't stay long enough to answer him. She was down the hall and in the study pulling books off of the shelves moments after she heard the name.

"Ward—Ward—Ward—." She was mumbling under her breath as she skimmed page after page. "Yes! Ward!" She slammed the book down on the table in front of her and a cloud of dust billowed around her. "William! William, come in here please!" She was yelling, but it wasn't necessary because he was already standing behind her. William, Tom, and Loraline had followed her into the room only seconds after she started tearing through the shelves.

"I'm right here. No need to yell."

She spun around at the sound of his voice. "Oh, yes. So you are. Sorry." She took the large open book up into her arms and read out loud the passage she had found. "Officials are still searching for a suspect in the brutal, almost animalistic, attack that left local man, James Ward, only twenty-seven years old, dead. Officials say that he died within seconds of the attack. Ward, a respected member within our community, is survived by a wife and two small children, twins, only five years old—." She handed the clipping to her husband. "This was from the McBain Tribune. This has to be them. It's the right time period, and I remember everyone talking about it. It was the biggest news in the Underground since, well, I don't even *know* when. The Wards were—are lycanthropes. James had been very involved in the Underground, prior to the shift in power. Then, when he got married he and his wife moved to McBain. After his death, everyone wondered if his wife would bring the kids back to Atlanta. She had grown up here, but they never came back. At least I hadn't heard about them moving back, until now. The woman's grandfather was also very well-known and respected in the Underground. He was actually a close friend of Granny Edith and Granddad Turner."

William was scanning the article when he realized who his wife was talking about. "Wait, you don't mean—?"

"Yes. Virgil Cummings." Elizabeth turned to her daughter who was quietly listening at the door. "You've heard the stories, sweetheart. You know our histories."

"But, mom—that truce has been in place since—God, who knows when. What could have made them—?" Then something hit her. Something Eric had said that first week he had returned to The Black Onyx and found her there, alive. He had said, *"—I took care of him years ago. They won't be coming after you or your family any longer."*

For years, Eric and Loraline disagreed about whether or not the truce between the Wenham coven and the Cummings clan would last. Eric believed that lycanthropes couldn't be trusted and swore a thousand times that not all of them had truly embraced the treaty. He swore they were living as shifters, not as mere humans. Loraline argued that how they lived wasn't her concern and that as long as they weren't harming anyone or feeding off of humans, vampires, or anyone else, then they should be able to live their lives any way they saw fit.

Her fear of what Eric had meant by *"I look care of him—,"* was the whole reason she had speeded up Alee's transition; however, somehow it had slipped her mind. "What did he do?"

"What did who do, darling?"

Loraline looked up to find her parents staring at her with wide questioning eyes. "Um, no one. Look, I need to run out for a while. I'll be home later, OK?" She didn't give them a chance to answer before she was out the door and down the hall. She needed to find Eric, and fast.

"Loraline, wait." Tom had followed her down the main hall and stopped her before she could open the large wooden door to the Underground.

"Tom, I don't have time. I need to find Eric."

"Please."

She turned and saw a desperation in his eyes that she had never seen before, even throughout the course of these past awful days. "Are you OK?"

"I can't just sit here. I need to help. Please, let me help. At the very least, don't take the tunnels. It isn't safe. Let me drive you there. If I sit here, I'm going to go crazy."

"Yeah, OK. That's probably a better idea anyway." They turned around and headed back up the hallway and out the front door to Tom's car.

Elizabeth and William were left, somewhat confused, standing in the study. However, Elizabeth didn't let it slow her down. Now that she knew who, or what, she was dealing with, she was ready to take action. Although they hadn't expected what came next, it was a pleasant surprise when a couple of hours later there was a pounding at the front door of the shop.

Elizabeth looked up at William, who was already making his way out the door. "I'll get it. You keep reading."

"Thank you, sweetheart." Her attention went straight back to the book in her lap as she sipped her herbal tea in front of the glowing fire in the fireplace.

When William walked back in with a passed-out Victoria slung over his shoulder, the teacup went crashing to the floor, shattering at her feet and splashing hot tea all over her skirt.

"I believe it's the Ward girl—the one from Aleerah's photos," he said.

"I can see that, but what is she doing here?"

"She was lying unconscious outside the door." He lifted her off of his shoulder and lay her on the couch across from Elizabeth.

Elizabeth's eyes were glistening. A subtle little grin, almost a sneer, made its way to her lips. "Like a present?!"

They stared at the girl for a while, unsure of what to do with her. "If she were our child, we would want her to be sent home," William suggested.

"Yes, but she isn't our child. She is responsible for the death of our child," Elizabeth snapped, "and hundreds of others!"

"We can't harm her. We don't even know what her part was."

"You're right." Elizabeth almost sounded disappointed. "We can't harm her, but that doesn't mean we can't get answers out of her." She moved quickly, pulling the coffee table out of the way, and clearing space on the rug in front of the couch. "A little truth-spell won't hurt." William moved to help his wife while she went to gather some oils off one of the shelves, along with a candle from the mantel. "Lock the door, please," she nodded to William.

Elizabeth placed the candle on the coffee table that was now just in front of Victoria's face, and knelt in front of the girl. She began by drizzling the oil onto the girl's forehead, and chanting, "Clarification I now require, let what is spoken be the words I desire." The candle sprang to life, and William knelt down alongside his wife, who continued the incantation. "The truth of your nature your plan does unfold. Unto me your secrets are told." Nothing happened—at least nothing she had expected, but she continued. "As of the earth so let it be that all that I seek be shown to me!" Victoria just lay there, in what appeared to be a peaceful slumber, and yet Elizabeth continued her chant, over and over.

It was almost an hour later when she finally gave up. "I don't understand why I can't get anything out of her. If she doesn't wake up, then—." she stopped almost as if someone had cut her off, but William hadn't said a word. "You—," she breathed. "*You* can get her to talk."

"Elizabeth, I—."

"Don't say you can't. You know you can. Our daughter is dead William. We have to do something."

"I don't even *know* if I can. It's been years since—."

"I know, but you have to. You have to try."

"What if I can't? What then?"

She just shook her head and laughed. "That's not even an option. You are who you are, what you are. That doesn't change and it doesn't just go away. You can do this. I know you can."

"But—."

"William—" She was only inches away from him, pleading. "—sweetheart. I was never ashamed of who you were, who you are. Granny Edith is gone now. My mother is gone now. I never should have hidden who you were. That was wrong of me and I see that now. But if our family has any chance of surviving, it could very well be because of who you are—what you are. You can do this." She smiled and squeezed his hands in hers. "Trust me."

"I do."

They moved quickly, yet silently, as they gathered the girl, a few fresh candles, and a small bag of white sand. Elizabeth didn't even bother to clean up her spilt tea and broken mug before they went straight to the kitchen, out the back door, and into the storm cellar under the old shed out back. They moved as if someone might be following them. To cover their tracks, they each took a different route through the yard. When they both had made it down to the cellar, William promptly locked the door behind them. With lycanthropes potentially about, you can never be too safe.

William gently lay Victoria down on the cold hard floor of the cellar, not looking as confident as Elizabeth seemed to be. "What if it changes me?"

Elizabeth just shook her head. "It won't. I won't let it." On her tippy toes, she stretched up and softly kissed him on the lips. "I'm not going to lose you. I promise. You are a good man, you always have been, and you are strong enough to control this."

He just shook his head, "I don't know how you can have so much faith in me, when I don't even have faith in myself."

"Well, I do. You have always been what you are; it has always been inside you. Ever since I have known you, you have been gentle and kind. Never once have you harmed a soul. If you could only see yourself the way I see you, you wouldn't be doubting yourself now." She grabbed him in her arms and pulled him close to her chest. "I love you. I love you. I love you."

"I love you too sweetheart." He drew back gently and looked down into her tear-filled eyes. "You're right, it will be OK. I know that now."

"Good." She kissed him again and smiled up at him. "Now, take this sand and get ready to show me what you've got. I'll get the candles lit so we can see a little better."

William smiled back, and then turned toward Victoria who was still motionless, sleeping on the cold floor.

The room was small—no more than ten or twelve square feet. The cement walls were bare. There was no furniture anywhere in the room. It seemed more like an empty closet than a room. Even the windows weren't really windows. They were mere slits of glass no more than six inches high and far above their heads, almost touching the ceiling.

Elizabeth lit the candles and placed them on the floor at her feet, then turned to the bare cement wall to the left of the door, pressed the palms of her hands against it, and closed her eyes. "When you find the door is locked all you must do is knock!" With a tight fist she knocked on the cement three times and before her appeared a small opening that hadn't been there before. Reaching in, she pulled out a leather satchel with a drawstring strap. As soon as the bag was free from the wall the opening quickly closed, leaving no trace of its existence. Turning toward her husband across the room, Elizabeth held the satchel out to him. "Are you ready?"

William had already taken off his shirt, socks, and shoes and had begun pouring a circle of white sand around

Victoria's sleeping body. He nodded and reached out his hand to take the bag.

Elizabeth didn't move. She was standing in awe of her husband, still in as perfect physical condition as the day she had met him. "Why undress?"

"It's a good shirt. Things might, well, get messy, and I don't want to ruin it."

"Oh." Her heart started to pound as she crossed the room and her hands trembled as she handed him the bag.

"Are you sure you want to stay?"

She took a deep breath, clearing her mind. "I'm not afraid. Not of you." With her right hand she stroked the side of his face and, again rising on tiptoe, she kissed him less softly than before. Her left hand went to his waist to steady her balance. The hard rippled muscles of her husband's body were not lost on her, and she took advantage of the hold she had on him before stepping back.

Their eyes were locked as he pulled a small vial of glowing blue liquid out of the satchel. "I'm only going to use a little. Just enough for this," he nodded down at Victoria. "But it won't take long for it to work."

"I'm not ashamed of who you are. With Granny gone, you don't have to hide anymore. Don't you want—?"

He just stared into her confident loving eyes and all he could feel was his own self-doubt, and self-hatred. "No. I'm not ready. Please put the rest back in the wall. Maybe one day, but not today."

"OK."

He put a single drop of the liquid on his tongue and quickly closed the bottle, dropped it back into the bag and handed it to his wife. "Go *now*—lock it up before I change my mind."

As he turned toward Victoria, Elizabeth went back to the wall and quietly recited the incantation again, "When you find the door is locked all you must do is knock!" She knocked, and the hole opened up again as if it had always been there. She placed the bag back inside, then said a silent prayer as she slipped the vial into her pocket and turned back toward William and Victoria.

He had closed the circle and was kneeling on the floor next to Victoria's sleeping body. Elizabeth noticed the muscles that rippled across his back slowly start to tense up. The skin between his shoulder blades started to stretch and pull, as he cried out in pain. He threw his head back, screaming as the skin tore open and blood started to pour down his back.

Victoria started to squirm on the ground as she began to wake up. William held her down with one hand as the other reached around to his back, pulling the loose skin off of the newly protruding nubs that had formed there. The more his back convulsed, the larger Elizabeth could see them growing. His screams soon stopped. He knelt within the circle and extended his newly formed wings. They weren't the soft and delicate white wings depicted in paintings of angels. His wings were jagged and edgy, with dark black and grey feathers. They looked ominous. The tips were covered with his own blood, dripping down onto the floor and seeping into the ring of white sand that surrounded him.

Elizabeth covered her mouth to stop a deep gasp, not wanting to make a sound. But it was too late. Williams turned his glaring eyes and sharp hungry teeth toward her, but she stood firm, without taking her eyes off of him. "You can do this!" Her voice was timid and unsteady, but she didn't show fear on her face. "William, you can do this. I know you can."

His eyes softened, and with a deep breath he nodded, before turning back to Victoria, who was staring in shock at the unnatural creature kneeling before her.

He didn't have to say a word. Fairies don't use spells in the same way that witches do; their power is more like the mind control of a vampire. He simply placed one hand on her forehead, and the other on her stomach to hold her down. She screamed, instinctively, but it didn't last for long. As he gazed deep into her eyes she settled into a relaxed state under his hold. Her breathing slowed and she looked content there on the cold hard floor.

William began channeling her innermost secret thoughts, and replayed them for Elizabeth to hear.

"Victoria, I'm shocked at you." It wasn't William's voice, though he was the vessel through which an older woman's voice was projected.

"You weren't there. You don't know. She came after us first!" That was Victoria. William was channeling a conversation Victoria had had. Elizabeth knew what he was looking for—any information about the attacks, but it wasn't going to be easy.

"You never, ever, kill a protected member of the Underground—not without cause, and not unless you are prepared for the consequences." A searing pain penetrated William's temples and he cried out, letting go of Victoria's stomach and gripping the side of his head.

"You are never to go to that shop again. Never Victoria, it isn't safe." He shook his head in frustration, "No, no that's not what I want."

"Fairies are mischievous creatures, and very vicious— not to be trusted." William's body shuddered and convulsed as he spoke the words. Elizabeth could see him fighting the impulse to lash out at Victoria's limp body.

Trying to calm him down before he did something they would both regret she called out to him, more strongly this time—to the husband she knew was still inside of the angry beast before her. "Focus William, it wasn't her, you know that."

William was only able to access pieces of the distant conversations. They weren't coherent enough for Elizabeth to make total sense of them, at least not until what he said next.

"They need to get close to the girl. If what I've heard is true, she's more powerful than even they could imagine. Once she is out of the picture it will be easy to take back what is rightfully ours." It was a man's voice.

"I agree. You heard him, you need to find a way to make Aleerah your friend, just watch your backs."

"But Mom—." It was the voice of a young man.

"But nothing! You're the ones who brought the Guardian bands to me. You're the ones who wanted to take back your

birthright. I was content living the life we have, but—. You're young, I can't ask you to do this and I won't make you. We can find others to help us if you two don't want to, but I have dreamed of this chance for years until I eventually gave up on that dream. You brought it back, you and your sister. Now that it is so close, I can't sit back and do nothing. But, if you still want to avenge your father's death, then you will do as I say—as we say. Please."

As if shocked by a powerful voltage, William pulled back from his grip on Victoria and gasped for air. His breathing was shallow—rapid—labored—hungry. He crouched on all fours, staring at the pulse in Victoria's throat. It had been well over thirty years since he had last feed the way fairies were meant to feed, and the raw cravings of his roots came rushing back.

"Are you all right?" It was a whisper now, but he clearly heard her, and he nodded as he turned back toward his wife, fighting against his ancient urges. "You're stronger than this William. I know you are."

"I'm fine." His voice was more of a guttural growl than anything else. Standing, he stretched his stiff body, and his wings spread out around him. With a deep breath in and out, he repeated, "I'm fine," and it actually sounded like he was now. His voice was back and he was able to focus again. He even smiled at her as their eyes met.

"It's their mother we're looking for," Elizabeth said. "She's working with someone, they are the ones in control. She may not have been in charge of the attack, but she's the one who was telling these kids what to do, and that's a start. If we find her, we can find the man she was with."

He nodded and, cutting the circle with his foot, he slowly stepped out. "I agree. It seems like Aleerah was her target, but she wasn't going to stop there. It sounds like she—they—had bigger plans." He absently waved at Victoria who was still moaning on the cold hard floor. "This one, she's just a pawn in her mother's game—her brother too. I don't even think they knew what was going to happen at the Founders' Celebration." Stretching his back, he took a deep breath as his wings folded themselves back down, and into the skin covering his shoulder blades. Only two small cuts remained, and even these had already started to heal before he cautiously stepped into his wife's waiting arms.

"Are you all right?" Elizabeth asked quietly as she ran her fingers across his back.

"It barely hurts any more. It's just because it's been so many years."

"And your head?"

"The headache will fade too. It will just take a little longer." He kissed his wife on the forehead, "I'm sorry if I scared you."

"You didn't." She didn't even think before she responded and he could feel the honesty in her answer.

"I love you."

"And I you."

He turned to gather his things from the floor while Elizabeth just watched. Hesitantly, she asked, "Do you want me to bind your powers again?"

"No." William just shook his head. "You were right, it's been long enough. It's time for our family to know. Jacinda died not fully knowing who or what she really was. I don't want that for Loraline, or for Phoebe. We've lost too many these past few weeks. I can't continue to lie to the family we still have." Then he looked deep into her eyes. "That is, if you will still have me."

Elizabeth didn't have to answer; she simply pulled the vial out of her pocked and held it out to him.

"You already—?"

"I've always trusted you. I loved you before I knew what you were and I've never stopped loving you." She wrapped herself back in his arms and that was good enough for him.

By the time they finished cleaning up and made their way back outside it was already dark. They weren't going to keep Victoria locked up in the cellar and, knowing what they knew now, they didn't feel there was any point to keeping her at all. After taking the leather Guardian band off her wrist, William drove her home. He left her lying on an old porch swing, snugly covered with a blanket he had brought along for just that purpose.

Just as he was pulling out of the Ward's driveway William was sure he saw someone leap out of the second story window on the side of the house and run into the woods out back. He rubbed his eyes and tried to focus, but when he didn't see anything he just attributed it to a lack of sleep.

Loraline wasn't a founding member of Atlanta by any stretch of the imagination, but being a Wenham, she had plenty of pull within the Underground community as well as the city above. When Tom and Loraline arrived at the square downtown and climbed up the courthouse steps, Loraline was greeted by a number of people she had known all her life.

"Good morning, Mrs. Wenham." It was Kim Dunham, the mayor's secretary. "I'm running out to get Mayor Ross some coffee. Would you—" She paused, looking curiously at Tom. "—and your friend like something?"

"This is my brother-in-law, Tom. Have you never met?"

"No, no I can't say that we have."

Tom held out his hand, but Kim didn't take it. "Well, it was nice to meet you."

Kim turned back to Loraline disregarding Tom completely, "Did you want that coffee?"

"No thank you, Kim. Have a good morning."

After a few steps Tom turned and made sure Kim was out of ear-shot before he leaned in closer to Loraline. "What was that all about?"

"I don't really know. Kim has always been a bit odd, but she really didn't seem to like you for some reason."

"Hey!"

"I'm just kidding. I don't know what's eating her today. Maybe the Mayor's in a bad mood." They laughed as they continued walking.

Christopher Plitt, the town's only judge, was coming out of the main doors as Tom was reaching for the handle. "Ah, Mr. Young and Mrs. Wenham, what brings you two down to my neck of the woods this morning?"

Loraline smiled softly. She had always been taught to respect her elders, and Judge Plitt reminded her of her grandfather in many ways. "We were just looking for Eric, sir. He was supposed to have a meeting here this morning. I was hoping it was here."

Judge Plitt and Loraline exchanged looks. "A meeting?"

"Yes. They called it early this morning. Had you not heard?" It was uncommon to discuss the Founders' business so openly, but Loraline knew that Judge Plitt, although not a member of the founding council, was very involved in their processes.

"No, no I hadn't heard." Looking from Loraline to Tom and back again, Judge Plitt asked, "Is something wrong dear?" Loraline could see the tension building in his shoulders as he straightened up, and his smile disappeared.

Not wanting to give away too much, but knowing that it was pointless to lie to Judge Plitt, she cleared her throat and nodded ever so slightly.

Judge Plitt was well-suited to be in his position, considering that he was a mind reader. It made it very hard for a suspect, or even a court witness, to lie. There was no need for juries in Atlanta. Judge Plitt was the judge and jury of all trials. However, to keep up appearances they always had a panel of jurors present—made up of members of the Underground.

"Then come with me, dear. Tom, would you like to come up, or would you rather wait?"

Tom looked at Loraline, "What do you prefer?"

"I'll be fine. How about I meet you back down here in a half hour? This shouldn't take too long."

"OK, I'll be back at the car, but if you need me just call."

Judge Plitt took Loraline's hand and led her into the building. They walked around the metal detectors instead of through them the way everyone else going into the building was doing. "She's with me," the Judge said, as he waved away one of the approaching guards.

There was yellow caution tape across the doors of two out of three of the elevator doors. "Construction is going slowly, but they did get the main elevator up and running just this morning."

"Really—it's taken that long?" Loraline watched as the numbers lit up above the door.

"Yes, but it's all right. My doctor says the stairs are better for my heart anyway," Judge Plitt chuckled.

When the elevator doors opened and Loraline stepped in, she noticed that the button for the ballroom level had been completely removed. She ran her finger across the empty spot and could feel her eyes well up with tears.

"I'm sorry for your losses. Your grandmothers, your sister, your niece—. They were amazing women. And your daughter, of course—." Their eyes met and there really wasn't anything else he could say. The elevator made the familiar dinging sound as it stopped at the top floor. "You're sure you want to interrupt this meeting?" She just nodded. "All right then, come with me."

He placed his hand flat against a plain white, square pad to the right of the door. In many ways Atlanta was still existing in the past, but in terms of technology they were light years ahead. The palm reader quickly identified Judge Plitt, and the doors opened, allowing them to exit the elevator cab. They stepped out into a small waiting area where a little grey-haired woman sat quietly at her desk. "Mildred, this is Loraline. She needs to speak with Mr. Chalkeus, right away."

"But, they just started—."

"Mildred, please. It's of the utmost importance," he said, glancing back at Loraline, who just nodded in agreement. "Mrs. Wenham may have information that could help our founders. Isn't that right dear?"

"I don't know if it—." Loraline wasn't really sure how helpful her information would be to the founders, but she knew that she needed to talk to Eric about it. She needed to find out if she was right about her suspicions. If this was the only way, so be it. "Yes. I mean, right, of course."

Mildred just glared at them across the desk, but slowly curled her lips into a submissive smile. "Yes sir." Her voice was shaky as she pulled herself out of her seat and grabbed the cane that was leaning against the wall behind her. She seemed frail as she made her way to the large wooden conference room doors and disappeared behind them.

Turning back to Loraline, Judge Plitt had a soft smile on his face. "You'll have to excuse Mildred. She's nearly four hundred years old. Although we try to make her comfortable, her kind were never really meant to survive that long."

"Her kind?" Mildred just looked like an old woman. Loraline would never have guessed she was over seventy, let alone nearly four hundred. "Is she a—vampire?" She said it quietly, even though there was no one else around.

He couldn't help but laugh. "No, not at all. Mildred is a fairy, dear. The average life expectancy for fairies is only about three hundred. I think, before Mildred, the oldest recorded fairy died at three hundred and twenty-nine. Mildred has somehow managed to live well past that. However, with age often come lots of health problems, of which Mildred has many."

The conference room doors creaked as they were pushed open and Mildred stepped out, slowly followed by Eric. He looked back and forth between Judge Plitt and Loraline. "Loraline?" He walked straight to her, and pulled her into the corner, the only place they could have even a hope of privacy. "What are you doing here? I thought I told you to stay out of the tunnels."

"I didn't take the tunnels, Eric. Tom drove me."

"Tom?" He quickly scanned the rest of the waiting room.

"He isn't here, he's waiting downstairs."

"In any case, that isn't even the point. You are well aware that I didn't just mean the tunnels. Now, why are you here?"

"I needed to ask you something." But she couldn't find the words without sounding like she was accusing him of something, and she didn't want Judge Plitt or Mildred to overhear her questioning him, to say nothing of the thoughts that were running through her head right then. Swallowing hard, she just came right out and said it. "Was it you who killed James Ward?"

If he had still been human his heart may have given out at that moment. His eyes widened as he glanced back over at Mildred and Judge Plitt who had been quietly talking together. They hadn't seemed to have heard Loraline's question. When he turned back to her, she already knew the answer. He didn't have to say anything, but he wanted to explain himself. He needed to explain himself. "I did what I had to do. He attacked you, and at the time I believed he had killed you. I was convinced he was still a threat to your family, to our daughter. I didn't have a choice."

"I told you that the truce had been in place for over—."

"*He* didn't uphold the truce."

"Yes he did! He wasn't the one who attacked me." She seemed so sure and so positive.

"Then who? How can you know for sure? All the threats before the attack and everything I could find led me to him." Eric knew that James Ward had been an active lycanthrope in the Underground. When his kind had been banned from any participation and their Guardian bands had been revoked, James had been extremely bitter. He had expressed his anger more loudly than most of the others. He had reason to strike out against the Wenham family and he didn't try to hide it.

"He was mad, but he had moved on. I promise you it wasn't him."

"Who then?"

"Eric, please don't make me do this. Not here. It's not important."

"Do what? If you know something you need to tell me. Please." When she didn't respond he took her hands in his, pleading, "Please, *talk* to me."

"Fine." A searing pain went through Loraline's temples, but it only lasted a second before it faded into a dull throbbing. She closed her eyes, trying to remember that night. "It was late. You had called to say you were going to be another couple of hours so I hadn't put dinner on yet. I was upstairs giving Aleerah her bottle and putting her down to sleep when the doorbell rang. I just figured it was another one of the neighbors' kids trying to sell us Girl Scout cookies, or candy for the marching band, but—."

"But what?"

"But it was your house. It was in your name."

Eric didn't seem to understand what that meant, or why that might be important, until it hit him, and then it was like a light turning on. "And I'm a vampire." Loraline just nodded. "So, any other vampire could just come in."

"That's right. No welcome necessary."

"It wasn't a shifter—it was a vampire. All this time, it was a vampire."

"I opened the door, but no one was on the porch. When I closed the door, he was there, standing against the wall across the room. I don't even know how he got in. I couldn't see his face. He kept to the shadows." She wiped a tear from her cheek. "He called me by name and I went to him. I didn't want to. I knew that I shouldn't have, but at the time I couldn't resist. I'm not even sure I really wanted to." When she looked up into Eric's eyes she could see the pain and anger he was feeling. "When I finally realized what was happening, I ran. He chased me through the living room and I made it upstairs. I wanted to get to Aleerah. I thought that if I could lock us in the bedroom, then maybe—but it was too late. He was too fast. He pinned me against the wall." Her hands were shaking and Eric quickly took them in his own, trying to comfort her. "I believed he planned to kill me, but I couldn't fight him. I wanted to—my brain was telling me to fight, to get away, but my body wouldn't listen. I just stood there, unable to do anything." She was silent for a few minutes, gathering her thoughts and strength, while he just waited. "When I woke up, I was at The Black Onyx with my family. They said I had been in the hospital, and that they hadn't heard from you."

"That isn't entirely true, I talked to Jacinda, and told her about Aleerah, but that still doesn't explain why you didn't contact me—why you let me believe you were dead—why you broke our bond."

"I did it for you. I was trying to protect you and Aleerah." Loraline took a deep breath as she looked over at Mildred and Judge Plitt, who were still talking quietly. "Don't you understand, Eric? He came after me because of you."

Nothing was making sense to Eric. Why would anyone, especially a vampire, attack her because of him? "Why? What could he have gained—?"

"The only thing I remember him saying, other than calling out my name, was—" She couldn't look at him. "—I won't allow any son of mine to be trapped like a caged dog."

"Son?" Eric knew that Loraline knew the story of his parents' death. Besides, he was over 700 years old, and even if he hadn't killed them after he was turned, there would still be no chance in heaven or hell that they had lived even a fraction of his life, or that their long-ago deaths would mean anything to their family's current-day descendants.

Then a spark appeared in his eyes—one that Loraline had never seen. "You know who it was, don't you?"

"Loraline, you must leave." She didn't move.

"Who is it? Who turned you?" she mouthed the words, as if she were shouting.

"You must leave, NOW!" He snapped his fingers toward Mildred and Judge Plitt, who quickly ran over. Mildred pushed the elevator door, summoning it instantly. As the door opened, Eric turned toward the older man. "See her out and then have security lock down the building. No one leaves!"

Loraline never took her eyes off him, but did as she was told, and left.

"Please, spare him his life." It was only a whisper from Mildred, as the elevator doors closed between them, but Eric didn't hear her, and if he had, he wouldn't have cared what she had to say.

10

"Why?" Eric yelled. He stood at the end of the conference table demanding an answer. The most powerful vampires in Atlanta lined the sides of the enormous table, but Eric's attention was focused on one man, Gregory Davis, who was seated at the head of the table opposite Eric.

Gregory Davis, born Gratianus, son of Drusus, was a prominent member of both the Atlanta community and the Underground. As the Atlanta High School principal, he was known and loved by just about everyone. However, in his role as the oldest founding member of the Atlanta Underground, he was both respected and feared. No one ever raised their voice to Gregory, and those who knew him as Gratianus never so much as looked at him in a way that showed even a hint of disdain or anger.

Eric's eyes were burning red. "What did you do?!" He leaned on the far end of the table with all his anger and energy pouring out of him in waves. "Leave!" He was whispering, but his voice rang out in an evil hiss, and everyone reacted instantly. They were out of their seats and hurrying out the door as quickly as possible.

Standing face to face with only a fifteen-foot solid wood conference table between them, Eric was ready to fight to the death if that's what it took. "You had no right to touch her, let alone try to take her from me!"

Gregory narrowed his eyes and cocked his head to the side as if he was just figuring out what was happening. "Are you talking about that pretty little thing you used to run around with? What was her name—?"

Eric slammed his fists down on the table, splitting the wood and sending slivers and shards of wood flying across the room. He grabbed a sharp piece of wood, about twelve inches in length, and leapt into the air. Racing across the table, he grabbed Gregory by the front of his shirt and flung him across the room. "Watch what you say old man." Eric warned him.

Gregory stood up, dusted off his pants with his hands, and turned toward Eric. "Have you forgotten who you're talking to? Don't forget that I taught you everything you know. I made you. I. Can. Destroy. You." His voice was like thunder echoing through the room and shaking the walls around them.

"Not everything." Eric winked, and in a flash he was gone. Gregory was left standing there in an empty room. "Some things *Loraline* taught me!" He appeared directly in front of Gregory with one hand on the older man's throat, holding him tightly in place against the wall. The other hand was pressing the tip of the wooden stake sharply against his chest. He didn't even hesitate before thrusting the stake into Gregory's heart, sending the man to his knees.

Gregory was old, and the wood alone wouldn't kill him, but it would paralyze him until Eric got the answers he was looking for—until he was *ready* to kill him. "Why did you try to kill Loraline?"

He didn't even try to deny it. "You're a vampire, Ermanes." He was struggling to get the words out. "You're not meant to be with a mortal."

"Don't call me that!" He spit the words at him. "Who are you to judge my life? What gives you the right to decide right from wrong?"

Gregory was flat on his back and a white film had already begun to coat his eyes. "I'm your maker—your father—. You're my s—."

"You are *nothing* to me!" Eric reached over and grabbed a silver butter knife that had been sitting on the credenza behind the table. Mildred had used it only moments before to spread jam on her morning bagel. Now, Eric used it, with a twist of his wrist, and thrust it into Gregory's chest right next to the wooden stake. It wasn't like in the movies. Gregory didn't burst into flames or turn to dust. It was much more straightforward than that. Within seconds of the silver penetrating his flesh his eyes went completely white, and every muscle in his body contracted until his body was as rigid as a corpse. He gasped for breath a few times, although his lungs had long since begun to fill with blood, and he choked, unable to cough to clear the unwanted liquid from his lungs. Gregory was paralyzed, helpless, and unable to fight back as he drowned in his own blood. It was sort of fitting—a vampire drowning on blood, the one thing that kept them alive. That is if you can even consider a vampire "alive."

Eric watched dispassionately. When Gregory finally stopped struggling, Eric knelt down and placed his hand over Gratianus' heart and whispered, "Your blood lives in me. You will be remembered." Then he pushed the silver knife as deep into Gratianus' heart as it would go. If it had been physically possible, a tear might have escaped as he wiped the blood off his hands and turned to leave.

Downstairs, Eric found Loraline anxiously pacing in the lobby outside the elevators. She threw herself into his arms. He was covered in blood, but she didn't care, or even question what had happened. On some level she already knew. The ride back to The Black Onyx in the backseat of Tom's car was quiet and long.

11

Alee was edging along in the shadows with her back pressed against the cool brick of the back wall of the house. She heard Damian's mother talking on the kitchen phone, and she ducked down, underneath the windowsill.

"No, no, she isn't home yet," Karen was saying. "Damian said he waited for her after school, but she never came out to the car. He came straight home and went to bed. He said he had had a bad migraine all day and spent most of the day in the nurse's office with a number of other students." She didn't sound worried, but she certainly wasn't happy either. "Yes, I know she's done this before. She's probably at Dani's house or something. I just wish she would answer her cell phone, or call to let me know she's OK. She's going through such a rebellious stage right now. Ever since the Founders' Celebration it's like she thinks she can do anything she—" Alee moved on, but failed to notice a small branch in her way. It made a loud cracking sound when she stepped on it. "Hang on, I just heard something out back. She might be home."

The back door opened just as Alee made it around the corner. "Victoria? Is that you?" The silence was Karen's answer and she went back into the house. "No, it wasn't her. Listen, I have to get up early. It isn't like this is the first time she's done this. I'm sure everything is fine—. OK, I'll call you when she gets in—. You have a good night too." Alee could hear the click as the phone was hung up, and then the footsteps as Karen headed upstairs.

It was a nice night out, so Alee made herself comfortable on the back patio, waiting for Karen to fall asleep. Before long, the only sounds Alee could hear from inside the house were two slow yet distinctly different heartbeats and the deep steady breathing of Karen and Damian as they slept.

Alee knew where Damian's room was, having visited him hundreds of times throughout their junior year. But she had never before visited with the intention of killing him.

She slowly moved in the shadows until she was directly beneath his bedroom window. *Why did you do it?* She wasn't expecting an answer, but what could it hurt to reach out to him one last time? She took a deep breath, not needing it— just building her courage. Then, turning toward the wall, she jumped up without any effort at all, and landed, balancing with her toes on his windowsill, and clinging to the window frame. She hadn't made a sound. His heartbeat was still calm and steady. She had to pause for a moment to pat herself on the back because, while she had imagined that move, she hadn't been a hundred percent sure it would work, and perching there on the windowsill she felt pretty awesome.

She slid the window open. Luckily for her he had never felt the need to lock it. Who enters a house through a second-floor window anyway, right? She slowly stuck her hand through the window, testing the water, so to speak. She had grown up watching horror films and, among other things, she had learned that vampires cannot enter someone's home without being invited. Apparently that wasn't true, because she had no problem waving her hand through the window. Maybe it was because she had been invited into this home so many other times, or maybe it was just something silly that had been made up by movie writers, or maybe it was because she was 'different' and it just wasn't true for her. She made a mental note to ask Eric later, although she knew that, in all honesty, it probably didn't matter.

She was at the side of Damian's bed in seconds. He was sound asleep, lying on his back. His breathing was slow and deep. He wasn't wearing a shirt, and she watched his chest slowly rise and fall with each breath. Alee could have easily killed him without even waking him, but the memory of Kyle falling to the ground dead at Damian's feet was burning like a fire inside her. She wanted to make him suffer. She wanted to make him scream. But most importantly, she wanted him to know it was her doing it.

With her left hand, she covered his mouth as she climbed on top of him, straddling him to hold him down on the bed. As soon as her body weight was on him, his eyes popped open. Fear, then recognition washed over his face. "Alee?" he mumbled into her hand, but she knew what he had said.

Her eyes were hollow as she slowly smiled. It was the most menacing smile Damian had ever seen. "Alee's gone!" With a quick snap, she turned his head to the side, leaned forward and sank her teeth into his throat. His blood ran quickly and was warm on her tongue. He struggled under her grasp and she could hear him whimpering in pain.

In seconds, his struggling stopped, and her grip on his arms loosened. Alee was caught off guard when Damian suddenly whipped his legs up and across the front of her body pushing her back and down onto the bed. He was on top of her in a moment and she lost hold of his throat. He didn't have the same healing powers as she did, so the bleeding didn't stop. It was a serious wound, but somehow he still found the strength to fight back. Alee kicked and struggled, but he had her pinned to the bed until, with a slight shift of her weight, she propelled him off of her and across the room.

He landed on his back against the far wall, and she crouched on the bed, ready and waiting for him to attack. When he moved toward the door, she beat him to it, slamming it shut, blocking his way. "Don't even try it Damian."

He turned toward the window and she could see his body start to shift as his legs and arms extended, hands and feet becoming paws—. In two lightning moves, she locked the window, and snapped the leather string of the talisman necklace that he always wore—stopping his transformation and leaving him with a burn on his neck. He probably could have shifted without it and still easily shift back, but the first rule of transformations was *always keep your talisman with you*. It grounded you to your human form. He stopped dead in his tracks. He turned, his eyes piercing and a low snarl in his throat. However, instead of fighting or attacking, he looked deep into her eyes, moving closer. He was only inches away, and she saw his face soften and his eyes fill with tears.

Kill him! Kill him! She told herself over and over in her head, but her feet were planted on the ground and she couldn't move.

"Alee, look at yourself. You lost your father. You've pushed everyone away. You've lied about your death, you've lost so many friends. Your mother was so devastated that she moved out of town just to—."

She shoved him away and moved across the room. She needed space, needed a second to catch her breath, needed to process. "What?" Alee hadn't heard about her mother, Martha, the woman who had raised her. The idea that Martha would leave town had never crossed Alee's mind. Alee had forced herself to move on, hoping that her mother would too. But she never imagined that she would leave. Secretly, Alee had always hoped that one day she could go home again and make things right. "What do you mean she moved?"

"What was she going to do Alee? You're dead. Alee's gone. You said it yourself, right!" It wasn't a question, it was a slap in the face.

Damian moved quickly and pinned her against the closet door. She didn't even try to get away. His warm hands on her arms held her tight, almost too tight, but the pain reminded her of why she was there. She looked up at him with fire red eyes. "Take your hands off me, or I'll do it for you." Her voice was calm, but the building anger inside her wasn't.

"I love you." It was only a whisper. Then, with both hands on her arms, he thrust her against the closet door again, so hard the wall shook and a picture frame fell to the floor next to her. Then, he kissed her.

She hated him for all he was, for everything he had done. Deep in her soul she wanted him dead. She wanted to kill him with her own hands—to drain his blood and leave him to rot—but instead she found herself kissing him back. It wasn't anything like their first kiss, which had been gentle and innocent. This kiss was urgent—forceful—almost savage. She was shaking—quivering from head to toe—and her lips were trembling under his embrace. She bit his upper lip, but it wasn't out of aggression or thirst, it was passion and excitement. As his grip loosened and he ran his hand up and down the side of her body, she felt the warmth of his flesh on her cold pale skin. She wanted more of it—more of him.

'I love you.' He wasn't speaking, but she could hear his thoughts again and again echoing in her head. After a while he stopped, slowly pulling away from her and dropping his hands to his sides. "I'm sorry. I never meant to hurt you, or—," Tears welled up in his eyes, and she could hear the sincerity and pain in his voice.

"Why did you do it?" She wanted so desperately to hate him, but, seeing him so vulnerable, she just couldn't bring those feelings back to the surface.

Damian stepped back. He looked at the ground and just shook his head. She waited, staring at him, hoping for an answer that might make her understand. She just wasn't expecting the answer he gave her. "Because of you." He looked up, and her black eyes had softened to the ocean blue he remembered. "I did it because of you." Taking a deep breath, he let everything out like a dam being broken by the force of a rushing river. "He had you, but he never deserved you. Then you died and he moved on so quickly—as if you didn't even matter—."

She cut him off, "But that was—."

"You! I know that now, but I didn't at the time, and it didn't seem right. It wasn't fair." His hands were shaking but his voice was clear and confident. "He got wrapped up in—.

"In what Damian?" she snapped. He just shook his head, looking down at the floor. "I know how you feel about my family, but they're my family whether you like it or not. Kyle accepted that! He accepted me—every part of me—without judgment—" A flash of anger returned, burning inside of her, and she rushed toward him, throwing him against the wall. "—and you killed him. WHY?"

It took Damian a minute to recover and stand up. "I did it for you. I did it because I love you." He wasn't lying, she knew that. Maybe that was why it hurt so much to hear him say it. Alee had once thought that maybe, just maybe, she felt the same way about him, but her heart belonged to Kyle, and Damian had taken him away.

"Stop saying that!" Her voice was a low rumble, but it projected all her anger and all her pain, as if emotions could be screamed through a microphone for the whole world to hear.

Damian wasn't afraid. Maybe he should have been, but instead of cowering he grabbed her by the arms and was yelling to get her attention. "I love you Alee! I LOVE YOU!" Then he leaned in to kiss her again. She could have easily gotten swept away in the moment again, but before his lips could touch hers she broke free from his grasp and slapped him across the face so hard it made his eyes water and his vision blur. When he was finally able to focus again, he looked around at an empty room and his curtains billowed in the breeze that wafted through the open window. He looked hard, and thought he could see a blur of motion in the distance, but he couldn't be certain it was her.

She ran until her feet ached and she couldn't push herself any more. She had no idea where she was going or what she was going to do. All she knew was that she had to get as far away from Damian as she could. She was angry—hungry— desperate. Every time she thought about Damian she could taste his blood on her lips and she longed for more. The burning in her throat grew worse and worse until she couldn't take it any longer.

She would have gone back to finish him off, but she knew he would be waiting for her. She couldn't take that chance. The streets were dark as Alee made her way through the town. It was easy to hide in the shadows and the darkened shop doorways. Atlanta had always been a town that shut down early. She had just assumed it was normal, but after being introduced to the real Atlanta, she realized it was just safer that way, at least for Atlanta's breathing residents. Knowing the town as well as she did, she knew exactly where to go. She headed straight for the downtown shelter. It would be full of homeless people by that time of night. No one worried about them or would be looking for them in the morning. In her mind, they were the perfect targets, if a target was something she needed.

Alee hovered outside the shelter for a while as people drifted in and out through the front door. Her body had started to shake uncontrollably, with tremors brought on by her hunger. She rubbed her hands vigorously along the sides of her arms and legs, hoping to make it stop. It was no use. She knew the only way to stop it would be to feed, so as soon as she saw the volunteer at the front desk turn off his computer and lock up the office, she made her move. Slipping in unseen was easy. She even explored the hallways for the perfect target without being detected.

Her first victim was an older woman lying asleep on her cot. The woman never even opened her eyes, and her already pale, wrinkled skin faded to a lifeless blue as Alee drained her. The old woman tasted bitter compared to Damian's blood or the animal blood Alee had become used to. It had an instant effect on her, unlike the blood of the dead bodies she had fed on after the Celebration. She felt more alive and alert than she had since she had woken up—dead—or as close to dead that you can get without actually being six feet under.

As she searched for her second victim, she didn't even consider the numerous children in the place. Although she was a vampire, she wasn't completely heartless. Killing a child was out of the question.

From across the room, in one of the private rooms, she could hear the slow, steady heartbeat of a dying man. She gripped the door handle of the locked room and slowly twisted the knob just past its breaking point and snapped the bolt.

She heard a hiss coming from somewhere off to her left. Spinning around, she bared her fangs and leapt straight out into the open air. She hit the wall with a loud crash, fell to the floor, and then quickly rolled back up onto her feet. She stood with her arms up guarding her face, and her knees slightly bent, ready to lunge at or away from, an oncoming attack. But it never came.

"You don't have to do this Aleerah." Jathan's voice was unmistakable. She knew it in an instant.

Alee saw it again—her mother being propelled through an open portal in the wall the night of the Founders' Celebration, and Jathan standing there silently amidst the chaos surrounding him.

"Why are _you_ here?" She spit out the words as she searched the room around her, but Jathan wasn't there. Her eyes were burning red and her tone was venomous.

"I've been looking for you. You're desperate but you don't have to do this." His voice was gentle—calming—yet Alee fought hard not to lose the anger she had built up. She needed to regain her strength. The only way she was going to be able to go back and take care of Damian was if she stayed focused and fed. "The Alee I know would never hurt these people."

She was still scanning the room but at the sound of her name, the name she had known as her own from childhood, she snapped. "What did you call me?" Since she had 'died' and resumed her life as Aleerah with her birth parents and a spell-cast new appearance, everyone other than her family and Kyle believed 'Alee' to be dead.

"I know who you are, Alee. I know what you are."

"You know nothing about me!" she spit back.

Jathan stepped out of a nearby shadow a few feet behind her. She screamed, startled, but the fear was short-lived. She lunged in his direction, only to have him disappear into thin air. When she turned around, searching the room again, he was leaning calmly against the far wall.

"Is this a game to you?" she snarled. She rushed toward him but again he was gone before she could reach him.

Finally, he raised his hands in front of him, as if in surrender. "Don't be afraid. I'm not going to hurt you."

"I won't give you the chance." Alee wasn't so sure that was possible, and by no means did she trust him. Jathan was a dream walker and as far as she knew, a very dangerous man—if you could even call him a man.

Dozens of events clicked together, and Alee realized that everything had started to spiral out of control when Jathan had come into town. Putting two and two together, she blamed him for Kyle's death—for Damian's change—even for the deaths at the Celebration. Her blood was boiling with rage as she looked at him with clenched fists, ready to attack.

"You don't want to hurt me?" She demanded, "Then tell me what you do want!" She had shifted her weight and slowly backed herself against a wall. Knowing, or at least hoping, that he couldn't come at her from behind made her feel a little more comfortable; at least it was somewhat rational in theory.

"I want you." He hadn't blinked or moved since showing himself. He showed no signs of preparing to attack and his voice was steady and calm. "I've always wanted you, Alee."

She was breathless as she shook her head, not fully understanding what was happening. *This can't be happening—*.

"But it is happening." He knew what she was thinking and her eyes went wide hearing him answer her thoughts.

"Get out of my head." He had crossed that line too many times. "This is your fault. All of this is your fault." She took off across the room with lightning speed and had him pinned against the wall before he could even blink. He didn't try to get away as she sank her teeth into his throat. Confusion struck her instantly, though, and she pulled back in alarm. He wasn't bleeding! There were no marks where she had bitten him. "What *are* you?!" She started backing away but he grabbed her arm to stop her.

"Not what, who!"

"What?" She wasn't focused on what he was saying—just wrestling to get out of his grip. "Let go of me."

"Alee, who am I?" His voice was calm and steady. "You know who I am. Who am I?" He wasn't making any sense.

"Jathan sto—."

"No! WHO AM I?" He looked deep into her eyes. His chocolate brown eyes brightened slightly, and softened into an emerald green color. His dark black hair slowly faded to a dusty brown. She was seeing him for the first time. She squeezed her eyes shut and shook her head as if trying to remove his image from her memory, but it didn't work. As soon as she opened her eyes he was standing there, as if he had always been there.

She didn't pull away. Instead she lifted her shaking arm, still wrapped in his warm embrace, until she could see the glow of her tattoo shining from beneath his fingers. When he lifted the sleeve covering his left arm, she instantly saw the shimmer of his tattoo. It was identical to hers and would have been impossible for anyone to fake.

It's not possible. Then their eyes met and she knew in her heart that it was. "Kyle?" It was a whisper so quiet even she wasn't sure she had actually said anything until he nodded. "But, you—" Tears escaped unchecked, and she couldn't make a sound. "—you died. I mean, you did die, right? I saw you—." She suddenly doubted herself.

"I'm so sorry you had to see that." He pulled her into his arms more tightly.

"So it's true?" He nodded, but looked down at the ground, avoiding looking directly at her.

"How? How are you—?" She was bordering on hysterics, yelling and crying at the same time. She was scared and overjoyed all at once. She was holding him so tightly in her arms that she almost crushed his bones. Suddenly, she remembered having actually broken his ribcage when she gave him CPR after she woke up and found him in the ballroom. "Wait, your ribs, I thought I broke them—." She pulled away and looked him up and down. "And I crushed your hand, but its fine now. How?"

"That wasn't me. I mean it was me, but it wasn't me."

"I don't—."

"I can explain. I can. Just not yet. Not here."

"What are—?" Then, like a light turning on, her eyes got wide and she pulled away—no longer afraid, but excited. "Are you a vampire? Wait, are you a ghost?"

Kyle just laughed, which broke the tension between them. "No, I'm not a vampire, and I'm not a ghost."

"Then how?" She was starting to calm down, but it was taking a lot of effort on her part.

"I promise, I will explain it all. Just give me time."

She nodded. "OK." Then, without even a second thought, she wrapped her arms back around him, buried her face in his chest, and let out a sigh of relief.

"It's really you, right? You're really here?"

"Yeah, it's really me, I'm here." He took a deep breath, "Isn't this freaking you out?" He was still holding on to her, afraid that at any moment she might turn and run. But she didn't.

"Sure, at first it was, but then—I'm a witch. I'm a vampire. Damian and Victoria are both, what? Shape-shifters. Now you've come back from the dead. That's what's happened, right? So sure, I'm freaked out—or I was, or maybe I should be—but with everything else—." When she smiled, it lit up the room, and she could feel his body relax.

"All things considered, I really don't think anything could surprise me, let alone scare me, at least not for long."

"Are you sure? I would understand if you turned around and left right now. It's OK if you're freaked out. You're kind of talking in hyper drive."

Alee nodded. "I'm sure. You didn't freak out when you found out about me. What did you tell me?" She looked into his eyes, "Oh yeah, 'I'm not going anywhere.' You meant it then and I mean it now. There is nothing you could do or tell me that will make me leave."

"Do you trust me?"

"You know I do," she whispered.

He took her hand, and started toward the door. "Then there's something I need to show you, but we need to find someplace we can go—someplace private."

"I know a place," she said, and just like that they left the shelter hand in hand, and headed down the dark city street into the night.

12

By the time they made it back to Granny Edith's house it was very late and Alee was exhausted. They had walked the entire way, hand in hand, not saying a word. Just being together was enough for both of them. They entered through the back door into the kitchen, with Kyle being super cautious not to touch or disturb anything. "Don't worry." Alee shook her head as she watched him looking at everything like he was in a museum. "Relax, no one lives here anymore. You're not going to get into trouble if you touch something."

He cocked his head to the side, as if confused. "This is your grandmothers' house, right?"

"Yeah, but—" She hadn't actually had a chance to talk to anyone about the fact that her grandmothers had both died. She hadn't thought it would hit her as hard as it did, and she was surprised when suddenly she was wiping tears from her cheeks.

"Alee?"

She took a deep breath, and turned to look him in the eyes. "Please, don't call me that."

"What?"

"Alee. I'm not her. Not anymore. I may look like her, but I'm not. Please, just call me Aleerah, OK? I know who I am now and I'm OK with that." He noticed that her eyes actually seemed brighter, almost glistening with life. "Actually, I'm better than OK."

"Then why are you crying?"

"I'm not. I mean, I am, but—it's not about that."

"OK. I'm sorry." He smiled, trying to show her he understood, or that he was at least trying to understand. "So, where are your grandmothers, then?" She could hear the concern in his voice. She worked to get her emotions under control.

Then she looked up at him and tried her best to smile. "They died. It was the night of the Founders' Celebration. The night you—"

"Oh, Alee—Aleerah, I'm so sorry." He reached out to her and wrapped his arms around her, holding her close to his chest. His hugs had always been the best. "What happened? I thought they got out."

"I don't know. I wasn't with them. I was—."

"What?"

"You were there in the ballroom. You called me. You were dressed like a waiter. You weren't supped to be there. Why were you there?" She finally pulled away, but not completely out of his arms, just enough to allow her to look up into his eyes.

"I'm so sorry. I didn't mean for any of this to happen. It wasn't supposed to be like this. They weren't supposed to—" Kyle's voice had faded to a mere whisper and Alee could tell that he was talking to himself, almost contemplating something, but she had no idea what it could have been.

"What wasn't supposed to be like this?"

"It's complicated." He pulled away and moved into the living room while Alee just stood in the middle of the kitchen watching him go. She wasn't sure if she was supposed to follow or let him have some time alone.

After a few minutes, she went into the living room. Kyle was kneeling on the floor in the middle of the room, holding a picture of her grandmothers in his hands, while silent tears rolled down his cheeks. He was obviously taking the news much worse than she had expected. She didn't know why. She didn't say anything—just crossed the room and knelt down in front of him, taking his hand in hers. They sat there in silence for a long while.

"I'm so sorry." She could hear the devastation in his voice, as if the world was crumbling around them and he couldn't do anything to stop it—as if he was even supposed to. Kyle had never been an overly sensitive guy, and he wasn't close to either of her grandmothers as far as she knew. It didn't make sense that he would be this upset.

"Kyle, it's not your fault."

"But, it is." When their eyes met she could see that he truly believed it was his fault. "If I hadn't—." He swallowed, holding back tears. "They wouldn't be dead. They shouldn't be—."

"If you hadn't—what? Kyle, there is nothing you could have done that could have led to their deaths." *And mine,* she thought. She sounded convincing and he wanted so badly to believe her, but she could tell that he still didn't.

Kyle lowered his head, in shame or sorrow—she couldn't tell which. Avoiding eye contact seemed to be a new thing with him, as did the crying. Kyle had always been such a strong guy, emotionally as well as physically. He usually told jokes in order to avoid showing any real emotion like pain or sadness. But, as she sat there waiting for him to say something, anything, she realized that there was something new about him. The longer she watched him the more she could see the soft white-golden glow that hovered around him.

"Kyle, you're—." She stopped herself, not really knowing how to describe it. Besides, she hadn't finished her studies on auras yet, and she had no idea what it meant. She knew that the white aura around her grandmother had been an indication that she was dying, but Alee knew that couldn't be the case with Kyle. He had already died.

He looked up at her. His eyes had softened but he wasn't crying any more. With a single finger he touched her lips. "Shhhh. Please don't be afraid."

Alee shook her head, as if to say, 'I'm not,' but didn't dare to speak.

Kneeling on the floor together, Alee watched as Kyle pulled his shirt up over his head, and she could feel all of her muscles tensing with excitement and a warm flush moved through her body. Then before her eyes—she wouldn't have believed it if she hadn't seen it herself—the most beautiful white wings unfolded from behind his back, stretching out at least five feet to his left and right. Kyle sat there watching her face, holding his breath as he waited for a response. He prayed she wasn't going to faint, or worse, run from the room screaming.

Alee blinked a few times, then slowly reached out to touch the soft feathers. "You're an—." As her fingertips gently glided over the top edge she could see out of the corner of her eyes as the full span of his wings started to curl forward, as if reacting to her touch. They were sitting close enough that pretty soon they were both wrapped in the warm embrace of Kyle's wings. "You're an *angel*?!" She was asking him, but she wasn't really expecting an answer. She already knew.

"I'm sorry."

"You're an angel." She knew it was true, but somehow it still seemed so impossible.

"I know." He just watched as she went from disbelief to knowing to understanding to accepting. "I'm sorry."

"Oh. My. God. You're an angel!" Alee clapped her hands over her mouth and shook her head. "I shouldn't say oh my God, should I? I mean, I shouldn't say God like that—. That's bad right? I mean—oh my God!" Then realizing what he had been saying she couldn't understand why he could possibly be sorry. "Why? Why are you sorry? You're an angel. You shouldn't be sorry for that." She felt such joy and happiness.

She felt safe. Yet she knew, somewhere deep down, like a whisper trying to be heard, that she should be worried or shocked, maybe even scared, but she just couldn't get herself to feel those things.

Then, looking him up and down, she started to see the subtle differences—aside from the soft white aura and the massive wing-span—that she hadn't already noticed. His eyes seemed brighter and his skin felt softer, almost like silk. His hair was fuller and shiny, but not in a greasy way. "Didn't you have a—." She touched the side of his nose where there used to be a small brown freckle. "Your skin is perfect. I mean, it's flawless. How is that even possible?" She didn't wait for him to answer before she was pulling away and out of his embrace. She stood up and walked around him, not afraid, but in awe. She wanted to take in every inch of him.

Kyle just sat there, kneeling in the middle of the room, not sure if he should get up, say something, or just give her time. He chose the latter.

She leaned down and ran her hand across his shoulder blades where the wings now protruded out of small little nodes in his back. "Does it hurt?" Kyle just shook his head. There was no blood, or even a sign that they had torn through his skin. "How—. Where do they—?" She was having a hard time completing a thought let alone constructing a full sentence, but he knew exactly what she wanted to know. He stood up, with his back still to her, and she watched as the muscles on his back contracted and released several times slowly pulling the wings back into their hiding place deep beneath his skin.

Then, in an instant, he released them again, and she gasped. "Wow."

"I'm sorry I couldn't tell you before." As he turned toward her his wings vanished as quickly as they had appeared.

"Don't be. You've told me now, but—." She closed her eyes, remembering the first time she saw him. They were in the office at Atlanta High, both waiting for new student orientation to begin.

"What is it?"

"How are you, you? I mean, Kyle—my Kyle—died. I get that, but you were you, or at least you were Jathan even when he, Kyle, wasn't dead." The more Alee talked the more confused she was making herself. "How could there be two of you?"

"There can't. That's why I had to appear as Jathan, instead of myself." He led her over to the couch to sit down. "It's funny. I was never a big believer in God or Heaven and Hell. I hardly ever went to church. I usually just slept in on Sundays." He tried to laugh, but it came out more like an uncomfortable cough. "But, I guess if demons are real then why not angels, right?"

"Demons?"

He cleared his throat and tried to avoid the question, quickly continuing on. "After I died, that night at the Celebration—after I watched *you* die—."

"Watched me die? How? I saw Damian kill you. You were bleeding out on the floor in front of me."

"Not the first time." He swallowed hard and shook his head, remembering that night. "I wasn't even supposed to be there that night. I kept telling myself that maybe if I hadn't shown up you wouldn't have died. I blamed myself."

Alee was shaking her head. "No. How can you even say that? If it hadn't been for you everyone would have died. No one would have made it out."

"That isn't entirely true. Yes, a lot of people died, but not everyone. Most of the people made it out before security managed to seal off the exits. Even your family survived. But, not you. You didn't get out—because you were trying to save me. I had to watch as you, and so many others, were trapped—locked in that basement to feed off of each other until every last one of you was gone. When I couldn't save you, I gave up. I'm not even sure who or what attacked me. I felt a sharp pain in my back and then—nothing." Tears were running down his face again. Alee reached up and brushed his tears away with the back of her hand. "That's why I had to come back. That's why I had to try to change it."

"I don't understand. What are you talking about?"

"All of this has happened already. We died, but I couldn't leave it at that. I couldn't let go. They kept telling me I had unfinished business here on Earth. It took me months of studying; and you know me—I don't like to study. Trying and failing, over and over again, until I finally learned how to use the windows to get back far enough to try and prevent it—to prevent the massacre. But it didn't work. I still couldn't do it. I should have focused on figuring out who had attacked, but I didn't. As soon as I got back and found you—you were all I could think about. I couldn't stop Kyle from going—my angel form can't exist in the same space as my human form, not for long at least—and you still died. I failed."

"You didn't fail, you saved so many others—." It was meant to make him feel better, to be encouraging, but all he heard was that he hadn't saved her. "And I'm just fine. I am what I am and I'm OK with that."

"But if I had figured out who was responsible, maybe the attack would never have happened. If I had thought of a way to stop Kyle—myself—from going. If I had gotten a message to him somehow, then maybe I wouldn't be—maybe we could still be together. I was so focused on the fact that the attack was going to happen that I didn't even think about *how* it happened. What if I was the reason they got in, the reason they made it past security. And even if I wasn't, then maybe, as Jathan, without Kyle there, I could have gotten everyone out. If Kyle hadn't shown up, and it had been just me, you wouldn't have been distracted." He reached out and softly tucked her hair behind her ears. "You never would have run to me, as Jathan, like you did when you saw Kyle. I should have stopped him, and now it's too late, I'm already slipping away. I don't get another chance and I don't know how much longer I can hang on here."

"Stop!" Alee stood up, pulling Kyle along. She took him down the hall and into the bathroom where they stood together in front of the mirror. "Look at yourself. Look at who you are. Can't you see what I see? You are beautiful! You are amazing and you saved so many lives that night, including mine!"

Kyle hung his head. "I couldn't save you."

"Yes you did! I'm a witch, I have been since birth even if I didn't know it. I'm a vampire, on some levels I think I always have been. It didn't matter if I died there in that ballroom or twenty years down the road, this was always my destiny. But, you have to believe me when I tell you that you are the one that saved me. It was your death that drove me to survive. Avenging your death was the only thing I could hold onto. It's the reason I'm standing here. It's the only reason I didn't give up that night. And it doesn't matter what you say, you didn't give up either. The fact that you're standing here right now is proof of that." Alee spun him around, with little effort, until they were face to face. "My heart may not beat as fast as everyone else's, but I am still very much alive, and that is because of you."

Kyle pulled her tight against his chest and wrapped his arms around her, not wanting to let go. "Thank you."

"I love you." She whispered back.

"I love you more."

"Not possible." On her tiptoes she tilted her head back and softly pressed her lips to his. He kissed her back, instantly, only harder and with more passion than she had ever known. She could feel her cool skin heating up under his fingers as they ran up and down her spine then slowly lifted the bottom of her shirt to explore the skin just above her jeans. As his fingers made their way to the front, just below her belly button, a slow exhale, more like a moan, escaped her lips. He popped the button, and it went rolling across the bathroom floor.

Alee's whole body started tingling with desire. Although self-control had been a strong suit of hers in life, she was still such a young vampire. To be so close to Kyle, wanting him so much, physically, and still craving the sweet taste of blood—Kyle's blood—the first human blood she had ever tasted—was almost too much for her newly acquired control. She was all but clawing at his flesh trying to control her impulses. Kyle didn't seem to mind though. In fact it was the exact opposite. He seemed just as enthralled with her.

She wrapped her legs around his waist as he lifted her up and carried her back down the hall to the living room couch. His weight was heavy on top of her, but she hardly noticed that. She felt the pain in her jaw as her fangs abruptly revealed themselves, telling her it was time to feed, and she struggled not to bite, and then, again, gave in and sank her teeth into his neck. He didn't realize what was happening until she pulled away and stood, wide-eyed, looking down at him.

"You don't bleed." It wasn't a question, but she did expect an answer.

"No."

As a human, Kyle's blood had been the sweetest, most amazing thing she had ever tasted, and being so close to him now, she could still smell it. But now that he wasn't human everything was different. "It's because you're an angel, right?" She was trying to understand. She needed to understand.

"Yes."

Her eyes narrowed, not in anger but in a sudden bolt of pain. "You said, that you were never really religious, that you didn't believe in heaven and hell." He just nodded. "You said that if demons are real, then why not angels." That got Kyle's attention. He sat up with a sudden urgency, but she didn't let him speak. "You're an angel. So, what does that make me? Who are the demons?" Kyle's eyes dropped to the floor. "Are they witches?"

Kyle shook his head, "Not all witches."

"Shape shifters, vampires, fairies—all of the above?!"

"Some, yes. It depends. The way they live their lives—*matters*." Their eyes met and Alee's were burning a fiery red. "Aleerah, I never meant—,"

"Yes you did."

"No! I don't see you that way. It's just that, in heaven—. When I first got there and you weren't there I told myself it was because you hadn't died, but you had, and I knew you had. It didn't take me long to figure it out. Some people—some beings—good and bad—they just don't make it to heaven. It isn't fair and I can't explain it." He tried to pull her into his arms, but she wasn't budging, and he wasn't going to force her. "They call them demons, but demons don't have to be supernatural beings like vampires or shape shifters. They can be human too. It all depends."

"Fine! If a demon is what you think I am, than a demon is what I will be." With that, she turned and was out the back door before he had a chance to protest.

Had Alee given him a chance, just a little more time to explain, Kyle would have told her that those weren't his feelings at all. He had never looked at her and seen anything less than perfection. He would have chosen her any day of the week and twice on Sunday, but she hadn't stuck around to find that out. Kyle knew he would have to find another way to reach her, but he wasn't sure how much time he had left. He could already feel himself slipping away. He hadn't meant to stay as long as he had, and he didn't think he could hold on much longer.

13

Phoebe woke up, shivering from the cold, startled to find that she was alone in the dark cellar. She saw that she was covered with dirt and sand, as she slowly pushed herself up from the floor. She got to her feet and stumbled to the door, only to realize that she was locked in. "Break down the door that keeps me in. Break through the lock and let me out!" She began chanting over and over, but nothing happened. Closing her eyes, she pressed both hands on the center of the door. She didn't really know if it was to help with the spell, or to just hold herself up. "When you find the door is locked, all you have to do is knock!" She knocked on the door, and then quickly tried again, but still nothing happened. She tried to force the door open, throwing her body against it again and again, but she wasn't strong enough to break through the lock, let alone the heavy wooden door. She didn't have the energy to try that for very long.

She gave up and used her shoe to break the glass out of one of the small windows high overhead. She found an empty crate and some of her grandmothers' old books, in the far corner and dragged them under the window. Climbing on the crate and stacked books she could barely reach the window to clear away the broken glass, pull herself up, and squeeze out through the window. She dragged herself onto the grass in the middle of her grandmothers' back yard and lay there for a few minutes. She was covered in cuts and bruises, which were illuminated by the light of a million stars. *What the hell happened?* Her head was throbbing as she looked around the yard. She had driven Petra's car, which was still there in the driveway, but there was no sign that anyone else had been there.

Phoebe made her way to her grandmothers' back porch, and up the stairs. Just as she was about to open the back door into the kitchen, she heard yelling coming from inside.

"Fine! If a demon is what you think I am, than a demon is what I'll be."

Phoebe didn't hesitate. She leapt off the porch and hid behind the tall bushes that lined the back of the house. Seconds later, she watched as Alee—Alee, not Aleerah! —rushed from the house and into the woods. She almost stood up to follow, but Alee was too fast. She disappeared into the woods before Phoebe had the chance to stand and call her name, uncertain as she was as to which name to use.

Phoebe didn't waste any time hopping back onto the porch and rushing into the house. She hoped to find her Aunt

Loraline, or maybe her grandmother, Elizabeth, the new family crone, but there was no one there. No one. It was very unusual. A thick cloud of fog filled the living room and billowed into the kitchen and down into the hall. "Hello?" She hesitantly called out. When no one answered, she went back out to the car and climbed in, turning the heat up as soon as the engine was running. *If no one's here, who was Alee yelling at?* Phoebe wondered to herself.

She knew that her father would be worried; she should have driven straight home. However, she was more interested in finding her aunt or her grandmother Elizabeth and telling them what had happened, or at least what she could remember of it—and more importantly, that Aleerah was still alive. So instead of going home, she drove straight to The Black Onyx.

"Grandma? Aunt Loraline?" She headed straight to the kitchen, but no one was there. "Is anyone home?" When she got to the study she saw her father asleep on the couch. "Dad?" she whispered.

He woke up at the sound of her voice and was wide awake in seconds. "It's four in the morning, baby. Where have you been all night?!" He should have been mad, and maybe he was a little, but she could tell by the sound of his voice, and the way he was hugging her, not wanting to let go, that he was more relieved than anything else.

"Dad, what are you doing here?"

"When you didn't come home for dinner I got worried. I waited up till about midnight, and then I headed here to find you. All I found was the den in a complete mess—broken glass on the floor, and no one home. I tried to reach you on your cell—I called your aunt and your grandmother. No one answered." He gestured to a pile of paper towels where he had cleaned up Elizabeth's spilt tea. "Why didn't you answer your phone?" She felt her pockets but her cell phone wasn't there. "Where were you?"

She swallowed hard, knowing that her father wasn't going to like her answer. "I was at Granny Edith's. You said I could go after school. I didn't mean to be there this late, and I'm sorry I didn't call, but I couldn't—and I don't know where my phone is. Something happened, and I—"

Tom let go of her and held her at an arm's length, looking her over. He was seeing her for the first time and realizing that she was covered in dirt, cuts, and bruises. "What happened to you? Are you all right?"

"I am. I'm fine, really. But, dad—I think I saw Aleerah. I think she's alive."

"What? Are you sure?"

"Yes. I mean, I think it was her. It was dark. Only—she was—Alee."

"Where did you see her?"

"She was at the house—Granny Edith's house. She was fighting with someone, or yelling at someone. I'm not really sure. She ran out the back door and by the time I got in the house whoever she was with was gone." Phoebe looked down. "There's something else."

"What is it?"

She wasn't sure what to say, or how to tell her dad that she couldn't use her powers any more. So she decided to show him. "Ignite," she commanded, attempting to throw a fireball into the fireplace—a simple spell—but nothing happened.

"Honey?" Tom was confused, and worried.

"Ignite!" She screamed it, trying to force something to happen. But it was no use. Her hands were shaking as she turned to her father. "I can't—. It's gone." He pulled her close and she sobbed into his chest. "What's happening to me?"

"I don't know, but we'll figure it out." They heard the back door slam shut and they both rushed to the kitchen, where they found Elizabeth about to prepare a cup of tea. "Oh, hello Elizabeth." Tom stammered, "I thought you might be Eric or Loraline coming home. It's late, or early, I guess. Is everything all right?"

"Yes, of course. There were just a few things William and I needed to take care of." Looking out the back door, Elizabeth hoped it wouldn't take her husband long to get home. She remained calm, even though her heart pounded at the thought of revealing her husband's biggest secret to their family. "Have you been here long?"

"I got here a couple of hours ago, but no one was home. Phoebe just got here."

Elizabeth jumped at the opportunity to take the focus off of what she had been doing. She quickly crossed the room toward Phoebe. "You just got in? Where have you been all night?"

"Grandma, I—." She looked at her dad and he just nodded, nudging her toward her grandmother. Tom was mortal and one of the few members of the Wenham family who didn't practice witchcraft. Over the years, though, he had learned a few things, and one of these was that it wasn't smart to try and keep secrets from the Wenham women.

Elizabeth knew from Phoebe's expression that something was very wrong, and her tone changed instantly from disciplinarian to nurturer. It was a gift that years of motherhood had earned her. "You're right Tom, it is early. No better time to start breakfast I suppose. Why don't you pull what we need from the refrigerator while Phoebe and I have a little talk?" She didn't wait for him to respond. She simply took Phoebe's hand and led her to the table. "Now, my dear." She smoothed Phoebe's hair behind her ears and wiped the dried dirt off her face. "What has happened?"

"It's my powers. I can't…" Phoebe closed her eyes, trying to hold back the tears, but it was no use. "They're gone."

"Are you sure?" Phoebe just nodded and looked down at her feet.

"When was the last time you used magic?" Elizabeth prompted.

"I don't—." Then Phoebe remembered that a couple of nights before she had been sitting in her room trying to come up with a plan. Absentmindedly, she had been playing with a candle and practicing a fire spell. "It was a couple of nights ago. I was in my room. I had been listening to music and practicing a fire spell." Elizabeth's eyes narrowed. She didn't like the girls to practice fire spells indoors by themselves these could be dangerous, and, if used carelessly, could cause a lot of damage. "It was nothing, really. Just small candles, I swear."

"You know how I feel—."

"I know. I won't do it again, I'm sorry. But, the point is, that night it worked just like always. But, when I tried a spell earlier this evening—." Her voice was shaking and her hands were still trembling.

"Nothing happened?"

Phoebe shook her head, tears welling up in her eyes again.

"What kind of spell was it?"

"It was simple, just a spell to unlock a door. I've done it a thousand times—" Elizabeth's stare froze, and Phoebe felt her own checks flush. She rushed on, not sure how much of the truth she should or shouldn't tell. "—when I've locked myself out of the car or forgot my house key." She was defending herself, but she could tell that her grandmother knew there was more to it than she was saying.

"Don't worry, we'll figure this out. I'm sure it's nothing," Elizabeth said. But even Tom, who turned now to look at her from across the room, could tell that she didn't really believe it.

"Now, tell me where you were all night and why you're covered in dirt—." She paused when she noticed something else scattered over Phoebe's clothing—white sand. Cocking her head to the side, she studied Phoebe's reaction. "And sand?! Phoebe, where have you been?" Everyone always joked that Elizabeth should have been a spy. Her ability to pick up on the little details was scary sometimes. Even Tom hadn't noticed the sand. He was just relieved that his daughter was here, and safe.

Phoebe quickly started to brush off her clothes with her hands, but it was no use, she was just spreading the dirt around. She gave up. "I was at Granny Edith's house. I'm sorry. I know I shouldn't have been there without asking you first, but Dad said—. I mean, I just needed to find something—and then she trapped me. I didn't even see—."

"*Who* trapped you?"

"Um—" Phoebe couldn't be positive that it had been Alee, even if every ounce of her instinct told her it was. "—I don't know."

"No Phoebe, you need to tell her." Tom was the dad everyone wanted. He was always able to make you feel better, no matter what had happened. Even if you failed at something or you did something wrong, he would find a way to encourage you to either believe in yourself or to do better the next time. "She can't help you unless you're honest with her, and neither can I."

"What aren't you telling me dear?"

Tom turned back to the stove and started cooking: eggs, bacon, French toast, and hash browns. It may have been early, but he needed something to keep him busy and awake. Besides, he didn't want to leave, but he wanted to give them a little privacy.

Phoebe took in a deep breath. She knew her grandmother would know if she was lying or withholding information, so there wasn't really any point in trying. "I think it was

Aleerah, but I couldn't see her, so I'm not a hundred percent sure."

"If you couldn't see her then why do you think it was her?

"I didn't see her at first, not when she had me in Granny Edith's cellar—."

"You were in the cellar?" Elizabeth cut her off.

"Um—. I went there to—."

"Never mind, we'll talk about that later." She exchanged a worried look with Tom. "You said you couldn't see her, so what made you think it was Aleerah?"

"I could smell her—the perfume she uses, I guess. The last thing I remember is her telling me something—." She looked down, deep in thought. "She said, I wasn't safe, I think. But it was later, when I woke up, that I realized what had happened. My powers were gone. I felt tired—drained— like she had sucked all the energy out of me. I was locked in the cellar. I got out through the window. I saw her leaving the house and running into the woods out back but I couldn't move to follow her. She was way too fast, Even if I did have the energy to run, I wouldn't have been able to catch her."

Elizabeth pulled her granddaughter close and tilted her head back and forth examining her neck. There, just behind her left ear, were two small puncture wounds. "She's bitten you."

"WHAT?!" Phoebe's hand went straight to her neck. She could feel the holes. They were already starting to close over with dried up scabs. "Why? Why would she bite me?"

Loraline and Eric had been cleaning up the mess left behind after Eric had killed Gregory Davis: his maker, longtime friend, and prominent member of Atlanta society. They had gotten back just in time to overhear Phoebe's account of what had happened, listening from around the corner. They walked into the kitchen at just that moment.

"To sedate you!" Eric had no doubt in his mind what had happened. It's what he would have done if he were in her shoes. The fact that his daughter had thought to do it too made him proud, if more than a little scared.

"What do you mean?" Phoebe asked, flustered at the addition to her audience. The fear was gone from her voice, though, and all that remained was anger and exasperation.

Eric tried to explain. "The venom in her fangs. Aleerah, if it *was* Aleerah, probably bit you only in order to sedate you. It's actually quite smart if you think about it. It would have made you sleepy, allowing her to cast a spell or something, temporarily stealing your powers—or borrowing them, depending on how you want to look at it." His attempt to lighten the mood didn't really go over very well with Phoebe, or Tom.

"Uncle Eric!" Phoebe was shocked at how casually her uncle had accepted the fact that Alee had most probably bitten her. But then again, he was a vampire. More importantly, why wasn't he surprised by the idea that Alee might still be alive?

Elizabeth, characteristically, went into problem-solving mode before anything had actually become a problem. "OK, if Aleerah is alive then she has to be planning something, and it must be big if she has gone to the trouble of taking Phoebe's powers." Pacing back and forth, she kept fiddling with a small strip of leather in her hand. "She's probably feeling betrayed by her friends—angry at what's happening." Then, realizing what she had been holding, she held the leather Guardian band out to Loraline. "If I were her, I would go after the ones I believed were responsible. I'd go after the shifters."

"I just don't understand why she wouldn't just come to us for help." Loraline was fighting off tears, leaning on her husband for support. "If she's alive, why is she hiding from us? It's been weeks."

Elizabeth laughed. "Because she's stubborn, like her mother, and probably thinks she can handle it all on her own." Elizabeth softly touched the side of Loraline's check. "But she's not hiding from us. In her own way, I think she's trying to protect us. She's a lot like you. She has your strength and your stubbornness. Both are gifts, in their own way."

Eric stood up and began to pace. "Not to point out the negative, but if she did survive the night of the Founders' Celebration, then we have more on our hands then just a stubborn teenager. I saw her die. I was there. I have my doubts that she was strong enough to survive, but if she did, then she's not only dealing with loss. She is also dealing with the blood lust of a newborn vampire. I'm not sure how well she will be able to control those urges on her own. She wasn't ready."

"Eric?" Loraline had just been trying to keep herself busy the last few weeks, trying not to lose herself in the grief of her daughter's death. Her head spun at the thought that Aleerah might be out there, not quite alive, roaming the streets seeking vengeance, or just hunting—feeding.

"I'm just saying, if it really was Aleerah, and I'm not convinced that it was, then we need to consider the possibility that we may be dealing with an Aleerah that none of us has ever met." Eric knew what he was talking about. He was over seven hundred years old, and he had seen vampires come and go, time and time again. "Being a newborn is hard enough when you've got the help of your maker, but doing it alone, and with Aleerah's unknown additional powers—. I just don't know."

"Will she survive?" Loraline's eyes were pleading, almost begging for him to give her some hope. "Can she?"

Eric couldn't stand to see his wife so scared, but he wasn't going to lie to her either. "I hope so. But honestly, I don't know." He grabbed a sports bottle from the refrigerator and downed the thick red liquid without heating it up.

"Well then, if she won't ask for help then we need to figure out what her plan is and be there when she realizes that she needs our help."

Tom brought plates and silverware to the table, and set out dishes of food, all the while listening carefully. He turned toward Loraline. "This family isn't going to lose anyone else, at least not without a fight. We'll find a way to help her. That's what we do."

They all took their seats at the table and, though it was too early for breakfast, none of them wanted to leave, so they ate.

William came in a little while later, intending to pick up his wife Elizabeth. When he saw the gathering in the kitchen, though, he knew he wasn't going anywhere. He joined the family, ate breakfast, and listened as the rest of them talked into the late morning hours about what Alee may or may not have done, where she might or might not have gone, and how she must be feeling. In the end, it all came back to vengeance—revenge—retribution. Justice, if you will.

Eric was convinced that Alee would try to punish Damian and Victoria for the role they had played in the Founders' Celebration attacks. Yet, when he brought up the idea of using them as bait to lure Alee home, William was the first to object. "No matter what they did, Damian and Victoria aren't to blame for what happened." Everyone's eyes, including Elizabeth's, turned toward him.

He was usually a very soft-spoken man, only speaking up when he felt very strongly about something. Now that he had everyone's attention, now that they were looking at him as if he had just told them the world wasn't round, he tried to explain. "It's true that what they did was awful; and yes, they should be punished. We all know that. But Aleerah is most likely out for revenge, and she isn't going to settle for just punishing them. If she is in fact a newborn, then she will likely stop at nothing to get what she wants. Damian and Victoria, they're just kids. They were used, like pawns in a game of chess. They were manipulated into doing the dirty work of others who held a grudge against our kind. They don't deserve to die." William's heart had started racing. *Our kind, our kind, our kind.* His words echoed back at him. What had he said? Beads of sweat appeared along his hairline. *Our kind, our kind.* He wasn't about to show them how nervous he was. These were his children, his grandchild, and he was determined not to be ashamed of himself, or what they might think of him. Still, deciding whether to tell them what he was, or even how to tell them, wasn't easy.

"What makes you so sure? How could you possibly know that?" Eric could hear the blood flowing through William's veins—saw the hairs stand up on the back of his neck. "What aren't you telling us William?" Eric's eyes narrowed in on the vein pulsing just beneath the skin of William's throat. Then it happened: it was subtle, and Eric was probably the only one who noticed. As Elizabeth tightened her grip on her husband's hand, there was a spark, a glint, a flash of fury that crossed William's face. Then it was gone. Eric had never seen William yell, or scream, or show even an ounce of anger in his life, but he hadn't been able to hide it this time.

"Dad?" Loraline was looking back and forth between her father and her husband, who seemed to be locked in a silent contest of wills.

"William?" Eric didn't flinch.

Elizabeth cleared her throat, trying to break the tension, or just divert everyone's attention. "Loraline, there is something your father and I want to—" She had to choose her words carefully. She knew this conversation could either end well, or extremely badly. "—*need* to talk to you about."

"What is it?" Loraline was hesitant. She had never seen her father so serious and she could feel Eric's eyes burning a hole into William as he stood beside her, not moving, not breathing, but simply waiting. The old vampires could do that, stand as motionless as a statue. It was eerie, but she had gotten used to it.

She had to say it quickly, like ripping a band aid off of an old cut; otherwise she might have lost her nerve. "Loraline, your father is a fairy." She held up her hands the second the word fairy came out of her mouth because everyone around her had their own shock reactions. They were primed to fire questions, accusations, suspicion, and even distrust. She was prepared to defend him with her life if she had to. "It's not a big deal, although we probably shouldn't have kept it from you this long. It was Granny Edith we really were hiding it from. We're telling you now and that is what's important."

No one could hide their surprise and alarm, and Phoebe most of all. "A fairy? A fairy—as in you feed on the flesh of little children?" She was upset and, being a teenager, she often didn't think before she spoke. But after all, this was her grandfather.

"Phoebe, stop," Loraline snapped, and then pretended to laugh, as if it was all a poorly executed prank. "He's not a fairy. Your grandmother is kidding." Turning to her parents, Loraline just shook her head. "Really, a fairy? With everything that has been going on, you really think pranks and practical jokes are appropriate?" She had never talked to her parents that way before, but then again they had never done something so tasteless before.

William stepped forward and took Loraline's hand in his own. "I should have told you a long time ago." His voice quivered as he spoke and his eyes glistened. Loraline suddenly realized that he seemed to have the weight of the world on his shoulders, when typically her father was the most light-hearted, stress-free man she knew. "I'm sorry." He took a deep breath before turning to his granddaughter, who was sitting on the edge of her seat. "Phoebe, not all fairies are evil. Not all the stories you've heard are true." Ashamed, his eyes drifted down toward the floor. "Though others are, I'm afraid, and that is why I choose not to live that life." Taking Elizabeth's hand back in his, he pulled her into his arms. "Everyone has free will and I chose your grandmother. She was the one thing in my life, until you kids were born, that made me sure of my decision. I've never looked back and I've never regretted it."

"Dad—." Loraline couldn't even finish before William cut her off.

William softly kissed Elizabeth's forehead, then stepped away and, with no effort at all, released his wings. They tore through the back of his shirt with a ripping sound that should have hurt, but didn't. "William, your shirt." Elizabeth sounded disappointed.

"It's fine, dear," he said, looking up at the faces of his family. Elizabeth turned to see that everyone, including Eric, was gawking at the vastness of his beautiful, yet eerie, black and silver wings.

"He isn't going to hurt you." Elizabeth nearly spit the words at her family, disgusted by their reaction. "He's the same man he has always been. What he is doesn't change anything. These wings don't change anything!" There were tears threatening to fall from her eyes as she tried hard to be strong.

"It changes everything." Eric wasn't scared, or even mad. He was focused. Before Elizabeth had the chance to respond, he was only inches away from William, studying his almost iridescent wings. "William, think about it. If you're a fairy, as it seems you are, then so is Loraline. So is Phoebe—" Phoebe's eyes widened and she was about to protest but Eric put his hand up to stop her. "—and so is Aleerah. How Aleerah survived when no other dhampir ever has—. It had to be in part because of your bloodline. We always thought it was because the Wenham bloodline was so strong and so pure, but fairies are known to live, what, into their hundreds right?"

William just nodded, but Loraline answered, "Three hundred. Three hundred years is the average lifespan of a fairy."

"How do you even—."

"I don't know, I just—I just do."

Everyone just stared at her. Eric finally broke the silence, turning back to William. "It must have been the strength of *your* blood that kept Alee alive all those years."

"But, fairies are also known to have—" He didn't want to offend his father-in-law. "—tempers. I've been where Aleerah is, and I know the confusion, temptation, anger—the *thirst* she's feeling. Having a fairy's temper on top of that—? Let's just say it could be a very dangerous combination. I'm not so sure we will be able to stop her." No one said a word as the extent of what was happening started to sink in.

"Dad—." Loraline looked twenty years younger, seeing her father for the first time. "Daddy, why didn't you tell us? How did you hide it?"

"When I met your mother I fell in love almost instantly. But, fairies and witches, they're not meant to be together. Our relationship was doomed to fail if anyone found out who, or what, I really was. In order to be with your mother I made the choice to live as a human. Your mother accepted me, wings and all, but I knew her family wouldn't. So I asked her to bind my powers. I knew that was the only way to have a life with her. When your sister and you were born, I had been living this life for so long that I didn't want you to see me as anything other than your father. Neither one of you had the physical traits of a fairy—." he shared a look with Elizabeth. "We thought—. We believed that since my powers had been bound when you were conceived, neither of you would be affected by my blood. Besides, our family isn't all that open to welcoming in other cultures." Eric's eyes widened and William responded genuinely. "Present company excluded, son. Yet, even you know how hard it was to gain the favor of Loraline's grandparents when you two first became involved."

"Something I'd rather not re-live." Eric had been acquainted with the Wenhams for many years prior to Loraline's birth. However, it wasn't until she had grown up and they realized what a strong connection the two of them had that his involvement in the family affairs became offensive to the family elders.

William took a deep breath; his heartbeat had slowed to its natural cadence, and he was finally feeling calm again. "I've been away from that life for so long it doesn't even feel like a part of me anymore."

"Then why are you telling us now?" Eric asked, not interrogating him, but merely trying to understand.

"There isn't a whole lot that people actually know about fairies. For the most part, fairies are a very private, hidden race. The ones you hear of, feeding off the flesh of babies, stealing the souls of the elderly, or haunting the woods and preying on the travelers, do not represent the majority of fairies." Phoebe's eyes were wide with both fear and intrigue. "The older a fairy gets, the more docile he becomes. Not weak or helpless, but less likely to fall victim to the desires and impulses that drive so many fairies to lead devastatingly vicious and reclusive lives.

"Fairies are much like the lone wolf that leaves the pack at a young age. It is rare to find fairies choosing to live in a community, let alone in harmony with humans. There is too much fear and hatred between the two. Neither race really trusts the other. That is partly because they do not fully understand each other."

Tom was listening quietly the whole time, taking in everything William said, yet he still couldn't wrap his mind around the enormity of the news. "But, why now? Why undo the binding spell now? What good could possibly come from that?"

"Telepathy!" Then, without any forewarning, he stopped speaking and burrowed his way into their minds. *All fairies have the power of telepathy. It's our primary source of communication. Though, when used with those of other races—.* He focused only on Tom, peering deep into his eyes. *—we can get into the depths of your memories, your thoughts, and we can unveil your deepest secrets: the thoughts, the feelings, the information you don't want anyone to know.'* Tom began rubbing his temples, as if he were starting to get a headache, and then fell to his knees. Phoebe quickly ran to his side.

"Daddy?!"

The pain stopped the second William looked away. "The process isn't very pleasant, though, for either party." William cleared his throat and took a long drink of water.

Thinking back to Mildred, Loraline remembered that although she was over four hundred years old, she didn't look a day over sixty-five, not that sixty-five was young. She had seemed so gentle and soft spoken, and Loraline hadn't made the connection when it happened. Now she remembered, though: how she and Eric had been talking in hushed voices there outside the founders' boardroom—how Mildred had been talking to Judge Plitt yet watching her and Eric with fierce intensity—how the migraine had hit in those same moments.

"Mildred." She said it out loud, but it was more of a thought than a comment.

"Excuse me?" William's ears perked up at the mention of Mildred's name.

"She works downtown, for the founders." Loraline felt Eric pull away ever so slightly, and she turned to him "You know her, don't you?"

Eric just nodded. He knew her, not only from her position with the founders, but also from long before. "I met her a long time ago. She was still young, maybe thirty, when she started working for Gregory. It was long before Atlanta had even been thought of." He shook his head, remembering so many times that she had been more like a mother to him than his birth mother ever had. However, as he grew into his role as a vampire, as he understood and accepted his new life, he was quick to leave her behind to grow old, to be Davis' problem instead of his own.

"Judge Plitt said she was over four hundred years old. She looks like she is still in her sixties." Loraline frowned at her father. "How old are you?"

"That's not important. What's important is Aleerah. If Eric is right, the lycanthropes are the least of our worries right now. We need to be focusing on Aleerah and bringing her home safely." William moved past his daughter and nudged Eric to follow him out the door and down the hall.

Elizabeth smiled as she leaned in and whispered it into Loraline's ear. "He was two hundred and eighty three on his last birthday."

"I heard that Liz!" William shouted back jokingly from down the hall.

Elizabeth laughed as she crossed the room to follow her husband down the hall. "You know I don't like it when you call me Liz!"

Tom, Phoebe, and Loraline were still too shocked and amazed to move let alone think, or try to take the discussion any further. They stayed back in the kitchen, quietly sitting together, finding comfort in not being alone.

14

Alee was hurt and angry as she ran through the dark woods. Her only intention was to finish what she had started. She would make Damian and Victoria pay for what they had done. If it proved her to be a demon, like Kyle had said, then so be it. She didn't really care anymore.

By the time she made it back to Damian's house, the sun was threatening to illuminate the sky off on the horizon. Alee didn't care. She was one of the lucky ones. She was a day-walker. The sun didn't have the same weakening effect on her as it did on other vampires. She had been afraid that it might, once she fully turned. Even Eric had warned her that once she became a full-blooded vampire she would be more susceptible to the vampire weaknesses. *"The older you get the less the sun will bother you, but when you first change it can be almost unbearable,"* he had told her.

"It's never bothered me before, and I'm half vampire now. Why would that change?" she had asked.

"I can't explain why it happens. I can only tell you what it will feel like. The sun won't kill you; it only weakens you. The longer you spend outside during the day the more tired you will become. You'll heal more slowly during the day or any time you're in direct contact with sunlight. That's why it's important to hunt between sunset and sunrise." Eric had knelt before her and stared into her eyes. *"Our people are at their most vulnerable during the day. I have seen many good men and women die at the hands of our enemies because they let their guard down, thinking they could handle the effects of the sun's rays."*

Alee had heard his warnings and taken them seriously. However, what she discovered, as a vampire, was nothing like what he had described. Her eyes were a little more sensitive to the light of the sun, but dark sunglasses fixed that—they just had to be darker than she would normally have selected. Her energy level never faltered, although she did find it easier to rest during the day, and hunting, for many reasons, was easier under the moon's glow.

She stood just inside the tree line about twenty yards behind Damian's house and stared up at his bedroom window. She could hear movement in the house and four clear heartbeats. *Four? Who else could be there?* Alee knew, as everyone else did, that Damian and Victoria's dad had died when they were young. As far as she knew Damian and Victoria's mom wasn't dating anyone. Damian had often said that his mother was adamant that no man could ever be as good as their father, so there wasn't a point in dating. Yet, there was an older male in the house that morning. Men's heartbeats, like their voices, resonate at a deeper level. It was one of the first things Alee had noticed in her training with Eric. Alee could hear the conversation clearly.

"I don't *know* what happened. Why won't you listen to me?" Victoria was crying as she pleaded with her mother.

"Then where have you been all night and why didn't you call?" Karen, their mother, was a stickler for the rules, but even Alee had been surprised when she had sent Damian and Victoria to school on the first day that it re-opened after the attack. It wasn't like people at the Celebration hadn't recognized Karen. It wouldn't have been hard to put two and two together and figure out that Damian and Victoria were also shifters.

"I don't—. I woke up this morning on the porch swing. I remember—I remember being in a cellar. It was cold. There was a man—a fairy."

"A fairy?!"

"A fairy?" Alee was confused.

"He—he had his hands on me—."

"A fairy did what?!" Karen was angry. She wasn't angry with her daughter but at the idea that a creature as disgusting as a fairy had done anything to her child. "Who was it? How do you know it was a fairy?"

"He had wings—black and silver wings like in that book you showed us. I don't know, I just knew."

What is she talking about, a fairy? Alee had dropped Victoria off at The Black Onyx and she couldn't figure out any reason she would be making up a story about a fairy. What possible advantage would that give her?

Karen was twirling Victoria around and around looking at every inch of her. "Did he hurt you?" She couldn't see any signs of cuts, bruises, or bite marks, but that didn't mean anything.

"No, I don't think so."

"Then what did he do?" Karen snapped. "I'm sorry. I'm sorry." She grabbed her daughter into her arms and just sat there for a while. "This isn't your fault. I'm sorry I yelled."

"Karen, it's going to be all right." It was the mystery man's voice. "Whoever it was didn't hurt her. If it really was a fairy he was probably just probing her for information, and since she doesn't know very much it isn't really an issue."

"I hope you're right, Jonathan. I never meant to put my family in danger, I only—."

"I know—" He cut her off before she could apologize. "—and I'm sorry for that. I've already called the elders."

"You've called the elders?!" Victoria chimed in instantly, and Alee could hear her heartbeat race with excitement. "Are they coming here?"

"How does she know about the elders?" Jonathan sounded concerned, and Karen didn't respond.

The elders, who the hell are they? Alee hadn't heard anyone in her family ever mention the elders before, but even without knowing who they were she didn't like the sound of it. She slowly moved across the tree line making her way closer to the house, while still staying hidden in the shadows. There were four of them, and although she was pretty sure she could take them individually, she wasn't so sure she would win a fight against all four of them at the same time.

"Um, hello! I'm a wolf. You didn't think Grandma would tell me about the elders? Hell, Damian has multiple animal forms, one of which is a wolf—."

"Victoria, you are nowhere near ready to join the elders if that's what you're thinking. Jonathan, tell her, please."

"Your mother's right. The elders aren't a bunch of teenage shifters. They're extremely dangerous and powerful. Before you go forcing yourself on them you need to learn to respect them. You also need to understand not only what they're about, but what it really means to be a shifter." Jonathan's voice was so familiar. Alee was sure she had heard it before, but she couldn't place it, and she couldn't think of a single Jonathan that she knew.

"Thank you for the advice, but you're not my father. I think—."

"Victoria!" Damian barked. "He's trying to help. Besides, he's been with us a hundred percent on this. If you go off all halfcocked and get yourself or the rest of our family into trouble then it affects him too."

"Seriously Damian, how well do you even know the guy? My God, he makes coffee for a living!" Alee had known Victoria to be impudent and sassy from time to time, but she had never heard her talk to her own brother that way.

"Victoria Charlotte Ward, watch your mouth!" Alee was leaning back against the shed in the Ward's backyard and now had a clear view into the living room as Karen snapped back at her daughter. "Mr. Sanders is my guest and while he is here you will treat him with respect or you will stay in your room. Is that understood?"

"Yes." Victoria sounded broken and defeated as she answered her mother.

Jonathan Sanders— Jonathan Sanders—. Where have I heard that name before? He makes coffee for a living? His name ran through Alee's head over and over.

"Jonathan, what made you contact the elders so soon?" There was a hint of fear in Karen's voice as she spoke.

"The attack on your son. He said it was a vampire. If that's true, then they're bringing the fight into your home and that needs to be dealt with."

"What do you mean the attack on Damian? When?!" Victoria sounded pissed, but no one was paying her any attention now.

Karen just ignored her questions and addressed Jonathan's assumption. "Jonathan, that's absurd. You can't possibly be serious. We attacked them first. How do you think the elders are going to react when they find out that we're the ones who started this?" Karen had had experience with the elders as a child and none of it was good. "They will not be as forgiving as you seem to think."

"I don't think they'll be forgiving, but they are the only ones who can help us now."

"What the hell is going on?" Victoria cut in. "And why the hell won't anyone answer me."

Karen was tired of her daughter's smart mouth and quickly put a stop to it. "Watch your language young lad—."

Alee remembered! *Jonathan Sanders*. "Java Jolt!" She gasped and quickly covered her mouth when she realized she had spoken out loud.

"Did you hear that?" Before the words were even out of Jonathan's mouth, Damian was halfway out the back door scanning the tree line.

Alee had ducked around the back side of the shed the second she realized what she had done. There was no way they hadn't heard her but she had no intention of getting caught. If spying through their windows wasn't enough to make them angry, she knew that attacking Damian earlier that evening was. She didn't want to find out what they would do if they found her. *"I cannot be seen. I cannot be felt. I cannot be heard. I cannot be smelt! I walk undetected for only those I grant to see. And as I have spoken so now shall it be!"* Her voice was hurried and almost breathless as she stumbled to remember the words.

"Alee?" Damian called out to her from the back porch.

Alee struggled to pull her clothes off and stash them in an old wooden barrel behind the shed. *"I cannot be seen. I cannot be felt. I cannot be heard. I cannot be smelt! I walk undetected for only those I grant to see. And as I have spoken so now shall it be!"* She clenched her eyes tightly shut as she chanted the spell one more time, just to be sure, before slowly opening them up. Lifting her hands in front of her face a silent sigh of relief escaped her lips.

"ALEE?!" Damian shouted as he turned the corner to the back side of the shed, but no one was there. Alee held her breath as she stood tight against the wall. He was less than five feet from her and staring right into her eyes, only he didn't know it.

Alee could hear the others gathering on the back porch. "Damian, is anyone out there?"

"No, no one—" He called back, but didn't move. "—but she was!" That last part was a whisper. He could feel her there, as if his body were being pulled toward her by an invisible string.

"You should come back inside Damian." Jonathan's voice was stern. Alee realized then that he clearly played an important role in what they were planning. He was calling the shots.

"Yeah, I'll be right there." Damian hollered back over his shoulder, waving him off. "Alee, are you out here?" It was only a whisper, but he was looking right at her, and it sent a chill down her spine. She stepped closer, careful not to make a sound. She was only inches in front of him. He couldn't see her, smell her, or even feel her unless she allowed it. He was so close, and she knew she could kill him right then and there if she wanted to. It wouldn't have been hard. A quick turn of his head would snap his neck like a twig. She was like a ghost in the night and could have been gone before anyone even realized what had happened.

Alee leaned forward, with every intention of killing him, but when it came down to it she couldn't do it. As her hands moved around his neck she could feel her body heating up almost instantly. Damian's eyes got wide, a reaction to her cold touch perhaps or maybe just his intuition trying to tell him something. Before he could respond, Alee pulled him close and pinned him against the wall, but instead of snapping his neck like she had planned, she pressed her lips against his and kissed him. Damian tried to cry out, but only for a second before reaching out into the empty air that held him there, to find her naked body, soft and smooth beneath his hands.

The kiss lasted longer than the last time. The warmth of his hands as they caressed the length of her back and finally cupped the checks of her butt, pulling her closer into him, made her body shiver with want and desire. "Alee—." She released him abruptly, his knees buckled beneath him, and he fell to the ground, breathless.

The leaves flew up in disarray and he heard small sticks crack under her weight as she ran off into the woods. "Wait, don't go!" he called after her, but she was gone. Damian pulled himself back up, straightened his clothing, and headed back toward the house.

"What are you doing?" Damian ran straight into Victoria as he turned the corner. She was eyeing him up and down. "Who were you talking to?"

Not really looking at her, he just shook his head. "Alee's back!" He pushed past her and headed straight toward the house without looking back. He could feel his sister's eyes boring a hole into his back the whole way, but he wasn't in the mood to try and explain what may or may not have just happened when he wasn't a hundred percent sure himself.

Victoria wasn't willing to be brushed off so easily. She grabbed Damian by the back of his shirt and spun him around so she could look him in the eyes. "You're sure?"

Damian just nodded. "As sure as I can be."

"Then we have to go after her."

Damian was shocked by his sister's lack of emotion. "And do what V, kill her?"

"What? NO! She's our friend! If she's back we need to *help* her. Besides, those witches may be hurting—."

"You don't understand," Damian interrupted. "They're not hurting her. She's one of them."

"What? What do you—?"

"Aleerah—Alee. She was right in front of us the whole time."

Victoria scoffed as she went past Damian, shaking her head. Their mother and Jonathan had already gone back inside. "That isn't even possible Damian." She was disappointed and it showed. "And, I thought you were being serious."

"I *am* being serious!" Damian snapped, but Victoria didn't stop walking. "I've known who she was since the night of the Founders' Celebration. But I didn't say anything because—."

"Because why? You thought you'd sound crazy? Well, you were right. You do!"

"Because you killed her!" Victoria stopped dead in her tracks and turned, half way up the back steps, to face Damian straight on.

Eyes narrow—if looks could kill, Damian would have been dead on the spot. "What did you say?"

"Because you killed her!" Damian watched his sister closely, afraid she might attack, but she didn't move.

"Explain."

"I can't really. Aleerah was there—so much fighting was going on all around me. Then I heard her voice. I would have known her voice anywhere, but I thought it was just in my head. She was screaming at me. 'RELEASE HIM!' But I didn't. It took me a second to realize that what I heard was real, and when I looked up—it was Alee who was standing there, but only for a few seconds. I saw you coming—."

"I wouldn't have attacked—."

"I saw you and I tried to stop you. I screamed, but you got to her first. She didn't even see you coming. She had no chance of surviving." Damian fell to his knees and tears ran down his face. "I didn't want to tell you. I didn't want to hurt you like that, but—,"

Victoria just stood there in shook. "I was at her funeral."

"But she wasn't dead!"

"I was at her funeral." It was all Victoria could say. She couldn't accept the thought that she actually could have killed one of her best friends. "I was there. I saw them bury her."

"No you didn't. You saw them bury her casket, nothing more." Damian had already had time to accept the fact that not everything you see in life is real and, even though it still hurt him to think of Alee's funeral, he knew that those memories held many of the answers he sought.

Victoria sat down on the porch steps. "We have to find her. We have to explain."

"Explain what? Explain that we're shape shifters and while we never meant to hurt her we had to fight for our rightful place within the Underground!" Damian sat down next to Victoria. "She's a witch and that alone doesn't make her our enemy, but—."

"But—? But what, Damian?! This is Alee we're talking about. The woman you love! Right? How can this even be a question for you?"

"Because, Victoria, I saw her die. I saw you kill her. Witches don't have the power to just come back from the dead, and—" Damian looked down at the ground. "—and it was her. Earlier this evening, it was Alee who attacked me."

"You said it was a vampire."

"I know." When Damian looked up and their eyes finally met, Victoria understood what he was saying.

"Oh my God!"

"Yeah."

"How—."

"I don't know."

They sat in silence for a while, just staring out into the thick trees that lined the back of their property. When the back door finally opened, they both jumped, startled by the interruption. "What are you guys doing out here?" Karen sat down between them and wrapped her arms around their shoulders, pulling them in for a hug, but neither one answered her. "Jonathan's getting ready to leave, and it's getting cold out here. Do you want to come back inside for some tea or hot chocolate?"

"Not yet, but we'll be in soon."

"All right, take your time." She kissed Damian's forehead and then turned and did the same to Victoria before standing and turning back to the house.

"Mom!?" Damian stopped her just as she was about to go into the house. "I love you."

"I love you too." Karen smiled at her children as she turned to head back into the house.

As the door shut behind Karen, Damian turned to his sister and she knew, by the look on his face, that he couldn't just let this go. Neither could she. They stood up simultaneously and without a word between them took off into the woods: two great wolves, speeding in the direction Alee had gone.

15

Not really thinking about what she was doing, Alee ran straight back to her parent's house. "What did I do? What did I do?" Still invisible, Alee was pacing in the woods behind The Black Onyx. She hadn't stayed around long enough to hear Damian and Victoria talking, so she had no idea what their plans were, but she knew she had to act fast if she was going to maintain the upper hand.

She longed to avenge Kyle's death, even though she was still upset that he had called her a demon, implying the same of all her family members, and all the others the lycanthrope had killed. However, every time there had been an opportunity, she had found herself pulled to Damian by an attraction she didn't even know she felt. So instead of killing him, she had ended up kissing him. She had to find a way to put those feelings aside, but she didn't know where to start. Then it hit her! If she was going to defeat the lycanthropes she had to utilize her powers as a witch, not just the physical strength she had as a vampire. Fighting wasn't going to do it, but magic could. Deep down, she already knew it, it was the whole reason she had taken Phoebe's powers in the first place. It just seemed that any time she got around Damian she lost her focus. Well, he wasn't here now!

Like the wind, she rushed into the shop, down the hall, and locked the door of the den behind her. She gathered supplies into a leather satchel that she plucked off a hook behind the door. She gathered white sand, five candles of varied colors, a handful of small potion jars individually labeled, and an old leather-bound book she pulled off the top shelf. It was the family's "Book of Shadows," or "Grimoire," as her grandmother always called it! She had no right to take it without permission; however, she didn't really care at the moment. Alee knew the spells it contained would be the only way to defeat the lycanthropes. Not wanting to be detected, she quietly dragged the satchel along the floor, so if someone showed up, they wouldn't see it floating along in the air like a balloon full of helium. She slowly headed out the door and down the hall to her bedroom. Once inside, she quickly cleaned up and got dressed. Staying invisible might have made things easier, but she didn't want another naked encounter with Damian, his hands on her bare skin was too much for her to handle and she wasn't sure she could resist him again. She wore black from head to toe. Just as she was lifting the window to make her escape, she heard him behind her.

"Aleerah!?" It was Eric. She had let her guard down, something Eric had taught her could get her killed. She stopped in her tracks, not saying a word. "Aleerah, I can help, but you have to let me." She wasn't so sure that he could and she certainly wasn't willing to put her father's life in danger too.

"No you can't. Not this time!" Then she was out the window in seconds, and running like the wind.

"ALEERAH, NOOOOO!" He shouted after her. He couldn't see her, she was too fast, but he could smell her, and that meant he could track her. He rushed out of the room and into the shop. It was only seconds before he was out the front door and quickly following his daughter.

"Aleerah?" Loraline had come running into the shop when she heard Eric yelling. However, by the time she got there they were both already gone and the door was shutting behind him. "Mom! Dad! Come quickly!" If Alee really had been there, Loraline was going to be damn sure she didn't get away again.

"Was Aleerah just here?" Phoebe came running into the room.

"Yes and she isn't getting away again." With her right arm, Loraline quickly swept the table in the center of the shop clean, sending crystals, stones, books, and more crashing to the ground. She unfolded a large map of Atlanta and spread it across the table. Elizabeth knew exactly what Loraline's plan was when she came in and saw the scene before her. She grabbed a scrying stone out of one of the nearby baskets, to help. Threading the stone onto a long leather necklace, she took her place across from Loraline at the map. Scrying works best with two witches of equal power. Loraline and her sister Jacinda had always had the best success in the Windham family but Jacinda was dead and Elizabeth was the only one who could take her place.

"What can *I* do?" Phoebe was at their side, but neither one of them was paying her any attention.

Tom took his daughter's hand and sat her down on the couch next to him. "Just let them do what they do best. You can't help them now."

"But I have to try."

"Please, let them handle it." Although she knew deep down there was no way she was just going to sit and watch, Phoebe smiled and nodded. At least her father could have peace of mind, thinking she would step aside.

Following Loraline's lead, Elizabeth watched as her daughter moved the crystal in a circular pattern above the map. Elizabeth lit the candles around the map as they chanted together. "Crone of wisdom and darkest skies let this crystal show us where Aleerah lies. From whence she goes, and whence she comes with our will so shall it be done! Crone of wisdom and darkest skies let this crystal show us where Aleerah—." They continued over and over again until, somewhere around a half hour later, the crystal came to a dead stop.

Elizabeth stared down at the map but, from what she could tell, the crystal was just pointing to a random street a few miles from the Atlanta High School. "Where is it? What's there?"

"It's the Ward house." William was standing behind Elizabeth, looking down at the map. "She's going after Damian and his family."

"Are you sure?" Loraline had hoped Alee wouldn't go after the lycanthropes alone but she wasn't surprised that she had.

"I'm sure." William knew exactly where the Ward family lived, having taken Victoria home. Telepathy, as a form of communication, wasn't the only advantage of being a fairy; they also used telepathy as a way to extract information, such as locations. That was how William had known where to take Victoria home, in the dark of the night. It was also how he knew now that the crystal was pointing directly at the Ward house.

"Tom, I have to go," Loraline said. "Will you stay here and wait for her in case she comes back?"

"Of course." Tom had gotten used to his place in the Wenham family and he understood that because he was only human that meant that he had to take a back seat during times like this. He was OK with that. He knew when and where to help, and no one saw him as weak because of it.

Loraline moved through the shop gathering a few tools: a silver stake, a pistol with a clip of silver bullets, and even a jar of fine-powdered silver.

Phoebe stood back, just watching, not knowing what to do, then it hit her—*the taking of blood*—and she ran into the kitchen.

William was moving through the room, gathering his own items. He glanced into Loraline's bag as she passed. "What is your plan dear? Do you want to kill the children, or get answers?"

"I don't know. I guess I want to protect my family. I want my daughter back!" Loraline was shaking as she set her bag down.

"Silver won't kill the lycanthropes, although it could hurt them pretty badly. However, it could get Eric or Aleerah killed if it gets into the wrong hands. Unless you're willing to risk that, you may want to leave those items behind."

"Then what should I take?" She hesitated, setting her bag down, and moved to look through her father's pile. "Mountain ash, rye, mistletoe—. What are these for?"

"Elizabeth, can you bring me a mortar and pestle from the kitchen?" Elizabeth headed toward the back of the shop. "Thank you dear." Then, turning to his daughter, he pointed to a shelf along the far wall. "Loraline, please grab a dozen or so of those corked glass vials and bring them over here." Loraline did as she was told even though she didn't know why.

After Elizabeth brought in the mortar and pestle, Loraline watched as her father quickly mixed all of his ingredients together and ground them to a fine powder. "If we can get close enough for the lycanthropes to breathe in the powder it will sedate them enough that we will be able to get answers."

"Sedate them? You mean like drug them?" Loraline was a little confused as to why her father wanted to drug their enemies instead of killing them, after they had taken the lives of so many.

"If you add a liquid element, maybe an oil, to the potion—it doesn't really matter which—if we can get it in direct contact we may be able to have it absorb directly in through the skin."

Elizabeth moved through the shop looking for just the right choice of oil. "Loraline, do you think you could come up with the spell?"

Loraline was still shaking her head, not knowing what she should be thinking of her parents at that moment. "I don't—I'm not sure. Yeah, I guess."

"Good, then get to it dear."

In a matter of minutes, Loraline had gone from the one in charge to the confused follower, not really knowing which direction to turn. It was clear that her parents had an entirely different agenda than she did. She just prayed that the desired outcome—her daughter being back home safely—was the same.

16

Alee had made her way back to the Ward's house, where she picked up Damian and Victoria's scent, leading away from the house and into the back woods. She quickly changed course and followed their trail until it broke off. Damian's scent was circling around, heading back to his house, but Victoria's continued farther into the woods. Alee followed Victoria's scent. When she found herself standing outside of Granny Edith's backdoor, she was only a little surprised.

"Victoria! I know you're in there!" Alee stood about thirty yards behind the house and yelled out to her. "Why don't you come out and face me."

The back door slowly opened, but it wasn't Victoria who stepped out. Jathan, with his dark black hair and deep brown eyes, hesitantly made his way out onto the porch.

"Ky—," Alee started to call, but his eyes got wide and he quickly shook his head to stop her from finishing his name.

That's when Alee saw her. Victoria had one arm around Jathan's upper body, holding him tight against her chest, with a knife tight against his throat. Her other hand held his free arm still so that he couldn't move.

"Tisk, tisk, Alee. I was coming here to talk—to work things out. To apologize. But, what do I discover instead? First you break my brother's heart for that idiot Kyle, and now Jathan? Seriously?"

Alee took a step forward. "The only reason you think Kyle was an idiot is because you could never get him to like you and I did." She raised an eyebrow and smirked. "Jealous?"

"Of you? Never!" Victoria retorted.

Moving a little closer, Alee was looking Jathan right in the eyes. "Jathan's never done anything to you, Victoria. What do you have against him? Why not just let him go? It's me you want anyway."

Victoria just scoffed. "And to think I actually came here to help you. I actually thought there was a chance we could be friends again, even after I found out you faked your own death. You let us all believe you were gone. We grieved Alee, we all did. You have no idea what you put us through, what you put Dani through. But, even with all of that, even knowing what you've turned into."

"What is that Victoria? What have I turned into?"

"Just look at you. You're obviously a vampire. I can smell death on you from a mile away. It's disgusting. Why Damian would even consider still wanting to be with you is beyond me. You're filthy—you're disgusting—you're nothing more than a corpse struggling to hold onto your humanity!" Jathan struggled in Victoria's grip, trying to get a hold on her. "Now, now Jathan, there's no need for you to defend your little girlfriend. I have a feeling she can hold her own!"

"You're damn right I can," Alee snapped. "but can you? I mean, you're only human right?" A smile spread across Alee's face as she saw Victoria's grip on Jathan loosen.

"That's what you think!"

"Then show yourself," Alee spoke calmly, turning her gaze toward Jathan. "It's OK to show yourself."

Victoria didn't catch the subtle change in Alee's expression, nor did she notice as Jathan slowly started to change. It wasn't until she herself had already begun her own transformation that she realized that Jathan was gone and Kyle was standing behind her. By then it was too late. She had turned and torn into Kyle's throat, snapping his neck with the pressure of her powerful wolf jaw.

Alee instantly reached out. "Talisman!" The leather necklace around Victoria's neck lifted up from beneath her shirt, revealing the small hand-carved heart-shaped wooden talisman "TALISMAN!" Alee screamed it this time, and the leather band it hung from snapped, releasing it from around Victoria's neck. The necklace flew across the air and Victoria dropped Kyle to the ground to reach out desperately for it. She stumbled trying to catch it before it landed in Alee's hand. A flash of fear crossed the wolf's eyes as Victoria struggled to shift back to her human form, unable to regain a hold on her humanity. Alee laughed, "Who's struggling now?"

Alee held the talisman up for Victoria to see, dangling it in front of her as if teasing her—tempting her to try to take it away. As Victoria leapt into the air, ready to fight for her life, Alee crushed the charm in the palm of her hand. The dark brown wolf landed with her front paws directly on Alee's chest, forcing her to the ground.

Victoria sank her sharp canine teeth into Alee's shoulder, and managed to tear a chunk of muscle right off the bone. Alee screamed in pain, but never let go of the hold she had on Victoria.

"With the power of mother and earth—" Alee was struggling through the pain, but already feeling her body beginning to heal itself. "—I bind your soul." She pressed the palms of her hands on the ground behind her and pushed the massive wolf off her with her feet and propelled herself into the air. "Within this beast—" Victoria pounced again, but Alee leapt to the right, taking a nosedive down the five-foot drop into the ditch below. Victoria was quick to follow, but Alee was waiting.

Just as Victoria's paws were about to hit the ground in front of her, Alee swung a thick tree branch as hard as she could, knocking Victoria backwards fifteen feet straight into the trunk of a large oak tree. Howling in pain, Victoria lay on the cold ground beneath the tree, not moving and no longer struggling. "—your soul shall keep."

Alee boldly stepped forward. No longer afraid, her chanting got louder, clearer, and more forceful even than before. "With the power of mother and earth I bind your soul! Within this beast your soul shall keep." Her eyes were pitch black holes into nothing and her hair was wild ebony flowing out all around her. Her skin was so pale and fragile it looked almost translucent under the light of the sun.

Victoria began thrashing around on the ground with great effort, as if her soul was trying to fight its way out of the wolf. Yet, the harder she struggled the more she cried out in pain. She had a large gash in the skin across her lower back, one of her back legs was broken, and her fur was already soaked in blood. Both Victoria and Alee knew that even if Victoria survived the injuries without the talisman that Alee had destroyed, she might never be able to return to her human form, at least not without help.

"I bind you! I bind you! I BIND YOU!" Alee sealed that fate as her voice rang out through the surrounding woods and echoed back at her. Lightning split the sky while thunder shook the earth beneath her feet. Victoria whimpered in pain and fear, but forced herself onto her three good legs and dragged herself through the woods, never once looking back.

The weight of everything that had just happened hit Alee all at once as the rain poured down, drowning her in what felt like a sea of tears. She fell to her knees and silently cried out in pain that was not purely physical.

When she woke up, soaked to the bone and still lying on the wet grass, she could hear voices coming from her grandmothers' house. She tried to pull herself up but Eric's hand on her shoulder stopped her. "You're not ready yet." She looked up into his eyes and then back toward the house. She tried again. Stubborn might run in the family, but when she saw Phoebe sitting on the distant porch with Kyle's dead body across her lap, the pain of losing him again flooded over her, and she collapsed back onto the cold hard ground.

17

As Loraline and her parents hurried off to the Ward house, Phoebe went in the opposite direction. In the rushed moments, when her aunt and her grandparents had been gathering their supplies, Phoebe had realized what she had to do. She ran to the kitchen and tore through the freezer until she found two sealed pouches of thick red liquid, one marked 'Eric' and the other marked 'Aleerah.' This blood was only meant to be used in case of a medical emergency, but Phoebe made the executive decision that this qualified as an emergency. She tossed the pouch marked 'Aleerah' into the microwave and quickly defrosted it. Then, before she could talk herself out of it, she gulped down half of the pouch. The rest she left on the shelf of the refrigerator before she ran out the back door.

She had to stop halfway to her car to keep from throwing up but she finally made it there. She sat behind the steering wheel and prayed to the goddesses, "I have no powers of my own, sweet goddesses of heaven and earth. Please show me the way, give me the strength, and help me to restore what family I have left."

As she put the car in gear and started down the road, she could feel a gentle pull in her gut. It wasn't the nausea she had felt before. Instead it felt almost magnetic, as if she were being led.

The "pull" led her to her Granny Edith's house, and she quickly parked the car and headed to the back yard. Not knowing what to expect, she was stopped dead in her tracks when she saw Kyle. He was lying lifeless on the porch, and a large brown wolf was rushing away from him and across the yard, following Alee into the woods. Phoebe dashed up the steps and scooped Kyle into her arms, but it was too late. He was already gone.

The phone rang five times before Loraline finally picked up. "What!?!"

"Aunt Loraline, it's me, Phoebe. I'm at Granny Edith's. Aleerah—I mean Alee—was just here, and you need to come fast."

Loraline hung up without even saying goodbye. Phoebe went back out to the porch to sit and wait with Kyle's lifeless form, not knowing what else she could do.

Alee lay unconscious on the forest floor when Eric appeared, as if out of nowhere, coming through the trees at the far end of the yard. He knelt down next to his daughter and slowly brushed her hair away from her face. He knew she wasn't dead because, although faint, he could still hear her heartbeat. He didn't dare move her though, just in case she had internal damage that hadn't healed itself yet.

It didn't take Loraline, Elizabeth, and William long to get there, and soon Alee was back inside, lying on the couch wrapped in one of Granny Estelle's old quilts, crying silently. Kyle was lying lifeless in the back bedroom, and Phoebe was pacing the living room as Eric talked through what must have happened with Loraline.

"—that doesn't explain the boy. I thought you said that he died the night of the Founders' Celebration." Loraline had her head in her hands fighting not to break into tears.

"He did. I saw him there. There's no way he survived."

I love you, Alee. Kyle's voice was only a whisper and as she looked around she could see a soft white glow standing down the hall, coming toward the living room.

I love you too. Alee looked around but no one else seemed to notice.

"But he did survive Eric. I'm not saying you're wrong, but you can't honestly be telling me his body has just kept all this time—and where? Where has he been if not alive and well?"

"I don't know, I DON'T KNOW!" Eric stood up, stretching, and taking in a deep breath he didn't really need. "I'm sorry. I didn't mean to yell. It's just that—"

It's not their fault. I hope you know that. It's no one's fault.

It's Damian's fault. This wouldn't have happened if it weren't for him.

"There's no need for apologies son." William walked through the kitchen door, crossing to his daughter. "Your daughter is safe and that's more than we could have hoped for." Turning to Phoebe he added, "Your father is on his way. You'll help him with the boy. His family should be notified."

Damian isn't to blame, Alee. He's a good guy and he truly loves you. Don't take this out on him. Even if none of this had happened today, I was already gone. I couldn't have stayed any longer. You have to forgive Damian. You have to move on.

"But, Grandpa, they already lost him once. We can't put them through that again."

I can't go on without you, Kyle.

Yes you can.

"She's right." Elizabeth said as she came through the kitchen door. "It will do no good to make them grieve all over again. We should bury the boy here, out back."

I will always love you, but you have to move on, for me. You have to let me go. You have to live your life and forgive Damian, because together you can be so much more than even we were. He was standing right in front of her now and, as he leaned down to kiss her, the light faded away. He was gone.

"No." Alee's voice was trembling and her whole body started to shake. "No. No. No."

"Aleerah? Aleerah, are you all right?" Loraline was at her side in seconds.

"No." She pushed herself off the couch and stumbled out from under the quilt as she made her way down the hall to the back room. She already knew what she would find—an empty bedroom—but it didn't make it any easier. She collapsed on the bed sobbing.

Her family quickly followed, but stopped short as they came into the empty room.

18

Tom couldn't see sending Phoebe to school that morning, and no one was going to argue with him. It was after two that afternoon by the time everyone had cleaned up, made their way back to The Black Onyx, and settled in for lunch. Elizabeth and Loraline busied themselves making more sandwiches then they could possibly need.

Everyone else sat around the table listening as, over a pint of B positive, Alee explained everything she had been through during the past several weeks. "—and then I tracked her to Granny Edith's. We fought, and she ran off."

"She just left? So she's still out there somewhere?"

"Yeah, but I don't think we need to worry about her anymore." Alee wasn't sure how her family would react to the fact that she had basically condemned Victoria to a life as a wolf. In many ways she was more dangerous now, but Alee doubted that Victoria would see it that way.

Eric handed her another sports bottle from the fridge, "How can you be so sure?"

"I can't, but I can guarantee she isn't going to be talking to anyone." She fiddled with the lid of the bottle and took a quick drink. "She can't." When her eyes met her grandmother's she had to look away. "I bound her powers. I broke the talisman that grounds her to her human body. She's stuck—in animal form, at least for now."

"You bound her powers? Alee—."

"I didn't know what else to do. She attacked me. She was going to kill me. She did kill me once. She killed Kyle, and who knows how many others." She looked around the room, and all eyes were on her. "I don't know why I even have to explain this to you, let alone justify it. You know what she did, what her family did. I didn't have any other options."

"There are always options—"

"No, Elizabeth, she's right."

"William?"

"She's right, and you know it," William said. "She may have had different reasons than you and I had for binding my powers, but she's right."

Alee wasn't sure she had heard him correctly "What?"

William continued talking without interruption. "The girl was dangerous. She wasn't going to stop until Aleerah was dead. Aleerah did what she had to do."

"I'm sorry, your powers?" Alee stared at her grandfather, not understanding. As far as she knew, he was just your basic run of the mill human like her Uncle Tom, Phoebe's father.

Elizabeth sat down next to Alee. "I just—. I know you did what you had to do but is there no way to help the girl now?"

Loraline stepped in. "Mom, I'm sure that, with time, Victoria will be able to find her way back on her own, or with her family's help. Until then, maybe what Aleerah did will help her."

"We have to talk to her mother. We need to see her family. They should know."

Forgetting about William for a moment, Alee snapped, "You didn't want to tell Kyle's family that he died but you want to run off and console Victoria's? Kyle was innocent in all of this. He was human, and if it hadn't been for me he would never have been caught up in any of it. His family didn't even get to bury his body. They buried an empty coffin because he was presumed dead after the "inclement weather." So many families buried empty coffins just so they would have a place to go to mourn the loss of their loved ones. Most of the families don't even remember what really happened, and those who should never have been affected, like Kyle's family, have been tricked into believing a lie. Victoria is anything but human and, at the very least, she's a murderer. Kyle was good. So good he was able to come back as Jathan—an angel—."

"Jathan was—?" Phoebe struggled to finish her question.

He was Kyle, yes! He was my angel and now he's gone." Tears were streaming down her face, "Victoria—there is no hope for her!" Kyle's last words ran though her head, *Damian isn't to blame, he's a good guy— forgive Damian, because together you can be so much more than even we were.* "Kyle said—."

"What, dear?" Elizabeth asked.

"Nothing. Never mind," Alee struggled to make sense of it. "I just don't think we can help Victoria. At least not yet." *Damian isn't to blame; he's a good guy—.* "Maybe Damian—I don't think this is his fault."

William stepped up to defend the boy, for the second time in two days. He knew, better than any of them, what Damian and Victoria had been through, along with their mother. "It's not the boy's fault," he said. "It's not Victoria's fault either, although she did take things too far. It isn't even their mother's fault. She isn't working alone. We just need to figure out who is behind all of this."

"And if I said I already know who's behind it?" But Alee was cut off before anyone had a chance to respond. The bell above the shop door rang, and the door crashed open.

Things happened quickly as ten vampires, dressed in all black and visibly armed with guns in hip holsters, moved through the shop and into the kitchen. No one even had time to react before Eric was yanked out of his seat and pinned to the floor.

"Ermanes son of Chalkeus, by the power of the founders you are being placed into custody until such time as your sentencing has concluded."

"Custody? Eric? Eric, what's happening?" Loraline was trying to pull the men off of him when she was scooped up by one of the guards who was obviously annoyed by her interruption.

"Ma'am, please let us do our job." He was easily holding her back with one hand as she continued to struggle.

"Don't think I don't know who you are, Sam" she spit in his face. "I know all of you, and I will make sure you all pay for this." The rest of the family was on their feet, wanting, but unable, to help. The remaining guards had formed a barrier around Eric and were moving him toward the door.

"Aunt Loraline? Dad? What's happening?" Phoebe was clinging to Alee's arm. Alee just stared at her father as he was yanked off the floor, his arms bound behind his back by silver chains. She could see a subtle hint of smoke as his flesh began to burn beneath the silver.

"Loraline, just stay calm. I will handle this." Eric didn't sound so sure, as they dragged him out the door, but he wasn't about to panic in front of his family. "The Council Guards are only doing what they've been told." Alee could smell the burning flesh now as well as the blood that ran down his arms and onto the floor.

"But you're a founder!" Loraline screamed. "They have to listen to you. Make them listen." Unheeding, they loaded Eric into the back of a large black van. Loraline twisted in the grasp of the intruder who was holding her back. "Get your hands off of me, Sam, or so help me goddesses I will—."

"Watch what you say Mrs. Wenham," the guard warned, holding her at arm's length. "A threat to a Council Guard could land you in custody alongside your husband, and then how would you save him?" Sam stayed behind as the others secured the van. "I can't say I disagree with Eric's actions,

Loraline, but he had to know they would get him into trouble."

"Loraline, explain," Elizabeth snapped.

"Not now mother." Taking Sam's hand in hers, she pleaded, "Sam, please. You've known Eric too long to believe he didn't have reason. He has stood beside you as a friend and as a brother. You have to help him. You have to help him. You have to help me to help him. Please."

"Stay put, Loraline. The only thing you can do for him now is to not cause him more problems. He will be held downtown in the courthouse. You won't be allowed to see him until after the sentencing, but I don't recommend coming. It won't be pretty." He turned back toward the van and started to leave. "It never is."

"Sam, please—." He moved with the speed that only a vampire can have and was in the van with the door shut before she could even finish her thought.

The van pulled out of the driveway and sped away as Loraline fell to her knees screaming. "Oh goddesses, oh goddesses, this is all my fault." Tears were pouring down her face as her father lifted her up and into his arms.

"Everyone inside." They listened, and followed as William carried his daughter into the study and lay her on the couch.

Elizabeth, as usual, busied herself with practical matters. "Phoebe, please get me the mortar and bring me some mountain ash, rye, mistletoe, and valerian root," she instructed, while she herself searched the shelves and quickly located a small leather-bound book on a lower bookshelf.

"William, if we can just calm her down, get her to sleep—. Maybe you can—."

"No, not Loraline. She'll be fine, and we *will* get to the bottom of this."

"But—."

"But nothing Liz! I will not probe her mind for answers. She'll give them to us herself when she has calmed down. When she is ready." William seldom raised his voice, and Elizabeth quickly backed down.

"Fine."

"Dad," Tom stepped up, putting his arm around Elizabeth's shoulder, "maybe Mom could give her just a little, to calm her down. Then maybe she can talk to us, on her own."

William was nodding his head. "I'm sorry," he said to his wife. "I'm sorry. I didn't mean to yell. He's right, make the potion, just not too strong." She hurried off to finish what she had started.

William called to Alee, who was standing quietly in the corner by the door, "Aleerah, come sit down please."

"I—."

"Please. I need your help." She did as she was told but her hands were shaking and no amount of rubbing them was helping. "Are you all right?" She shook her head but couldn't get the words to come out. "Tom, Aleerah's in shock, can you—."

"No," Alee whispered, shaking her head, "Not shock." Her eyes were burning, her throat was starting to clench, and she realized she needed to feed. She could still smell her father's burning flesh and, although the thought made her sick, the smell of the blood running down his arm had awoken her hunger in a way she hadn't felt in weeks.

By the time William realized what was happening, it was too late. Alee had grabbed Tom by the throat and had him pinned to the wall as she sank her fangs into his wrist. He was trying to pull her off with his other arm, but his struggling quickly stopped as she drained him.

"NOOOOO!" Phoebe dropped the mortar and herbs as she entered the study. She flung herself at Alee, pulling her off of her father. It would have been a great plan, if Phoebe were more than humanly strong, but she wasn't, and so Alee just turned her hunger toward her.

Tom sank to the floor, still breathing, but not conscious enough to help. William rushed to Tom's side while Loraline grabbed her daughter and Elizabeth pulled Phoebe out from underneath Alee. "Oh goddesses, what's happening to her? Mom, what's happening?" Loraline cried.

Phoebe was OK—she was shaken up, but she hadn't lost enough blood to be anything more than scared and pissed off.

Elizabeth moved Phoebe away from Alee, who was still struggling in her mother's grasp. Elizabeth quickly grabbed a silver chain from a shelf above the fireplace and tossed it to Loraline. "Put this on her."

"No, it will—."

"Just do it!"

Loraline fastened the chain around Alee's throat and, instantly, Alee's screams became screams of pain, and not hunger. She grabbed at her throat, but wasn't able to get hold of the necklace long enough to break it free. Phoebe ran to the kitchen and came back with the last three bottles of blood. She quickly rolled them across the floor to Alee, but Alee was so focused on the searing pain around her neck that she didn't even notice them. Loraline grabbed the first bottle and took Alee into her lap and began to feed her like a baby

"Shhhh. You're OK. Everything's OK."

"The hell it is," Phoebe snapped. "As if we don't already have enough to deal with, now this!"

By the time the second bottle was gone, Alee had stopped shaking and was sitting on her own, calmly drinking. Loraline took the necklace off of Alee's neck as she finished the third bottle. All eyes were on her, watching, waiting to see how she was going to react.

"I'm fine." She slowly got up, "Really, I'm all right. I know sorry isn't enough, but I am."

"No, sorry isn't enough. Look what you did to my dad. I've already lost my mom and Petra. What the hell happened to you?" Tears were flooding her eyes, threatening to pour out, but Phoebe wasn't about to look weak. "I get that you're a vampire, big deal. That doesn't give you a free pass to feed on whoever you want, whenever you want. Pull yourself together and start helping—"

"Phoebe!" Her father cut her off sharply, but she just gave him a look.

"No, Dad!" she turned back to Alee, "You pull yourself together and start helping this family instead of being part of the problem, or get out."

"Phoebe! Aleerah isn't the problem. This wasn't her fault."

"How can you say—?"

"She hasn't fed—not enough—and she's still too young to handle the cravings on her own. We've all been busy. We forgot to treat her like the newborn she is. This isn't her fault, it's ours. She's been dealing with this all alone for weeks, but now we're here and we need to take some responsibility too."

"But, I just—"

"Just let it go Phoebe. I'm fine, you're fine, and she's going to be fine too. Aren't you Aleerah?"

Alee nodded, just watching Tom as he pulled himself off the floor and made his way to the couch. "Well, at least it got Loraline to stop crying. You see, there is some good that came out of this." He held up his wrist, which had already begun to heal. "Oh hey, look at that. Vampire saliva really does help you heal faster, cool."

"Yeah, cool. She bit me earlier and now you. Let's just hope we don't wake up in the morning with fangs and a craving for blood." Phoebe was still watching Alee like a hawk.

"It doesn't work that way, Phoebe."

"No, Alee? It doesn't work that way? How do you know how it works?"

"Because, you can't be turned just by being bitten. It takes more than that." Turning to Tom, "You won't turn, I promise. Neither will Phoebe. My dad said there has to be an exchange of blood. I drank yours, but you didn't drink mine. So, you'll be fine."

"But—." Phoebe's mind wandered back to standing in the kitchen, guzzling the pouch of Alee's blood. "But if he had drunk your blood and then you bit him and drank—."

"Then yeah, if he had died he might—."

Phoebe quickly turned back to her dad, trying not to think about Alee's blood or the possibilities it could lead to. "Dad, I think you need to lie down." He didn't lie down, but he did lean back on the couch and close his eyes.

Just then Elizabeth closed the space between her and Alee. "Aleerah?"

"Yes?"

"Your necklace, the one with the Wenham pentagram, where is it?"

Alee's hands went straight to her neck. "Oh—I lost it." She hadn't actually lost it, but it was easier than telling them that it had burned through the skin of her throat just before she yanked it off and dropped it onto the blood-covered ballroom floor.

"Hmmm. We'll have to get you a new one. Maybe a leather necklace this time, or gold."

"That would be nice, thank you."

19

Eric sat huddled in the middle of a small silver cage. His arms were no longer restrained behind his back—being surrounded by silver was restraint enough: he wasn't going anywhere. The burns on his arms and wrists had already begun to heal, although it would take much longer for them to heal completely. Nothing hurts a vampire quite like silver. That's why silver bullets are banned in Atlanta—for the civilians anyway. Silver is standard issue for the Council Guard and they know how to use them.

Aside from the cage, the room was empty. A single light bulb hung from the middle of the ceiling, flickering on and off as if the power could go out at any minute. There were no pictures on the walls, no windows, no furniture around the room, not even a rug to cover the cold cement floor.

Empty. Alone. Eric knew this room well. He had led the Council Guard for many years. There was always one founding member on the Guard—Head of Security, if you will. For years that had been his calling and he had been good at it. However, after leaving Atlanta to start a new life with Loraline, he had had to step down. After returning to Atlanta, he was thankful enough to just be welcomed back into the Founding Circle, and he didn't push his luck by requesting his old job back. They had survived for years without him; he had to trust they knew what they were doing. It turns out they did.

The cage was just as he had left it, with maybe a little more dried blood coating the bars, but that was to be expected. It would have been hard for any vampire to clean the cage without getting burned himself, so why bother cleaning it at all. Eventually, the blood would all dry up on its own.

With only five square feet of space, there wasn't enough room to lie down and, at six foot two inches, there was no way for Eric to stand up. So he sat, legs crossed, back straight, and head held high as he waited. He knew that eventually the founders would come. They always did. It was just a matter of time.

20

"They had no right to take him." Loraline was pacing behind the couch.

"You still haven't told us what he did. Maybe if you explain what happened, we could figure out a way to get him home."

"Mom, it's not as simple as that. Eric—, I—. Crap." She stopped pacing and took a seat next to Tom on the couch. "The attack, after I had Aleerah—, it was Greg—. Gregory Davis."

"What?!" William bolted upright in his seat.

"I didn't know it at the time. Believe me, I would never have been able to bite my tongue all these years had I known. I never saw his face, and he either disguised his voice or maybe he did something to make me forget, I don't know. All I know is, over the years I remembered things about that night—details. I remembered him saying, 'I won't allow any son of mine to be trapped like a caged dog.'"

Everyone just listened—waiting.

"I guess I never thought about it much, but then when I told Eric, he knew instantly—. He never even hesitated for a second. Huh, Gratianus son of Drusus—such a big name for someone as weak as he really was."

"Sweetheart, what did Eric do?"

Loraline laughed, "What do you think he did, Mom? He killed him. Vampire law says he was within his rights to kill him. Gregory had no right to lay a hand on me—I was taken. I belonged to Eric. Eric had hungered for revenge for years and to finally find out who it was—that it was his own maker. What else could he do?"

Elizabeth stood in the corner, like a statue made of marble, not blinking, not even breathing. "Death. There won't be a trial, not for him. Gregory was the oldest Founding member. Killing him will cost Eric his life." Her voice was void of all emotion, empty and distant.

"Unless we get him out first."

"William! You know we can't do that. Would you risk all our lives?"

"He is our daughter's husband, our granddaughter's father. Haven't we lost enough of our family? Would you not risk anything to save what little we have left?"

"I—."

"Call the others. Tell them it's time to stop mourning and start fighting. Elaine and Robert need to get on a plane tonight and be here by morning. Melissa and Michelle need to go down to the courthouse and see what they can find out. Tell them not to be seen! I'll call Wayne and tell him to get your Aunt Ellen out of bed, cleaned up, and over here right away. Julia has enough to do dealing with Luvena, but Jaclyn and Jeanne—they're your cousins and they should have been standing at your side throughout the last few weeks. I don't know what has happened to this family, but it is time to pull it back together."

Everyone just stared at him in silence—in awe.

"Now!"

Elizabeth fished her cell phone out of her pocket and headed into the hallway. William made his way into the kitchen to use the house phone.

"I'll call Jaclyn. I'm sure Jeanne will be at her house anyway." Tom followed Loraline into the shop, leaving Alee and Phoebe alone in the study.

"Wow." Alee said while watching her family bustle about.

"Yeah—. Wow." Phoebe quietly watched in awe.

The girls sat in silence for a while as everything sank in. "Who's Luvena?" Alee finally asked.

"She's Julia's daughter. She has autism. It's pretty severe I guess. She's two years older than you, I think, but she can't really do anything for herself. Plus about a year ago, she started developing her powers. Since she is basically a toddler stuck in the body of a young adult, she's pretty scary to be around."

"And, who is Julia again?"

"Wow, you've been around for how long? OK, Julia is Jaclyn's daughter. Jacyln is Grandma Elizabeth's cousin, her Aunt Ellen's daughter." Alee was just staring at her like a deer in headlights. "Never mind. They're not around enough for you to remember anyway. Maybe I can make you a cheat sheet or something. You met them all during the new moon ceremonies, but those things aren't always the best time to mingle. Trust me, I have a feeling we'll be seeing a lot more of them soon enough."

"Yeah, about that—."

"What?"

"What if I can't—? I mean, what if I—."

"What? What if you freak out again and start feeding on the family?" Alee just looked away. She was already feeling bad enough about what had happened. "Yeah, that would suck, so just don't do it, OK?"

"You don't get it. I have no control over it. It's not like I meant for that to happen."

"That's not entirely true. You have some control. You just need to be better about eating. Seriously, Aleerah, I'm not going to bottle feed you, but if I have to force you to eat, I will and it won't be from my vein. You already bit me once, and besides I already drank your blood. I don't think I need to test my luck any more. I don't want to wake up a vampire if something bad happens one day."

"Wait, you what?" Alee was watching closely as Phoebe tried desperately to avoid eye contact.

"It's nothing. I did it to help find you and it worked. How did you think I found you so fast? I don't regret it. I'd do it again, even knowing now that it got me one step closer to being a vampire myself."

"I—. Thank you."

"Forget it."

Phoebe got up and held her hand out to Alee. "Come on. I'm sure there's more we can do than just sit in here. In fact, if you're up to it, I think I have an idea."

21

"Wait, explain to me again what we're doing in the tunnels."

"Well, Grandma Elizabeth and your mom are busy gathering the family, right?

"Yeah, I guess."

"So they aren't going to have time to babysit us. That means we have time to actually do something. Sitting at home isn't going to help and none of them are going to listen to the two of us. I'm just a kid and well, you're—new to all of this."

"Hey!"

"In their eyes."

"Whatever."

"Aleerah, listen to me. They won't take us seriously, even though between the two of us we can actually get your dad out. They will just see us as two kids without enough experience to do anything useful. Well, I happen to know that isn't true."

"You do, huh?" Alee watched as a grin spread across Phoebe's face.

"Yup, I do. Come on." Phoebe pulled Alee around a corner and into a small hole-in-the-wall shop. The walls were covered from ceiling to floor with racks of clothing, stylish—not like the typical Atlanta street wear, but more like what you might see in the movies.

"Yeah, I'm not sure I'll ever get used to the idea of an underground city below Atlanta. I just don't get how no one ever notices—how I never noticed." She pulled a black leather belt with metal spikes all around it off of a rack and held it up to Phoebe. "What do you think? Can I pull this off?"

"Um, yeah, maybe not. Just think of the tunnels as an underground mall." Then, looking around, Phoebe spotted a young girl in the back of the store. "There she is, come on." She pulled Alee to the back of the store and through a curtain into the dressing rooms.

"What do you want, Phoebe?"

"Nice to see you too, Marie." Phoebe and Marie stood eye to eye, neither one willing to back down.

"Hey, I've seen you before." Alee was trying to place where she knew Marie from. "Yeah, we had Lit class together."

"Oh yeah?"

"Yeah."

"Well, I don't remember you. Sorry!" The sarcasm was oozing out of her like pus from an infected wound.

"OK, well, nice to meet you."

"Not really." Marie was done chatting with Alee. She turned back to Phoebe, obviously annoyed. "What is it you need Phoebe? I don't have all day, you know."

"Cut the crap, Marie. This place is dead so you have nothing better to do. Plus Aleerah and I need a makeover – tracker style!"

"Are you serious? I could get into a lot of trouble for that."

"You're not going to get into any trouble. No one will ever know. If, and it won't happen, but if we were to get caught I'd tell them we got everything from my sister's stash."

"But, she—"

"Yeah, she's dead, I get it. They even came and cleaned out her room, but that doesn't mean I can't tell them they missed a few things!"

"Why do you need it?"

Phoebe hesitated, *how much do I tell her? I know I can't trust her, but*—. "Aleerah's dad has been taken by the Counsel Guards."

"Oh crap—. Eric?"

"Hah! So you do know who I am," Alee said with a smirk on her face.

"Fine. Yeah, whatever."

"So you'll help us, right?" Phoebe asked.

"I don't know, Phoebe."

"Well, I do, and you owe me."

They were silent for a while. Alee didn't know if they were still fighting, or what. "Fine, go in room one. I'll get you what you need." Then she was gone and Phoebe was pulling Alee behind another small curtain, into an even smaller dressing room.

"We're both going to change in here?"

"Yeah, so get over whatever shyness you have, because we're not going for the little miss nice girl look right now." Phoebe started undressing as if it was the most natural thing in the world to disrobe with another girl standing so close you couldn't avoid touching.

"Petra was a tracker, right?"

"Yup."

"But, you're not, right?

"Not officially, no."

"But you have a plan?" Phoebe nodded. "And, it involves, what, pretending to be trackers?"

"Sort of." Phoebe was down to only her panties and bra when Marie swung the curtain open.

"Here, put these on. When you're done come to the front for the rest." She eyed Alee standing there still fully dressed hugging her shirt like it was a security blanket. "What's her problem?"

"She's just shy."

"Yeah, well she better get over that real quick if you're planning what I think you're planning."

"No—, not like when we went in after Matt—"

"Hey, we agreed never to mention him again." Marie's checks flushed. Alee wasn't sure if she was mad or just embarrassed, but she made a mental note to ask Phoebe about Matt some other time when her father's life wasn't on the line.

"Right, I know. Sorry. Anyway, this is totally different. She'll be fine. She can handle herself."

"Whatever, not my problem." She turned, closing the curtain as she walked away.

When Phoebe turned back to Alee she just shook her head. "Yeah, she's right though. The deer in the headlights routine isn't going to work. You've been on your own for weeks now. You're a full-blooded vamp and you look like a lost puppy dog. After what you did to my dad back there and what you almost did to me—, I think you can handle yourself. So snap out of whatever this is and put on your big girl panties so we can get ready to go save your dad!" She sifted through the pile of clothes Marie had brought in and handed her a stack. "Here, get dressed."

Alee did what she was told without complaining. As she stepped out of the dressing room Alee got a good look at herself in the full-length mirror. "Wow." She took a few seconds to size herself up and down, like you would someone you're about to fight.

"Yeah, yeah, you're hot. Now let's go."

"No, seriously. I've done the whole makeover thing before. I've reinvented myself twice already, but this—."

"What?"

"This is just different." A smile spread across her lips, showing more fang than she normally allowed. "I could get used to this."

"Well, goody. I'm glad you're comfy in your new clothes but you're not a tracker so this is a one-time only clothing loan for you."

"Not you?"

"Nope—" she walked through the curtain into the main shop, not taking the time to explain any more. "Marie, we're ready. What else you got for us?"

"Just the usual paraphernalia." She placed a small black case on the counter and two black armbands. "You do know how to pick a lock right?"

Phoebe just laughed. "I don't usually need tools for that, magic you know."

"Yeah, well where you're going, magic isn't going to help you. Take the kit, you'll need it." Phoebe threaded her belt through the loops on the black case and refastened it tightly around her waist. "Other than that, just wear the bands. Upper right arm. And if anyone asks—."

"We didn't get them from you. Got it."

"Right." Marie started back toward the back of the shop. "Good luck Phoebe." She was gone before Phoebe had a change to thank her, although Alee didn't even know if she would have. She wasn't sure if Phoebe and Marie were friends, enemies, frenemies, or just unimportant to each other, but none of that really mattered right then.

They left the shop looking a thousand times more menacing than they had going in. Alee still didn't know the plan, but that was about to change. "Stand up straight and look straight ahead. If you thought you got attention the last time you were down here with your little glowing tattoo, believe me, you haven't seen anything yet. Try not to draw attention this time, please."

"Sure thing. Trust me, I don't want that kind of attention right now."

"Right now? So—. What. After dear old dad is safe, you want to come back down and do a little flirting with the—."

"Shut up, Phoebe!"

"Yeah, sorry—too soon." Then, pulling her around a corner where she could try and explain, "So, your dad is being held at the courthouse. It's actually pretty creepy down in the cellar there. They have the equivalent of dungeons, but they call them interrogation rooms. Problem is, they don't interrogate anyone. They're not looking for answers. If you get locked up, you stay until they clean you out, not let you out."

"You die there?"

"Yup, pretty much."

"How do you know all this?"

"I was a stupid kid once." Alee had to swallow back a laugh. "Yeah, yeah, whatever. Anyway, a few years back, a friend of mine got taken in because he had been doing magic in public."

"Matt?"

"Yeah, Matt. He broke too many of the founders' rules. Marie and I decided to get him out, but it didn't work. By the time we seduced our way past the guards and found him, he was already gone."

"Gone how?"

"Dead. The vamps had tied him up and fed on him for days. No blood left meant no life left." Alee noticed her shudder as if she were trying to shake away the memory. Unfortunately, there were some memories you just can't get rid of no matter how hard you try.

Alee didn't know what the acceptable length of silence was before moving on from a conversation like that, but they didn't have time to waste. "So, what's your plan? If we don't want to get there too late this time, what do we do?"

"Well, we're older this time, so we won't be seen as kids. Plus, in these outfits we look the part. We should be able to get past the first set of guards rather easily. They aren't the brightest of the bunch." She pulled Alee down the corridor and continued walking. "Once we're in the back, you'll need to do whatever it is you do to make us all invisible and shit."

"What? Me, why me?"

"Because that isn't a talent I have and I know you do." She stopped, and stood eye to eye with Alee. "Which reminds me, I've been meaning to talk to you about that. Did you enjoy your little snack in Granny Edith's cellar? You never did thank me by the way."

"How did you know—?"

"That it was you? I put two and two together. That's twice now. Don't let it happen again."

Alee was more embarrassed in that moment than she had been in the dressing room. "I won't, and I'm sorry. Again."

"Whatever, I'm over it. Just messing with you. But, no seriously—how did you do it? You can do it again right?"

"Of course. I mean, I think so. If nothing else, I can use the shadows to conceal us."

"Nope, not going to work."

"Why not?"

"We'll be in vamp central." She pulled Alee around yet another corner. This one led to a tall set of stairs. "Come this way." They started up the stairs. "You won't be able to use any of your little vampire parlor tricks around these guys. It has to be witchcraft."

"I know the spell I used but I don't know if it will work for both of us. Besides I don't know how to make our clothes—I mean I was always—"

"Naked?" Phoebe turned eyes wide open, "You're joking right?"

"What if I can't—?"

"No what ifs—you have to, and I'm keeping my clothes on, so figure it out."

They were almost to the top of the stairs when Phoebe stopped. Her voice was almost a whisper now, "Once we reach the top the guards will see us. I can get us past this first set, just don't say anything. After the door closes behind us it's your turn. Make it count because we only have one chance. We'll need to stay close. I can lead us to the cellar but we'll still need to find his room. You'll need to use your connection with your dad to find him." Alee started to shake her head but Phoebe just continued. "Just concentrate on him. Think about him and you'll know where to go. Once we know what room he's in I'll get the door open and we'll get him out. Just don't be surprised if we have to fight our way out after that. Once his cell is open they'll know we're here and they'll come for us."

There was a loud bang as a door up ahead slammed shut. Both girls jumped.

One of the guards started toward the top of the stairs, "Jimmy, did you hear something?"

"Yeah, your mom screaming as I sucked the life out of her."

"Yeah, really funny. It might have worked about two hundred years ago."

"Whatever, mom jokes are always funny!"

Phoebe started up the last flight of stairs with Alee right behind her.

"Who are you two?" One of the guards stepped in front of them as they stepped off the stairs and walked toward the doors. He was tall and lanky, but what size he did have was all muscle. He looked like he was built for speed, Alee figured if they got into trouble and had to run, this guy would catch them without even breaking a sweat.

"We're new!" Phoebe nodded down at the band around her arm.

"You got a name new girl?" The other guard stepped up. He was shorter, by about six inches, but somehow he seemed bigger. Maybe it was the fact that his shoulders were almost as wide as he was tall. He worked out, hard. Alee wondered if he was compensating for shortcomings in other areas of his life or if working out just came with the job. Either way, she didn't like their odds if it came to a fight.

"Phoebe, and you?"

"Jimmy."

Phoebe took a step closer to Jimmy, closing the gap between them and slowly ran her hand down the front of his chest. "Nice to meet you Jimmy. Maybe you can spot me at the gym sometime?"

"I uh, yeah, OK sure."

"Well, we better be getting in—meetings, you know."

"Right, yeah. Hey Bobby, open the door for the new girls."

The tall thin guard—Bobby, apparently—went back to the doors and used what looked like a plastic hotel key card to unlock the doors. They swung open automatically and Phoebe stepped around Jimmy and started toward the door.

"You coming A?"

"Yeah, right behind you." Alee hurried to catch up, and once the doors were shut tight behind her said, "A?"

"I don't care if they know my name, but if they heard yours—. Well, let's just say with your dad in the slammer, you've probably been tagged. Better to just avoid anyone recognizing you if we can. But hey, it's your turn now. So, get to it. Work that magic!"

"OK, but we'll be talking about Jimmy later." Phoebe blushed and quickly turned away.

"Cute right?"

"Yeah and I'm guessing somewhere in the range of two hundred years old. So, kinda gross too."

"I'll tell your mom you said that."

"Shut up."

"Whatever, he didn't look a day over eighteen." When Alee thought about it, it was true. He must have been turned around eighteen or nineteen and he hadn't aged a day since. Alee wondered how weird it was going to feel in a couple hundred years when she still looked in the mirror and saw the same reflection staring back at her. "Aleerah? Hey, Aleerah, where'd you go? Wake up."

"What? Oh yeah sorry. I'm ready." She took Phoebe's hands in hers and softly started to chant. "We cannot be seen, we cannot be felt. We cannot be heard, we cannot be smelt! We walk undetected, for only those I grant to see. And as I have spoken, so now shall it be!"

Phoebe chuckled, "We cannot be smelt? Wow, you really do think of everything don't you?"

"Shut up." Alee smacked her on the shoulder. "Why don't you try helping?" She started the chant over and Phoebe joined in, "We cannot be seen, we cannot be felt. We cannot be heard, we cannot be smelt! We walk undetected, for only those I grant to see. And as I have spoken, so now shall it be!"

The door behind them started to open and they quickly turned together and were standing face to face with Jimmy and Bobby.

"See Bobby, I told you, you're nuts. No one's here. Just an empty hallway, look for yourself." Bobby took a step in, cautiously looking around. He sniffed the air. A few more steps and he stopped only two feet from Alee.

"Yeah, OK but I still say I heard something."

"Whatever, let's go. We shouldn't be in here anyway."

Bobby stepped back into the lobby and shut the door behind him.

"Oh crap, that was close." Phoebe was laughing. "They really couldn't see us. This is so cool."

"Yup. Which is weird because like I said, I've never been able to do this fully clothed before." Alee's heart was racing faster than it ever had.

"Wait, you weren't kidding before? You really were naked?"

"Don't judge!"

"Nope, not judging. Just a little surprised. You seemed so shy back in the dressing room, but—." She stifled a giggle. "Never mind. Hey, I don't get it."

"What?"

"How come I can see you, but they couldn't?"

"I don't know, I guess it's just part of the spell. '—for only those I grant to see.' I guess because we did the spell together, we can see each other."

"Wow, that's actually pretty smart."

"I don't know how smart it is, it just kind of happened that way." Phoebe just stared at her. She wasn't sure what to think of Alee. Magic just seemed to come so easily for her and it didn't seem fair.

"Come on, we need to hurry." She grabbed Alee's arm and started down the hall. "Just up ahead there's an elevator that goes down to the cellar. Stay against the wall: they have cameras that detect body heat."

"Um, hello—vampire – I don't think I'm going to set off any heat sensors."

"Right, I forgot. I guess it's just me."

They hurried into the elevator as someone was stepping off and quickly backed all the way against the wall. Phoebe pushed the button that said C3.

When the door finally opened, after what felt like too long of a ride, they stepped out into the cellar. To Alee it looked more like a tunnel someone had dug in the ground with a shovel way too small for the job. The floor was uneven and the earth walls seemed to close in around them.

"You need to figure out where he is Aleerah. Just concentrate. Which way do we go?"

Alee looked around. There was a tunnel straight ahead and two others off to their left and right. "I don't know."

"Concentrate."

She closed her eyes and thought about her father. She thought about the first time he had taken her hunting. The way he had smiled down at her after her first kill. *"It's in your blood. It's who you are."* When she opened her eyes it was as if she was being pulled down the hall. "This way."

"Are you sure?"

"I'm positive. Come on." Without thinking about Phoebe, Alee took off, running in the direction of her father. Phoebe didn't have the speed that Alee did and wasn't able to keep up. By the time Alee got to the door, Phoebe was still running and almost out of breath.

As Alee reached for the doorknob Phoebe yelled out to her, "Silver, don't touch it!" but she was too late.

Alee screamed as her hand started to smoke. The skin was already bubbling up and peeling away. Phoebe clasped her hand over Alee's mouth, "Shhh, you can't scream. They'll hear us even if they can't see us. You need to be quiet."

Tears were starting to fill Alee's eyes, "I—, it—."

"I know it hurts, but your hand will heal; *you* won't, if they find us here."

"OK, I'm OK." She wasn't, but it felt better saying it.

"I got the door. You just stand guard." Phoebe kneeled down and pulled the black case off her belt. Inside there was an assortment of small metal rods and what looked like knives. She began picking at the lock, trying each tool one at a time, but nothing happened.

"Hey, Phoebs?"

Phoebe looked up, confused or just taken aback by the casual way Alee had referred to her. "Phoebs, really?"

"What? Fine. Hey, Phoebe? Can I ask you something?"

"Sure, what?" Phoebe laughed.

"Why would vampires have silver doorknobs? That doesn't make much sense does it? I mean, what's the point in putting in doorknobs you can't even touch?"

"Yeah, I have no idea. Maybe that's something you need to ask dear old dad when we find him."

"Yeah, OK."

Finally, after about five minutes, there was a quiet click and the knob turned in her hand. "Oh thank you, goddesses," she whispered.

They slowly pushed the door open and peeked inside. It was a dark empty room with only what looked like an empty cage near the back wall.

"Are you sure this is it?" Phoebe asked.

"He's here," Alee said, nodding to the cage.

Alee moved into the room and Phoebe pulled the door closed, making sure not to shut it all the way, locking them in. Alee crossed to the cage and found Eric curled in a ball on the floor in the center of the small cage. "Dad?" He didn't move. "Dad?" Not a sound. "Dad. DAD wake up!"

Eric rolled over just a little too far and burned his arm on the bar behind him, "Shi—." He bit his tongue as he looked up at his daughter. "What are you doing here?"

"You can see me?"

"Of course I can see you." He got to his knees, forgetting about the burn momentarily. "How did you get down here?"

"Phoebe and I—,"

"Phoebe's here too? Where?"

Alee turned around and saw Phoebe still standing by the door, peeking out as if she were preparing herself for the guards to rush in, but no one was coming.

"Hey, Uncle Eric." She waved her hand, a casual gesture, but she was faking anything but casual right then. "We've come to save you."

"You have to go, both of you. Aleerah, you need to get Phoebe out of here, fast."

"We're not leaving without you."

"There is no way you'll be able to get me out of this cage. I can't leave, but you can. If you stay and they find you, they'll kill you too." Eric reached his arm through the bars and grabbed his daughter's hand. His arm started to burn but he didn't let go. "I can't lose you again. Please, you have to go now."

"No!"

"Aleerah!"

"I'm sorry but we came all this way. I'm not leaving without you."

"Sorry Uncle Eric, but I'm with her. I say we get you out of that cage and we take our chances with the guards."

Alee was shaking her head, "We won't have to. I know another way out." She pulled her shirt off over her head and started wrapping it around her hands. "First, we need to lift the cage—."

Phoebe was doubtful. "How are you going to do that when you couldn't even open the door? It's silver; you guys can't touch it and there is no way I can lift it."

"You might not be able to lift it, but we can." She looked at her dad and he had already figured out what she was doing and had begun wrapping his shirt around his hands.

"I don't know why I hadn't thought about this. The cage actually isn't that heavy but the silver burns quick. That's the whole reason I always locked the prisoners in naked."

"You what? Never mind, you can explain later, when you tell me why vampires would install silver doorknobs in their own buildings."

"It actually made sense at the time" Eric said. "The shifters were the ones in charge of—this area back then."

"This area? You mean the dungeon in general or—punishing prisoners?"

"Aleerah, I don't think this is the time."

"Right." Alee stood facing her father, ready to grab the bars. "On three." He nodded. He was ready. "One, two, three." They both grabbed the bars and started lifting the cage slowly up. It wasn't too heavy, but it certainly wasn't light, and in addition to the heavy lifting, the shirts weren't doing much to protect their skin.

"You got it?" Eric asked.

"Yup, go." Her voice was strained as she tried not to drop the cage on him as he ducked down and rolled out into the open room. She dropped the cage only a second after he cleared the opening.

Eric was at her side, unwrapping her hands in seconds. "Are you OK? Are you all right?"

"I'm fine. It's fine." He knew she wasn't but he was so overcome with emotion that he didn't know what else to say. He wrapped his arms around her as tears rolled down his cheek.

"Um, great Hallmark moment and all, but we really don't have time for you two to catch up right now." Phoebe was standing at the door peeking out. "So, if we're not going out the same way we came in, what's your plan?"

Both Phoebe and Eric stood watching as Alee leaned up against the wall, pressing her hands into the cold earth. "Open a door to the other side and grant us access where we can hide!" It started slowly at first but a mist filled the room, as the wall seemed to separate, breaking apart right beneath her hands. "Open a door to the other side and grant us access where we can hide!" The opening was large enough for them to walk through and dark enough that even Eric hesitated.

"Where does it go?"

Alee shook her head, "I don't know. Last time it took me to Granny Edith's." She nodded to her cousin, "Phoebe shut the door. It's time to go."

Phoebe swallowed her fear, shut the door, and made her way to Alee's side.

"Take my hands, we'll go in together." The three of them stood hand in hand as they stepped through the hole and put their faith in the goddesses.

22

Back at The Black Onyx, everyone was so busy they hadn't even noticed that Alee and Phoebe were gone. It had only been a couple of hours, after all.

"You really think you can get her to take you to him?" Loraline asked her father.

"Mildred and I go way back. She may not like me very much, but I still think she'll listen to reason."

"I'm not sure I agree with you. She was pretty upset when Eric—you know."

William pulled his daughter into a hug, "You have to understand, Gregory and Mildred have been together for longer than you can imagine. One day, if you make the choice to really be with Eric, you'll understand." He pulled away, to look in his daughter's eyes. "I'm not telling you what I think you should do. I'm just telling you that a lifetime with someone isn't very long, but when you're talking hundreds of years—well, that takes work. They made it work, not everyone can." William looked over at his wife, Elizabeth, who was quietly listening now. The look on her face told him that if it were possible for her to have more than just a lifetime with him she would, but mortals couldn't be turned into fairies. It didn't work the same way as vampirism, you either were or weren't born a fairy. "Mildred can be stubborn sometimes, but she is a reasonable woman. She had to have known that what he did was wrong, and I believe she will do the right thing in the end."

Elizabeth joined them, "Let's just get Eric out. I'm not losing anyone else."

Just then, Tom burst into the room with Melissa and Michelle right behind him. "Loraline, Elizabeth—"

"—there's trouble at the courthouse," Melissa finished, seeming awfully calm considering the news. "Someone got past the guards and it wasn't us. The courthouse has been barricaded and the founders have issued a citywide lockdown."

"A what? They can't do that." Elizabeth snapped. "Who got past the guards? Did you find out anything useful?"

"I'm sorry Aunt Elizabeth, but we couldn't get in. By the time we got there the lockdown had already begun. We weren't even able to use the cloaking spell to sneak past the guards. We talked to the guard at the main entrance. We pretended to be seeking counsel from the founders. He told us it would have to wait until next week. He said that an alarm had gone off somewhere inside the facility and that everyone was being detained until further notice." Melissa and

Michelle shared a look that Loraline couldn't read. "There is one other thing."

"Well, spit it out."

Melissa nodded to her sister. "I believe Phoebe was there."

"What do you mean you believe Phoebe was there? Phoebe and Aleerah have been here, in Aleerah's room, all day." Elizabeth went to the study door and leaned out, "Phoebe? Phoebe get in here please." No answer. "Aleerah, can I see you for a minute?" Still no answer. She snapped back into the room. "When did the girls leave? Did anyone see them leave?" Tom, William, and Loraline just shook their heads.

"I don't think Phoebe would go—,"

"She has done stupider things, Tom." She pointed to her niece, Michelle, "You tell me everything. Tom, you find Phoebe and Aleerah." He didn't wait to ask how she intended to have him find them, instead he quickly left the room, pulled his cell phone out of his pocket, and headed for his car.

"When we got there, two of the guards were being questioned. We overheard one of them mention a couple of new trackers who had shown up. He said one of their names was Phoebe. Apparently, there was no record of any new trackers, which led to a lot of screaming and one of the guards being dragged off into the facility. I'm guessing he isn't coming out any time soon. When we made it up the stairs the other guy—Jimmy, I think his name was—said that we'd have to wait till next week to see the founders. He's the one who told us about the alarm. After that, we came straight here."

"Could you sense her there at all?"

"No. I tried, but our magic wasn't working at all. After the alarms went off, they must have done something to protect the site from magic."

"Granny Edith." Elizabeth spit her name like it was a curse word.

"Liz, what's wrong?" William was at her side.

"It was years ago. I knew it would come back to bite us." She was pacing now. "Granny Edith and Grandpa Turner worked with the founders to develop a sort of magical protection spell. It was only supposed to be activated in cases of extreme emergency."

Michelle was now pacing right behind her, "What did it do?"

"What do you think it did? It prevented anyone from using magic to break into the courthouse.

"To get into the courthouse?" Melissa asked, the curiosity thick in her voice.

"Yes, why? What are you thinking?"

"It's just that, if someone got past the guards, and if that someone was Phoebe and Aleerah, they could still have potentially used magic once they were inside the courthouse, right? And, maybe to even get out."

"I'm not—."

"Maybe they got Eric out already," Loraline breathed— hopeful, for only a second. "But, why didn't they come home? If they did get out, why didn't they come home?"

Melissa shrugged, Michelle just shook her head. Who could really know what had happened, surely neither of them.

"If they got him out, they will find a way to let us know. Maybe they're afraid it would be too dangerous to come back here. Where else would they look for him?" At that moment, the front door to the shop burst open, for the second time that day.

"Go, go, go." A large man in all black was yelling. Three other men dressed exactly the same flooded into the room. Although there were only four of them, they seemed to fill the shop and take up more space than Loraline, Elizabeth, William, Tom, Melissa, and Michelle. Sometimes, size really does matter.

Moving through the shop and spreading out to search the rest of the house, the Guards acted as if they didn't even notice the Wenhams.

"Excuse me. Excuse me. You can't just come into my house and—."

"Ma'am, unless you want to be taken in for obstruction of justice you'll let me do my job."

"Obstruction of justice?" Loraline stared up into his crystal blue eyes. "How is it justice that you can burst into my home without my permission?"

"Ma'am, I'm only going to tell you one more time to please step aside and let me do my job."

William grabbed his daughter's arm and pulled her out of his way. "Can you at least tell us what you're looking for, sir?"

The Guard looked him up and down, the way men do when they're trying to figure out if the other man is a threat. Obviously he didn't think much of William, because he answered. "We're looking for Ermanes." Then, back to Loraline, "You know, Loraline, your husband, the traitor."

"He isn't a traitor!" She almost hit him, but William held her back.

"Eric isn't here. He was taken away this morning by some of the other Council Guard members," William said, in his calmest voice.

"Call Sam." Loraline pleaded, trying to sound calm, but failing. "Call Sam Hubbard, he'll tell you."

"I know he was taken this morning. Hell, we had him locked up, but obviously, if we're looking for him again, he isn't locked up anymore." He pushed his way past them and down the hallway. "Now, move out of the way, and stay out of the way."

The guards didn't stay long. The Black Onyx wasn't very large; it took the Guards only about ten minutes to search every nook and cranny. They didn't leave a single room or closet unopened.

As soon as the door closed behind them, Loraline rushed to the window and watched them drive away. When she knew it was safe, she let out a sigh of relief. "They got him out. I don't know how, but they got him out." Tears were starting to pour down her face but she didn't care.

Alee, Eric, and Phoebe, still holding hands, stepped into an empty room. The walls were dull beige and the carpet was a burnt umber shade. They could have been almost anywhere, but they weren't. They were here, and both Eric and Alee knew where it was.

"Oh." Eric and Alee said simultaneously. Eric quickly turned toward his daughter, Alee, who had already started trembling.

On the verge of tears, Alee let go of their hands and walked out of the room.

"What's going on? Where are we?" Phoebe stared up at Eric who had stopped breathing as he watched Alee leave. Only the oldest vampires were able to go so still that they appeared to be statues. Eric was that old. "Uncle Eric? Hey, snap out of it." Phoebe shoved him toward the door, "What's going on?"

"We—. She—. This is the house she grew up in." He quickly made his way out the door and down the hall to where Alee was standing in the middle of the kitchen.

"Well, not the first place I would have picked to hide, but OK." Phoebe was talking to herself since no one else had bothered to stick around. She took her time moving through the house before she found Eric and Alee in the kitchen.

"He said she left," Alee said quietly, "but I— I don't think I really believed him."

"Who? Who said she left?" Eric asked. "Where did she go?"

Alee tried the faucet, but the water was turned off. The light switch did nothing as she flicked it up and down, over and over again. "Damian. He said my mom couldn't handle my death. He said she moved away." Alee looked at Eric then and fire burned in her eyes. "You said—. You all promised that she wouldn't feel it. You said she would move past the grief and move on with her life." Tears were streaming down her face but she wasn't going to give in to the pain and sadness. She clung to her anger, like a life raft in the ocean.

"No. No. We never said she wouldn't feel the pain. She had to grieve. She had to believe you were dead." He tried to take her hand, but she pulled away. "Aleerah, she never would have stopped looking for you if she thought, even for a second, that your death wasn't real. We had to make sure that she knew, without a doubt, that she had lost you."

"NO!" Alee shouted. "Not like this." She pushed past him into the living room. "You drove her away. You made her leave me. You took her away from me." She fell to the floor, on the living room carpet where their old couch used to sit, and wept. She couldn't control the pain any more than Eric could take it away. She cried for what felt like hours, but was probably only minutes. When she had finished, her voice was hoarse and her eyes were red and swollen.

"I'm so sorry Aleerah." Phoebe was kneeling beside her, brushing Alee's hair out of her eyes. "I'm so sorry."

Alee looked around, but didn't see Eric anywhere. She took a few deep breaths and could feel the anger slipping away. "I know you're still here," she called out. "I can feel you—." She wiped the last tear from her face. "Even when I can't see you, I can feel you."

"You're part of me, Aleerah, and I won't apologize for that." He still hadn't come into the room, but she could feel that he was closer.

"That didn't give you the right—."

"She wouldn't have accepted you, once she knew."

"You don't know that." Alee stood up and made her way around the corner. Eric was standing on the steps leading up to her old room. "You don't know, not for sure. She was my mother, and she loved me. She knew more about me than you think, and she would have accepted me."

"It's nice to think that, Aleerah, but she was also a fierce warrior. She was vicious in her vengeance toward all vampires, shape shifters, fairies and, frankly, anyone who wasn't 'human.'" He made finger quotes when he said human. "The only reason she didn't kill you when she first found out what you were was because she knew that it would be a death sentence. Sure, she grew to love you. She told herself that you could live a normal life—that you didn't have to be a witch if she just protected you." Eric took a cautious step forward. "But Aleerah, it wouldn't have mattered how much she protected you. You are who you are and nothing could have changed that. Just as she is who she is and nothing, not even you could have changed that."

"I just—."

"I know." He went to her and she let him pull her into a hug. She felt safe and, more than anything, she knew, even if she didn't want to admit it, that he was probably right.

She started to say that she was sorry but before the words could come out of her mouth he put his finger to her lips and hushed her. "No apologies. You owe me nothing. It is I who owe you an apology. I should have been there for you all those years. I should never have let them take you away. You shouldn't be feeling this pain right now, and Martha and David shouldn't have had to suffer."

David was her father, the man who had raised her. He had died shortly before the Wenhams had faked Alee's death. *His* death wasn't pretend, though. They had called it an accident, but Alee knew better. It had been punishment. Years overdue, according to Alee's great grandmother, but punishment nevertheless.

She shook off the memory of her father's death, pushed away the pain of her mother's leaving, and settled herself. "I can't forgive you yet, but I want to. I know that someday I will. I just hope you're patient enough to wait." Eric didn't say anything; he just held her tighter. Even Phoebe came over and joined in the hug, until Alee pushed back and started up the stairs. "Mom may be gone, but not everything is."

Upstairs in her bedroom closet, she knelt down and started to pry up one of the floorboards. She reached inside the gap, searching, and pulled out a black velvet bag. Inside was a silver dagger—the one she had gotten from Jacinda so long ago along with a book of beginner spells. It was the same book that Dani had purchased on their first visit to The Black Onyx. Alee began flipping through the pages, when Phoebe recognized the book, having flipped through it many times while hanging out at The Black Onyx as a kid. "Um, you know those spells aren't real, right?" she said.

Alee just looked at her.

"Aleerah, that book is just for wannabe witches—young girls who think that being a witch is cool, or sexy, or whatever. Those spells don't actually work. If they did work there's no way Aunt Loraline would have sold it at the shop or that Granny Edith would ever have approved it."

"These spells do work," Alee said under her breath, still flipping through the book to find the one she was looking for.

"I don't—."

"Phoebe, they work. You just have to have the magic inside you first. Maybe they won't work for little miss normal, but believe me, they work." She found the page she was looking for and quickly handed it to Phoebe. "That's the one!"

"I don't understand." She was looking at the book as if she was missing something but couldn't figure out what.

"What is it?" Eric asked from across the room where he had been quietly waiting. Watching.

"A love spell." She just shook her head. "Aleerah, why do you want to do a love spell? Who—. Who do you want to put a love spell on?"

"It's not a love spell. At least not in the way you think." She took the book and read, "Does he love you? Is it real? This spell will separate puppy love from the real deal!" She looked up at Phoebe as if that was supposed to explain it all.

"Um, OK—."

"Phoebe—" She looked back at Eric, who was still watching attentively, but with some carefulness, not wanting to push too much. "—Kyle told me, before he—. Kyle told me that Damian isn't a bad—."

"Damian?" Phoebe snapped. "You're not seriously telling me you're considering—."

"Hear me out. Kyle said that what happened wasn't Damian's fault, just like Grandpa William said. Kyle said that Damian is a good guy and that he loves me. He told me to forgive him."

"Aleerah, you can't honestly think that Damian had nothing to do with all of this."

"No, I'm not stupid. I know he played his part, but that doesn't mean he had a choice. Kyle said I have to forgive him. He said that together Damian and I—, that we could be so much more than even he and I were." She looked back at Eric who had already started to move further into the room. "I don't know what all that means, but Kyle came back to save us, and he did it. He loved me more than life itself. He would never push me toward Damian unless he honestly believed there is good in him." She left Phoebe and went to her father. "Eric—Dad, you have to believe me. I think Damian is the key to making things right. If he really does love me, then he will help us."

Eric nodded, "You really believe that?"

"I do. I'm young, but I know what love is. I know how powerful it can be. I have to believe that if Kyle was right—, then Damian isn't going to hurt me."

"He helped his sister get the Guardian bands."

"I know."

"He helped lead the attack the night of the Founders' Celebration."

"I know that too, but I don't think he understood what would really happen, what impact it would have on everything—everyone."

"OK. I'll trust you." He reached out to Phoebe for the book. "I want you to explain what you have in mind, but first, let me take a look at that spell. I may be just a vampire, but I've learned a trick or two over the years."

Phoebe handed the book to Eric as Alee pulled her toward the door, saying "I just need to check one more thing before we go."

24

Less than three hours later, Phoebe was headed back to The Black Onyx to gather the troops. She was driving Alee's old chrome-colored 1985 Chevy Camaro.

Just as Alee had suspected, her mother hadn't wanted to take it with her when she left. *"It'll be here, I know it will. Mom knew how much I loved that car, and there's no way she would have wanted to keep it around, reminding her of me all the time."*

"I don't know Aleerah."

"Trust me." When Alee finally got the door to the old garage open, there it was. Martha had covered it with an old black tarp, but the keys were still in the glove box, just where Alee always left them.

Phoebe promised to be gentle with it, but as soon as she pulled out of the driveway and felt the power of the engine humming around her she couldn't help herself. She gunned it down the road and made it to The Black Onyx in half the time it should have taken.

Eric and Alee were headed into the tunnels of the Underground, but they wouldn't be alone for long.

It had taken less persuasion than anyone could have predicted—even Alee, who already knew that Damian loved her. She just hadn't been a hundred percent sure that he would work with her.

The phone only rang once, and Damian picked up.
"Alee?"

"Hey."

"Hey yourself."

Neither one of them would go as far as saying it was like old times, but it wasn't as awkward as it could have been, either.

"Did you really mean it when you said that you love me?" She had stepped out of the room, for privacy, but it was only the illusion of privacy. Eric, being a vampire, would have been able to hear the conversation even if she had gone all the way downstairs.

"You know I did." He was protecting himself—she could feel it—keeping up a metaphysical wall so that she couldn't get inside his head.

"Then I need your help. I still believe that vampires and shape shifters can share this town. I don't agree with how you—. I don't agree with what happened at the Founders' Celebration, but I understand why you did it." She could hear him moving or settling into his seat. Then she could feel him starting to let go of some of the control he was trying to maintain. "I have questions. I need to understand what really happened."

"What do you want to know?"

Alee knew that this conversation would either push Damian away or bring them closer, it all depended on how she worded what she said next. "How did you do it? I mean, how did you get into the ballroom?"

"I—. I mean, we took the back staircase." He was whispering.

"I already know that part. What I want to know is how? How did you get passed the guards and down into the stairwell in the first place?"

"Alee, please don't make me explain this. No good can come out of your knowing this." He was pleading, which only made Alee more insistent.

"If you want me to be able to trust you, then you need to tell me."

"Fine. We had planned to get in early, we were going to take the uniforms of the catering company members, but when we got there they had already gone in. We were too late and we almost had to cancel our plans—or at least postpone them. We sat outside, up the road, and watched as the guests were arriving. Shortly after the streets had emptied I noticed Kyle and your cousin, the young one with black hair—."

"Phoebe."

"Right. They were hanging out at the front of the building for a while, but instead of going in they made their way around the back. I decided to follow them. Phoebe led Kyle through a window on the lower level. The lock had been broken. I'm not sure how she knew about it, but it didn't seem like it had been the first time she had gotten in that way."

"Stick to the story. I don't need or want to know about what Phoebe might or might not have done. I just want to know about that night."

"I'm sorry. It's just that—." Damian went silent.

It was almost a minute before Alee spoke up. "Are you still there?"

"Yeah, I'm here. Sorry." He cleared his throat and continued. "When I followed them through the window it led to a back hallway. From there we were able to get into the stairwell without anyone noticing."

"What about the guards?"

"There were a lot of guards stationed out front and in the main lobby by the elevators, but there was no one in the back stairwell. It was almost too easy. I remember thinking that something was wrong, that it must have been a trap. But, it wasn't."

"No, it wasn't." Alee looked around and back over her shoulder, she was still alone. "Thank you. I know it was hard for you to share that, but I needed to know. I guess it doesn't matter now, it's just that Kyle died worrying—wondering if it had been his fault. I just needed to know the truth." She took a deep breath and swallowed back the lump that had formed in her throat. "Listen, I'm still new to all of this, but I can see that some of the founders are too set in their old ways. There are changes that need to be made, and I think that if we—you and I—work together, maybe we can make that happen."

"Alee, I don't think that—."

"It wouldn't be just us. I know we're not strong enough alone. My father and my cousin are here with me. The rest of my family will help too. I need to know if you're willing—if your family is willing to help." He didn't answer for a long time, but she could hear him breathing. "Damian?"

"Alee, I don't know. There's more to it than you could possibly imagine. There's more history between my family and yours than you know. I just don't know if my mom would—. Besides, we have enough to worry about right now. Victoria has gone missing, and not that that is entirely a bad thing, but we haven't been able to reach her."

The image of Victoria, in wolf form, running off into the woods, flashed into Alee's mind. "I know, and that's my fault. I'm sorry, but I—."

"What do you mean that's your fault?"

"Damian, I didn't have a choice. She was going to kill me."

"What did you do?" He didn't sound mad but there was hollowness to his voice that she had never heard before.

"I didn't kill her if that's what you're asking."

"What did you do then?"

Now it was Alee's turn to be silent. She didn't know what to say, or how to say it in a way that it wouldn't ruin any chance she had of getting Damian back on her side. "I— I was coming to your house. I wanted to—. I don't know what I wanted. You guys were there and when I figured out where she had gone—to my grandmothers' house—well, she attacked me, I took her talisman. I broke it. I shouldn't have I know, but I didn't know what else to do."

"But, she's alive?"

"Yes, she's alive. She's just still in wolf form. I don't think she knows how to change back, without the talisman, but even if she does, I—. I bound her powers. I don't think she can change back. She looked scared, or angry. I'm not sure, maybe both."

Damian laughed unexpectedly, "Victoria is strong. If you say you didn't kill her then I believe you. She may not have changed back yet, but she'll find a way, binding or no binding. If I were you, I wouldn't be around when she does. She isn't going to be happy." His laughter trickled through the phone, sending a shiver through Alee's body. It was the old Damian again. The one Alee had spent so many late nights with, pretending to study but really just talking. "You remember that time Dani borrowed her red dress for the dance and spilled soda down the front? Victoria freaked out so bad her date left her there to find another way home"

"Yeah, I remember."

"Well, I have a feeling that will look like nothing more than a child's temper tantrum compared to how pissed she's going to be after this."

"Damian, I understand if you can't—."

"Are you kidding? I wouldn't miss this for anything. Besides, she isn't blameless in all of this. None of us are. So, if you can move passed what I did then I can move passed this. You're right, there has to be a way for us to work things out. I'll talk to my family." All of a sudden she felt him, as if he was standing right behind her. She turned but no one was there. He had dropped, or rather broken down, all of the walls he had built to keep her away. Instantly, he was there in her head and she was in his. *"Kyle came to me."*

"What?" She was surprised, but somehow knew she shouldn't have been. Kyle had told her to forgive Damian and to move on. *"What did he say?"*

"That you love me too. That together—"

"We could be more than even he and I were."

Phoebe's voice came from behind her. "Aleerah, you still on the phone?"

"Um, yeah. Sorry. I'll meet you guys downstairs in a minute." She took the phone into the back bedroom and shut the door behind her. "Damian, I do love you. I think I always knew it, but—. Let's just get through this and then we can see what we are to each other. OK?"

"Yeah, so where do we meet you?"

"Do you know about the Underground?"

"Yeah."

"Meet me there."

"How will I find you?"

"You just will." She hung up the phone and headed downstairs to catch up with Eric and Phoebe. She quickly shared the plan and they were on their way.

It didn't take Phoebe long to drive back to The Black Onyx in the Camaro, and, although her family wasn't really excited about the idea of working with the shifters, they trusted that if Eric was going along with it, then it must be the only option.

Alee and Eric went straight to Granny Edith's house. Alee needed to feed, and Eric insisted that fresh animal blood was going to give her more strength than cold blood from a refrigerator at The Black Onyx. Alee didn't argue. Besides she wasn't really in the mood to explain that she had already drank all of the stored blood at The Black Onyx after attacking her uncle.

Eric and Alee didn't have to hunt for long. The large deer and two smaller foxes they caught were enough to give Alee the energy she needed.

By the time they got down into the tunnels, Alee was on high alert and ready to fight. They made their stand at the most central location within the Underground. The closest exits led up to the courthouse, the hospital, the records department, and, just down the main hall about a quarter of a mile, the high school.

They were surrounded by vampires, witches, fairies, and other preternatural creatures busying themselves shopping, eating, and just enjoying their day. Little did they know that Alee and Eric were there with the intent of starting a war.

Alee knew the instant Damian entered the tunnels. She could feel him like a warm energy filling the room and then he was in her head, *"Alee?"*

"Damian." She was nervous and excited all at once. *"Where are you?"*

"We came in through the coffee shop entrance."

"The Java Jolt?" She chuckled to herself and Eric stared at her, confused. "Sorry, he's here, Damian and his family." she told Eric.

"So are Loraline and the others," Eric said.

Alee looked around, but didn't see her family anywhere. "I don't see—." But then she felt Phoebe, as if she were tied to her by an invisible rope.

"Trust me, they're here. They're ready." He looked at his daughter. Dressed in black, she looked strong and confident—more like her mother than ever before. She looked around, frowning. "Are you OK? What's wrong?" he asked.

Alee was scanning the faces of everyone around her, searching for Phoebe, wondering how she could feel her as if she was holding her hand. "I don't know. It's Phoebe—I feel like—."

"Like she's standing right beside you. Like you could reach out and touch her if you wanted?"

"Yes, why?"

"You've drunk her blood, but that shouldn't connect you so closely." He was asking without asking.

"She—Phoebe said that she drank my blood. To find me. Could that—?"

"Yes."

They sat in silence a few more minutes, but Eric knew they couldn't wait long. "In time the bond may weaken, if not—." He looked down at his daughter, "then maybe you will learn to appreciate your connection. But Aleerah, know that Phoebe is now more a part of you than just cousins can be. With the exchange of blood you take on partial responsibility for her, for her safety."

"But I—."

"I can explain more later, but right now we need to focus on what we can here to do. Are you ready?" She took a deep breath and nodded. "Then let's do this."

Alee stood up on the table they had been sitting at and pulled the hood off of her long auburn hair. "You know who I am." She wasn't yelling, but her voice carried through the tunnels. "I am the daughter of Ermanes son of Chalkeus. The blood of the Wenham coven flows through my veins as does their power." A crowd instantly began to gather around her. "My mother is Loraline, and my grandmother is Elizabeth, crone of Wenham coven." The crowd grew as more and more people came out of the shops to gather around her. "I am the dhampir!" She was the only surviving dhampir in history, and that fact alone gave her power. It gave her *clout*.

There were murmurs throughout the crowd as she continued. "The founders have taken liberties to which they are not entitled." A few people were nodding in agreement. Then, in the back of the crowd, she saw Damian. His eyes, a misty grey, seemed to peer right through her. Then he smiled, and she could feel the warmth of his energy crawling up her body and wrapping around her, as if it were a physical entity of its own. She shook it off, trying to regain her focus. "They have imprisoned my father without cause—."

"I heard he escaped," yelled a man at the back of the room.

"I heard they killed him," yelled another man off to Alee's left.

People started to yell back and forth throwing out what they thought, or what they had heard had happened. "He burned." "They hung him." "I heard he fought and killed ten Guards."

No one noticed as Eric stood up. No one noticed until he was standing on the table beside her. "I ask you, do I look dead? Do you believe me to have burned?" The crowd went silent.

"I told you he escaped" yelled the man in the back. The crowd went wild. The cheering and screaming filled the tunnels and echoed off the walls around them. "Aleerah is right. The founders have abused their powers."

"But, you're one of them. You're a founder!" It was an older woman sitting only a couple of tables away. Her voice was raspy but held a certain strength of its' own.

"And as a founder, I can see clearly the faults of my comrades. If we are to right their wrongs, we must do it together. We must forgive the mistakes of the past and move into the future with new hope—and new allies!" The noise of the crowd died down and people listened tentatively. Eric continued. "For many years, we have stood our ground, forcing out all those who would challenge us—abandoning them as if they didn't belong." A few people cheered and others hung their heads in shame. "It was my daughter who showed me that those we so recklessly deserted should be welcomed back into the fold." Gasps filled the air.

"You would have us, what, recognize the shifters again? After what they did?"

"I would have us admit that we have all made mistakes. I would have us accept that without them at our sides we are not whole." A few people pushed their way out of the crowd and left, mumbling their contempt as they went. However, the majority stayed. "Our society can be so much more, so much stronger, if we all unite and work as one. We were that strong once—not that long ago. Have we forgotten so easily the way things were?"

"I haven't forgotten." Karen was standing in the back of the crowd, her son at her side, and about fifteen or twenty others around her.

Alee leaned in to her father's side and whispered, "It's them."

"We haven't forgotten either." Elizabeth and William said proudly from the other side of the crowd, with Loraline, Tom, and Phoebe standing next to them. Just behind them stood the rest of the surviving Wenham coven.

Eric nodded for Loraline to join him and Alee on the table. She did so without question. "My family will stand side by side with any of you who are willing. Together, we can make the changes this town needs." He scanned the crowd that surrounded the table, and made eye contact, as he demanded, "Who will stand with me now?" A few hands went up while others nodded. He said again, "Who will stand with me now?" More hands went up and people began to cheer. And yet again, "Who will stand with me now?!— UNITED!" Eric cried fiercely, and the tunnel erupted in cheers and screams.

They needed a revolution and that is exactly what they got.

25

Eric raised his hands, and everyone held back their enthusiastic cheers as he explained what he planned to do. With their help, he planned to take over the town and push out the founders. Immediately, a few vampires stepped up to stand in his support, in front of the table, facing the crowd, and they were quickly joined by a small group of witches, a few fairies, and several of the shifters—one of whom was Damian's mother Karen. In total there were twelve supporters already—a small army willing to fight at Eric's side.

Then things changed.

It started slowly at first, with a few muffled screams of fear replacing the excitement. One by one, someone or something was picking off those at the back edges of the crowd. No one had noticed at first, and then a young girl let out a gut-wrenching shriek as she was being dragged away.

Eric flew off the table with such force that it went toppling to the ground, sending Loraline and Alee down with it. "Stop!" He shouted at the figure dressed in all black with a hood shading its face. The coat was identical to the one Eric was wearing, and unmistakably marked the wearer as one of the founders. The fact that a founder had come himself to do the dirty work that was normally given to the Guards surprised Eric. "You can't hide, not while wearing the mark of the founders."

The figure stopped, holding the screaming girl. He casually tossed the girl aside, and she ran into the crowd, grasping for anyone who would help her.

The figure called out to Eric, "And *you* cannot rebel, not while wearing the mark of the founders." He laughed a guttural laugh that sent a chill down Alee's spine.

Eric reached down and ripped a small golden pin—the founder's pin—off the chest of his coat. "This means nothing to me now." He threw it at the feet of the hooded man. "Face me like a true warrior so you can die with dignity, or hide and die with shame."

The cloaked man started to laugh, but Eric didn't give him a chance to respond. With speed that only the older vampires possess, Eric was on top of the other man, pinning him to the ground. A soft growl reverberated from Eric's chest, sending the crowd into thunderous applause. He reached down and *through* the other man's chest, yanking his heart out and lifting it high above his head. "With shame you came here hidden, and with shame you now die." Blood trickled from the heart and down Eric's arm. The crowd went silent, waiting to see what would come next.

Eric nearly forgot the crowd behind him as the smell of blood filled the air around him. He lowered the heart to his mouth and bit down, draining it of blood, and then, dropping it to the floor, he licked the still-warm blood off his hand and stood to face the crowd. Once again, the crowd roared with excitement and praise.

A few of the shifters, one lion and one tiger, shifted effortlessly and tore at the lifeless body at Eric's feet. Before others had the chance to change form, the body was all but gone. Only scraps of clothing and bone remained. When they shifted back, blood stained their faces and they looked into the crowd with pride. "We will stand behind no one any longer," the werelion said. Then turning to Eric, "—but we will stand *with* you" He held his hand out to Eric. "Name's Ethan, but you can call me Little E."

Eric took in the other man, all six foot six of him. "Little E?"

"Yup."

"OK then, it's good to meet you Little E." He turned to the other man, who was still wiping the blood from his face, and held out his hand. "And you are?"

"Samuel, but call me Sam."

"Sam," Eric nodded, and shook his hand. Turning back to address the crowd, he said, "Little E and Sam have made their choice, as have others. Now I ask all of you. If you are ready to fight for what we rightfully deserve and if you are willing to stand with us, then step forward—because the battle begins *today*."

Most of the crowd stepped forward, with the exception of a few of the older members—not because they didn't believe in the cause, but because they felt themselves too old to fight.

Damian wove through the crowd to Alee's side. Leaning close, he whispered, "Kyle gave me something, but I think it was yours to give, not his."

"What do you mean?"

He didn't answer, but instead rolled up his sleeve. There, on the inside of his wrist, was a glowing infinity symbol, identical to the one the goddesses had branded Kyle with. She stared at it in awe, and when she lifted her own sleeve her tattoo had also started to glow. "That's not possible." She looked up, meeting his eyes, "How is it possible?" She took his hand in hers and instantly the vine that wrapped around her lower arm started to grow. Not only did it wrap its way up the rest of her arm; it stretched to his, and slowly made its way around his wrist and up the rest of his arm. "Oh my goddesses. That never—."

"Happened with Kyle." He finished her thought.

"No."

"Aleerah?" Loraline stood behind her, mouth agape.

"It is time!" Eric yelled from the other end of the room, and all at once the crowd started to move as one body, like a huge ocean wave. Everyone was swept up into the crowd-wave as it moved toward the long steep steps that led up to the courthouse.

Alee and Damian hastened to the edges of the throng, and made their way, hand in hand, to Eric and the rest of their families. When they arrived at the bottom of the courthouse steps, everyone had gathered in groups. The vampires stood in the center with the witches all gathered on one side, and the shifters on the other. Others, smaller crowds of fairies, nymphs, and jinn gathered too. However, the Wenhams all gathered together, just behind the mass of vampires and Damian never left Alee's side.

26

Everything seemed to move at an alarmingly fast pace. The doors at the top of the stairs burst open and the Guards poured out, spilling down, as the vampires and shifters charged forward. Alee and Damian, and the rest of Alee's family, stood their ground as the others surged forward around them. They quickly formed a multi-coven power circle. Loraline pushed Alee into the center of the circle, "Call the elements, do it quickly."

"But, I have no candles."

"You don't need them. Only you can do this Aleerah. Do it now!"

No pressure here, Alee thought to herself. She looked back to see Damian standing only a few yards away and reached out to him. "I need you."

He made his way to the center of the circle and took her hand. "I'm here."

She smiled as his hand wrapped around his. She centered herself, trying not to focus on the fighting and bloodshed going on just yards ahead.

"This might hurt." It was only a whisper, and she didn't give Damian a chance to respond before she closed her eyes and reached out to the elements. Not knowing what the compass directions were here in the Underground, she reached, not with hands but with powers. She reached out to the elements, psychically calling for their help. "Air, you are the wind that pushes us along our path." She had called numerous circles since joining the Wenham family, and the words, so familiar now, just flowed out of her, "You encourage us through hard times. I welcome you into our circle." Wind that had no natural place so deep underground blew around the circle, sending a chill through the crowd. Alee's hair blew back with the wind, away from her face, revealing her eyes as black as night.

"Fire, you strengthen us when we feel we have been defeated. I welcome you into our circle."

It is believed that all who follow the wiccan faith have a special personal connection to at least one of the elements, and when Alee called fire to the circle, it was clear who among them was aligned with fire. A soft orange, almost reddish glow surrounded four or five of the women standing in the circle, and above Alee there appeared a bright golden fire—. "Oh my—." those nearest to Alee whispered. Instinctively, they reached out, as if accepting the fire, knowing that it couldn't or wouldn't harm them.

"Water, you cleanse and clean us. You give life to the earth and nourishment to our bodies. I welcome you into our circle." As if the ocean had mystically appeared around them, a salty fresh scent filled the air. A lacy mist wrapped itself around Alee and many of the others throughout the crowd.

"Earth, you give life, food, and shelter to all living things. From you we were born and to you we will one day return. I welcome you into our circle." The sweet smell of freshly cut grass and newly opened roses wafted up from the ground under their feet.

Alee slowly turned and gazed out, not at the wiccan sisters and brothers around her, but at the elements that also danced around the circle, clinging to those with whom they felt a connection. She didn't need a mirror to tell her what she looked like just then. She already knew how strong her connections to wind, fire, water, and earth were. But even this display of unearthly power was nothing compared to what was to come.

Alee released Damian's hand and lifted her arms to the sky, seeing beyond the walls and ceiling that held her beneath the ground. She reached through the earth above and into the open sky and called out, "Spirit, you are our conscience. You help guide our choices to good rather than evil. I welcome you into our circle." The walls started to shake and bits and pieces of the ceiling started to crumble down into the circle, but no one moved. "Complete this circle and do unto our enemies as they would have done unto us!" The last was a command, shouted to the heavens, and with it a burst of sunlight flowed into the Underground through what had just been the ceiling.

Spreading out, the cracks in the ceiling didn't break the circle because no line had been drawn. As if tied together with an invisible band the undrawn circle moved and spread with them, protecting not only them, but the others who were there fighting for them. Shifters were using their claws like blades, and blood was everywhere staining walls, ceiling, clothing, and faces. Fairies were feasting openly for the first time in centuries. Vampires fought vampires and the Founders' Guards were scattered throughout the tunnels, dead, having faced the true death.

As the sun crept in through the ceiling, hitting the bodies of the dead, the dead vampires' bodies burst into flames, burning until nothing but ash was left.

"Nothing burns like a dead vamp." Little E was standing next to Alee, wiping the blood from his face with the back of his hand. He looked calm and somehow happy, considering the fight that was still taking place.

"What?"

He smiled down at her, "They should have been too old to burn by sunlight, but you—you pack a punch little lady." Then, turning to watch the few small fights still in progress, he took a deep breath, and said, "I haven't felt this good in decades. Thank you."

Before she could respond he was gone, dashing out into the crowd until he was lost in a sea of blood, fur, claws, and fangs. "You're welcome," she whispered to no one at all.

Just then, arms wrapped around her from behind, but they weren't threatening. "That was—amazing." She turned in Damian's arms and laid her check against his chest.

"It was, wasn't it?"

"Yeah, yeah it was. How did you—?"

"It wasn't just me. It was us." Her powers had always been strong and with Kyle they had been even stronger, but nothing she had ever experienced in the past came close to what she had been able to do with Damian there in the tunnels. *Together you and he can be so much more than even we were.* Kyle's words ran through her head again and she looked into Damian's eyes, remembering how it felt as the elements flowed through her. "Did it hurt?"

"No." Damian pulled her in and hugged her even more tightly as they stood there watching the fighting die down.

When all their enemies had been killed or had fled, they slowly continued their way up the courthouse steps. It didn't take long before all of the founders were accounted for, and Eric knew exactly what he had to do.

Standing before the founders, now caged and chained, Eric announced, with genuine sadness in his heart, "Sometimes, the only way to change the future is to first embrace the past." Then, he pulled a large metal chain that hung from the ceiling above him. Fire filled the cage from the grated floor beneath them, and screams of terror and pain filled the room as his brothers and sisters of centuries past burned at his hand.

27

"Eric." He didn't look up from the ever-growing stack of papers on his desk when Loraline walked in.

"Eric, it's been ten months since the founders died." She stood at the door as he slowly lifted his eyes to hers as if the weight of the world was on him.

"You mean since I killed them!"

"Fine, since you killed them." She closed the distance between them. "You only did what you had to do to protect us." Moving around his desk, she took his face in her hands and pulled him close. "You saved us all."

"I killed my maker. I killed my brothers—my sisters—my friends."

"You saved your family and you saved our town." She kissed him softly on the lips, then pulled away. "In the last ten months you have restored the shifters to their rightful place as Guardians. You not only found, but also invited back into the Underground, the two remaining dream walkers. You rebuilt a Founding Council with representatives from seven of the different communities. You even issued an open invitation to any reapers, something that would never have been heard of in the last one hundred and thirty years." At that, he looked up. "You have not just restored our community, you have made it better. Now it's time to stop hiding in this office and be the leader you were born to be."

"I'm not hiding Loraline." He stood and walked to the windows that overlooked the town. "I'm coping. But you're right. There is much to do before the Founders' Celebration next month."

"You're still going through with it?" She was surprised and didn't try to hide it.

"Our daughter has convinced me that to avoid it would be detrimental to morale. However, instead of celebrating one hundred and thirty-one years, we will be celebrating a new beginning. We will be letting go of the past and seeking a new future. The Council and I have chosen Aleerah as the orator."

"Aleerah?"

"Yes."

"But—." At a loss for words, Loraline lowered herself into one of the leather armchairs across from Eric's desk.

"She'll be fine darling. She will be safe. I promise."

"It's just that, she's been through so much and I'm not sure she has fully recovered."

"There is no better choice, Loraline. Aleerah is strong. She is brave. She is the only surviving dhampir. That has to prove to you that she is more than we could ever have imagined." He sat down in the chair across from hers. "Besides, we will all be there with her. We aren't limiting the Celebration to only those of age any longer. All members of the Underground, old and young, will be invited."

Loraline didn't know what to think of the changes, but she believed that Eric had earned his responsibilities and the respect due him. She didn't protest from that point on. When the night of the Celebration finally arrived, she was in awe of his strength and that of their beautiful daughter as well.

***

Aleerah stood in front of over two hundred members of the Underground community and silence filled the air around her. Her flowing red hair was like a crown around her flawless porcelain skin, and her long silk gown was overshadowed only by her new hematite pentagram charm that hung from her neck on a golden chain. "By now you all know me. Just a few short years ago, I was only a child, naive to the ways of our world." Her eyes sought out Damian, sitting only ten feet away, and her body grew warmer. "Now I stand before you, not as a child but as your equal. I stand before you with joy in my heart, for what we have accomplished, and for what we will accomplish together in the years to come."

Cheers filled the once-silent room and the walls shook around them.

"It wasn't long ago, only a year to this day, when we were told to celebrate. It didn't happen then, but today it can.

Today we celebrate for good reason. Our city is thriving and it is because of each and every one of you. It is because of your commitment to the changes that had to be made. Tonight, celebrate! Celebrate everything we have accomplished together—celebrate the lives we have built here—celebrate the strength we have created within our new-found community."

She lifted her glass high above her head and toasted each and every one of them. "A toast to the night walkers among us, to our wiccan sisters, to our fairy friends. A toast to the dream walkers, to the sirens, the arachnes, and the reapers we welcome, but hope never to face. And last, but certainly not least, a toast, and a loving welcome back, to the shifters. Your absence from our community may not yet be forgotten, but your homecoming shall always be remembered."

The crowd cheered again as tears of joy and shouts of encouragement filled the room.

Alee raised her hands and her voice one last time. "We have lost many to get to where we are today, but their lives were not lost in vain. We will live on, and they too, in our hearts, will live on forever.

The End

BONUS MATERIALS

BONUS MATERIALS

Q&A WITH NINA SODEN

Where did the idea for the Blood Angel Series come from?

Honestly I don't really know. I started writing these short—really short—scenes. Some are included in the Blood Angel Series books, others aren't. Then the characters just kind of came to life in my mind. I figured I might as well put them onto paper and before I knew it I had hit 90,000 words and over twenty chapters and I was looking at an actual novel. From there I couldn't see just saving the story on my computer. I decided to go all the way with it and get it edited and try to indie-publish it.

How and why did you start writing? And what inspires you?

I've written poetry for years, as far back as I can remember. I also dabbled in screenplays. I wrote a full-length feature film called *Pro Bono*, about a woman who killed her husband. It was a bad title and it never went anywhere except on my bookshelf, but it was a good learning experience.

In 2005, I self-published a collection of my poems in a book called *Private Words Unspoken,* which is still available online. It was my first experience with Indie publishing and it led me to start exploring some of my other story ideas.

I started writing AWAKEN, the first book in the Blood Angel Series, in late 2010, and after a lot of re-writes I finally published it in July 2012. BEGINNINGS, book 2, didn't take as long to write. I think the idea was so fresh in my mind that I already knew what was supposed to happen. I wrote the first draft in about two months. It went through about seven rewrites before finally being published in May 2013. I started book 3, REVENGE, shortly thereafter.

What made you choose Atlanta, Michigan as the setting for your book?

I grew up in Michigan and, as a child I spent most of my summers in Atlanta, Michigan. It's a very small town and only had one stoplight when I was little. I haven't been back in years, and I am sure it has grown and changed a lot since then. But, I associate so many of my best childhood memories to the time I spent there that it just seemed natural to have it be the setting for my series. Of course, I took liberties with the description and changing the layout of the town. Yet, even with the changes I made, it still feels like the same small town to me.

What characteristics did you keep in mind when you were developing the main character, Alee— or should we call her Aleerah?

She was born Aleerah, but having grown up as Alee for the majority of her life she relates more to the name Alee, at least until book 3.

When writing Alee I wanted her to be strong yet insecure, fearless yet hesitant. So many young girls are stronger than they believe, and I wanted the readers to relate to her. I wanted Alee to be able to bring out, in my readers, their courage and strength that maybe even they didn't know they have.

How has your childhood influenced your writing?

My childhood was full of adventure! My family did a lot of vacationing together. By the time I graduated college I had visited almost all 50 states throughout the United States.

I think that growing up in such a close family unit I didn't have a fear of expressing myself. My parents supported me, no matter what. When I told them I wanted to be an artist, they bought me painting supplies. When I said I wanted to move to California and be an actor, they helped me pack and load the moving van. When I told them I was writing a novel, they asked if they could be the first to read it, and have since purchased many copies sharing them with family and friends.

Having that kind of support, throughout your entire life, can really help develop your passions. For me, those passions have always been creative. I think that if it wasn't for the amazing childhood I had I wouldn't feel as free and open to write the stories I do.

What authors have inspired you?

Well, as a child, the first author that got me really excited about reading was Dr. Seuss. He used words so playfully that each page was more like a song than just words on a page. As a kid I enjoyed the Hardy Boys books, Nancy Drew, Encyclopedia Brown, and the Babysitters Club. However, reading didn't actually become an obsession of mine until high school when I discovered Stephen King.

Now, I am pretty much addicted to the supernatural stories. I have fallen in love with the Anita Blake Series by Laurell K. Hamilton and had a hard time putting them down while I read the complete series. I also really enjoy reading Rachel Caine, Lauren Kate, Stephanie Meyer, L.J. Smith, Suzanne Collens, and of course the inspiring indie-author Amanda Hocking.

Are there any words you'd like to impart to fellow writers? Any Advice?

Don't give up. If writing is something you really want to do, then do it. There are so many people who never finish—or worse, they never start—because they feel like they'll never get a publisher or that people won't buy their book. Sure, the dream of most writers is to get a great publisher, have a team of dedicated people marketing their book, do book signings around the world, and have their book on the best sellers list. But if your dream isn't the fame and fortune, but to just get your idea on paper and have your book published, then there are options. Indie-publishing is a great alternative to traditional publishing. Sure, you as the author have to do a lot of the legwork to market your book and get it seen, but believe me it's a great feeling to finish your manuscript and hit [SEND] knowing that in just a few days your eBook and paperback copies will be ready and available around the world for anyone who wants to read them.

So don't give up. Know that it takes a lot of hard work, but also remember that anything is possible if you set your mind to it.

What message would you like your readers to hear directly from you?
Thank you! I can't say it enough, the idea that anyone would want to read my books is amazing and thrilling to me. So, thank you, to all of my readers, from the bottom of my heart. Thank you for indulging and supporting my crazy dreams of being a writer.

Where can readers find out more about you and your books?
I invite all readers to "follow", "like", and "subscribe:

Blog: http://www.ninasoden.wordpress.com
Facebook: http://www.facebook.com/BloodAngelSeries
Twitter: http://www.twitter.com/Nina_Soden

~ Nina Soden ~

NINA SODEN'S BLOOD ANGEL PLAYLIST

I don't usually listen to music when I write. Most times, I need everything around me to be so still that I can hear my own heartbeat. But, there are times, particularly when I'm writing relationship-building chapters, that I need music that reminds me of the characters. So, here is a list of musical artists that I leaned on throughout the writing process for the Blood Angel Series:

1. Jason Mraz's
2. John Mayer
3. Lifehouse
4. Maroon 5
5. Mat Kearney
6. One Republic
7. Pink
8. Plumb
9. Zac Brown Band

I'm sure there were others, but these are the ones that come to mind right now as I type.

the weghan family tree

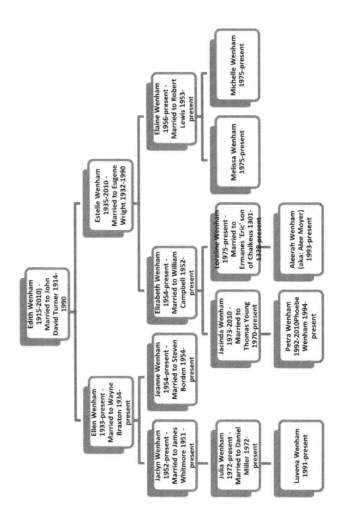

~ Nina Soden ~

GLOSSARY OF SUPERNATURAL CULTURES WITHIN THE UNDERGROUND COMMUNITY

(Not all of the following supernatural cultures were mentioned in the Blood Angel Series, but all were researched and considered throughout the writing process. Many where in the original drafts, but taken out throughout the editing process.)

- **ANGEL.** A supernatural being or spirit who possesses retractable wings, and often appears in human form. They have the ability to travel from realm to realm with ease, as well as the ability to manipulate time. However, they cannot exist in the same location as their past "living" self.

- **ARACHNE.** Creatures with spider-like abilities. They appear to be human, but have double-irised eyes. They have an infectious bite that can turn their victims into arachne. The only way to kill them is through decapitation.

- **DHAMPIR.** The child of a vampire and a human. Dhampirs have powers similar to those of a vampire, but without the usual weaknesses. (Note: Alee/Aleerah, the dhampir in the Blood Angel Series, was not only the child of a vampire but her human parent was also a witch, and to top it off her grandfather was a fairy. Therefore, her powers far exceeded those of a traditional dhampir.)

- **DREAM WALKER.** Appearing in human form, a dream walker can enter and/or manipulate ones' dreams. This is done for the sole purpose of persuade desired behavior in his victims. They are able get into the mind of their victim, even while the human is still awake, manipulating what they believe is happening around them. Oftentimes the dream walker appears to their victim as 'familiar', but this is an illusion created when they alter their victim's perception.

- **FAIRY.** Fairies usually appear in human form; however, in their true form they have wings that retract into their shoulder blades. Although they can survive on the same foods that humans eat, many choose the more grotesque lifestyle of living off of the carcasses of humans—oftentimes children.

- **LYCANTHROPE.** A person affected with lycanthropy. Unlike a shape shifter, a lycanthrope can only take the form of one animal. After their first transformation they are physically and spiritually bonded with their spirit animal.

- **LYCANTHROPY.** The magical ability to assume the form and characteristics of an animal.

- **MESOMORPH.** A human physical type that is marked by greater than average muscular development

- **NIGHT WALKER (VAMPIRE)**. Immortal creatures that suffer from bloodlust and feed regularly on the blood of other humans and/or animals. Aside from having retractable eye-teeth, which they use to rip through the skin of their victims, vampires have enhanced senses, varying based on the age of the vampire.

- **REAPER (DEATH)**. Neither ghost nor angel; it is the reaper's job to collect the souls of the recently dead.

- **SHAPE SHIFTER**. Humans who have the ability to shift into animal form. Unlike traditional werewolves, the shape shifter's transformation is not controlled by the lunar cycle. They have the ability to change forms at will. However, unlike the lycanthrope, the shape shifter, if strong enough, can take the form of multiple animals— and the strongest among them can also take the forms of other humans.

- **SIREN**. A type of shape shifter, able to change its appearance depending on his/her choice of victim. Once a victim is selected the siren will appear to him/her as their ideal mate, be it sexual or platonic. The siren calls its victim through the sound of its voice—many believe through song, but others believe it is through manipulating the victim's mind into hearing what or who they want to hear.

- **SKIN WALKER.** A person with the supernatural ability to turn into any animal he/she desires.

- **THERIANTHROPY.** The mythological ability of humans to metamorphose into animals through shape shifting.

- **TRACKER.** This is a rare form of witch who possesses the ability to locate those they seek, even without a blood connection as is required for vampires to do the same.

- **VAMPIRE (NIGHT WALKER).** Immortal creatures that suffer from bloodlust and feed regularly on the blood of other humans and/or animals. Aside from having retractable eye-teeth, which they use to rip through the skin of their victims, vampires have enhanced senses, varying based on the age of the vampire.

- **WARLOCK.** The male equivalent of a witch.

- **WEREWOLF.** Humans who turn into wolf-like animals, monthly, during the full moon. Typically the human is thought to black out, having no control over what the wolf does. Werewolves have enhanced abilities such as speed, strength, stamina, increased senses of smell and hearing. They have an infectious bite that can turn other humans into werewolves.

- **WITCH.** A woman of wiccan belief who claims to possess magical powers and who practices sorcery. Light witches are said to practice white magic, making their connection through nature. Dark witches are said to practice black magic, making their connection through the Devil.

BLOOD ANGEL SERIES
BOOK CLUB DISCUSSION QUESTIONS

- How did you experience the series? Were you engaged immediately, or did it take you a while to "get into it"? How did you feel reading it – amused, sad, disturbed, confused, bored, all of the above?

- Describe the main characters—personality traits, motivations, inner qualities.
  - Why do the characters do what they do?
  - Are their actions justified?
  - Describe the dynamics between the characters.
  - How has the past shaped their lives?
  - Do you admire or disapprove of them?
  - Is there a character that reminds you of yourself or a person you know?

- Do the main characters change by the end of the series? Do they grow or mature? Do they learn something about themselves or life in general?

- Is the plot throughout the series engaging—does the story interest you? Is this a plot-driven series: a fast-paced page-turner? Or does the story unfold slowly with a focus on character development?

- Talk about the book's structure. Is it a continuous story or interlocking short stories? Does the time-line move forward chronologically or back and forth between past and present? Does the author use a single viewpoint or shifting viewpoints? How did these aspects effect your reading experience?

- What is the main theme or topic that the author explores? Does the author use symbols to reinforce the main ideas? How does the author approach the main theme or topic differently from other authors you've read?

- Is the ending satisfying? If so, why? If not, why not and how would you change it?

- If you could ask the author a question, what would you ask? Does this series inspire you to read other books by the same other? Would you recommend this series to fellow readers?

26715192R00165

Made in the USA
Columbia, SC
19 September 2018